Praise for *Daddy Lenin*

"Guy Vanderhaeghe's *Daddy Lenin and Other Stories* is the work of an assured writer who needs no pyrotechnics to keep us reading. Each story is superbly crafted, razor-sharp, wickedly funny. The reader is carried along in the hands of a master, a seasoned professional at the top of his game."

– Governor General's Literary Award Jury Citation

"*Daddy Lenin* wrestles with the seemingly intractable divide between modernity and postmodernity, between masculinity and postmasculinity, in a way that is direct and vigorous. It is an entertaining return to the form that launched its author's literary career."

– *The Globe and Mail*

"Masterful, these often lighthearted, comic scenario peppered, and nonetheless dark-tinged stories showcase the author taking a few confident steps from his pensive historian persona toward another as an amused pupil of human foibles.... Vanderhaeghe's penned-in guys . . . might have a bit of foolishness in their DNA, but that makes them all the more engaging."

– *Vancouver Sun*

Books by Guy Vanderhaeghe

FICTION

Man Descending (1982)
The Trouble with Heroes (1983)
My Present Age (1984)
Homesick (1989)
Things As They Are (1992)
The Englishman's Boy (1996)
The Last Crossing (2002)
A Good Man (2011)
Daddy Lenin and Other Stories (2015)

PLAYS

I Had a Job I Liked. Once. (1991)
Dancock's Dance (1995)

GUY
VANDERHAEGHE

DADDY
LENIN

And Other Stories

EMBLEM

To Sylvia

Library and Archives Canada Cataloguing in Publication
is available upon request.

ISBN: 978-0-7710-9916-8

Typeset in Sabon by M&S, Toronto
Book design by Kelly Hill
Cover image: © Image Source / Corbis

Printed and bound in the United States of America

McClelland & Stewart,
a division of Random House of Canada Limited,
a Penguin Random House Company
www.penguinrandomhouse.ca

1 2 3 4 5   19 18 17 16 15

Penguin
Random
House

CONTENTS

The Jimi Hendrix Experience

IT'S THE SUMMER OF 1970 and I've got one lovely ambition. I want to have been born in Seattle, to be black, to be Jimi Hendrix. I want a burst of Afro ablaze in a bank of stage lights, to own a corona of genius. I ache in bed listening to "Purple Haze" over and over again on my record player; the next night it's "All Along the Watchtower." I'm fourteen and I want to be one of the chosen, one of the possessed. To soak a guitar in lighter fluid, *burn baby burn*, to smash it to bits to the howl of thousands. I want to be a crazy man like Jimi Hendrix.

What I didn't know then is that before my man Jimi flamed his guitar at Monterey, he warned the cameraman to be sure to load plenty of film. This I learned much later, after he's dead.

It's not a good time for me. After school finishes in June my father moves us to a new city; all I have is Jimi Hendrix, Conrad, and Finty. I don't know what I'm doing with these last two, except that with school out for the summer I lack opportunities to widen my circle of acquaintances. Beggars can't be choosers.

Finty I meet outside a convenience store. He introduces me to Conrad. There's not much wrong with Finty; born into a normal family he'd have had a chance. Conrad is an entirely different story. Finty proudly informs me that Conrad's been known to set fire to garbage cans and heave them up onto garage roofs, to prowl a car lot and do ten thousand dollars' worth of damage in the wink of an eye. He's a sniffer of model airplane glue, gasoline. That stuff I don't touch. It's impossible to imagine the great Jimi Hendrix with his snout stuffed in a plastic bag. Occasionally, I'll pinch a little grass from my big sister Corinne's stash in her panty drawer, have my own private Woodstock while Jimi looks down approvingly from the poster on my bedroom wall. I tell myself this is who I am. Finty and Conrad are just temporary way stations on the big journey.

Conrad scares me. His long hair isn't a statement, just a poverty shag. His broken knuckles weep from hitting walls; he's an accident willing itself to happen. The only person who comes close to scaring me as much is my father, a janitor who works the graveyard shift in a deadly office complex downtown, midnight to eight in the morning. A vampire who sleeps while the sun is up, sinks his teeth into my neck at the supper table, goes off to work with a satisfied, bloody grey smile on his lips. So far as he's concerned there's only one lesson I need to learn – don't be dumb when it comes to life. I hear it every night, complete with examples and illustrations.

I'm not dumb. It's my brilliant idea to entertain ourselves by annoying people because that's less dangerous than anything Conrad is likely to suggest. The same principle as substituting methadone for heroin.

The three of us go around knocking on people's doors. I tell whoever answers we've come about the Jimi Hendrix album.

"What?"

"The Jimi Hendrix album you advertised for sale in the classifieds in the newspaper."

"I didn't advertise nothing of any description in any newspaper."

"Isn't this 1102 Maitland Crescent?"

"What does it look like? What does the number on my house say?"

"Well, we must have the right place then. Maybe it was your wife. Did your wife advertise a Jimi Hendrix album?"

"Nobody advertised nothing. There is no wife anymore. I live alone."

After my warm-up act, Finty jumps in all pathetic with misery and disappointment like I've coached him. "This isn't too funny, you ask me. Changing your mind at the last minute. I promised my sister I'd buy your album for her birthday. A buck is all I got to buy her a lousy second-hand birthday present and then you go and do this. We had to transfer twice on the bus just to get here."

"His sister has cerebral palsy, mister." I hang my head like I can't believe what he's doing to the poor girl.

Conrad says to Finty, "I got fifty cents. It's yours. Offer him a buck and a half. He'll take a buck and a half."

"I ain't going to take anything because I don't have no Jimmy Henson record. I don't even own a record player."

"I've got thirty-five cents," I tell the man. "That makes a buck eighty-five. He *needs* the album for his sister. Music is all she has in life."

"She can't go out on dates or nothing," Finty says, voice cracking. "It's the wheelchair."

"Look, I'm sorry about your sister, kid. But I'm swearing to you – on a stack of Bibles I'm swearing to you – I don't have this record."

"Maybe you've forgotten you have it," I say. "Does this ring a bell? Sound familiar?" And I start cranking air guitar, doing "Purple Haze," no way the poor wiener can stop me until I'm done screaming hard enough to make his ears bleed.

One afternoon we're cruising the suburbs, courtesy of three bikes we helped ourselves to from a rack outside a city swimming pool. You can feel the heat coming off the asphalt into your face when you lean over the handlebars and pump the pedals. Conrad's been sniffing and the toasty weather is steaming the glue in his skull and producing dangerous vapours. Already he's yelled some nasty, rude remarks at a woman pushing a baby carriage; now he's lighting matches and flicking them at a yappy Pekingese on somebody's lawn, driving the dog out of its tiny mind. The lady of the house is watching him out her front window, and I know that when she closes those drapes, it'll be to call the cops.

Conrad is badly in need of structure, a sense of purpose at

this particular moment, so I point to a bungalow down the street, a bungalow where every shrub in the yard has been trimmed to look like something else. For instance, a rooster. I definitely recall a rooster. It's easy to guess what sort of a person lives in a house like that. Prime territory for the Jimi Hendrix routine.

Finty and Conrad take off with me in a flash, no explanation needed. We pull up on our bikes, leave them on the lawn. There's a sign on the front door, red crayon on cardboard: ENTRANCE ALARMED. PLEASE ENTER AT REAR. The old man who comes to the door is dressed like a bank manager on his day off. White shirt, striped tie, bright yellow alpaca cardigan. He's a very tall, spruce old guy with a glamour tan, and he's just wet-combed his white hair. You can see the tooth marks of the comb in it.

"We have come to inquire about the album," I say.

"Yes, yes. Come in. Come in. I've been expecting you," he says, eyes fixed on something over my head. But when I turn to see what's caught his interest, there's nothing there.

"This way, this way," he urges us, eyes blinking up into a cloudless sky. For a second I wonder if he might be blind, but then he begins herding us through the porch, through the kitchen, into the living room, his hands flapping down around his knees like he's shooing chickens. Finty and Conrad are giggling and snorting. "Too rich," I hear Conrad say.

The old man points and mutters, "Have a seat. Have a seat," before disappearing off into the back of the bungalow. Conrad and Finty start horsing around, scuffling over ownership of a recliner, but it's already a done deal who's going to claim it. Like the big dog with the puppy, Conrad lets Finty nip a bit before he shoots him the stare, little red eyes like glazed maraschino cherries left in the jar too long and starting to go bad. Finty settles for the chesterfield. Big dog flops in the recliner, pops the footrest, grins at me over the toes of his runners. "Right on," he says.

I don't like it when Conrad says things like "Right on." He's not entitled. He and Finty aren't on the same wavelength as people like me and Jimi Hendrix. Conrad would be asking people for Elvis Presley albums if I hadn't explained that the types whose doorbells we ring are likely to own them.

Finty is into a bowl of peanuts on the end table. He starts flicking them at Conrad. Conrad snaps at them like a dog trying to catch flies, snaps so hard you can hear his teeth clear across the room. The ones he misses rattle off the wall, skitter and spin on the hardwood floor.

I'm wondering where the old guy's gone. My ear is cocked in case he might be on the phone to the police. I don't appreciate the unexpected turn this has taken, the welcome mat he spread for us. I'm trying to figure out what's going on here, but there's this strange odour in the house that is creeping up into my nostrils and interfering with my thoughts. When I caught the first whiff of it, I thought it was the glue on Conrad's breath, but now I'm not so sure. A strange, gloomy smell. Like somebody's popped the door on a long-abandoned, derelict fridge, and dead oxygen and stale chemical coolant are fogging my brain.

I'm thinking all this weird stuff when Finty suddenly freezes on the chesterfield with a peanut between his thumb and middle finger, cocked to fire. His lips give a nervous, rabbity nibble to the air. I scoot a look over my shoulder and there's the old man blocking the entrance to the living room. With a rifle clutched across his chest.

Conrad's heels do a little dance of joy on the footrest.

The old gentleman pops the rifle over his head like he's fording a stream, takes a couple of long, lurching strides into the room, crisply snaps the gun back down on a diagonal across his shirt front, and announces, "My son carried a Lee-Enfield like this clear across Holland in the last war. He's no longer with us. I thought you boys would like to see a piece of history." He smiles and the Lee-Enfield starts moving like it has a mind of its own, the muzzle sliding slowly over to Finty on the chesterfield. One of the old guy's eyes is puckered shut; the other stares down the barrel straight into Finty's chest. "JFK," he says. Then the barrel makes a lazy sweep over to Conrad in the recliner. "Bobby. Bobby Kennedy."

Some nights I turn on the TV at four in the morning when all the stations have signed off the air. I like how the television fizzles in my ears, how my brain drifts over with electric blue and grey snow, how the phantom sparkles of light are blips on a radar screen tracking spaceships from distant planets. Similar things are happening in my head right now, but they feel bad instead of good.

"Get that out of my face," Conrad orders him.

The old man doesn't budge. "I could feel John and Bobby giving off copper right through the television screen. Lee Harvey Oswald could feel it and Sirhan Sirhan could feel it. I think, as far as North America goes, we were the only three."

Conrad squints suspiciously. "What kind of bullshit are you talking?"

"And you," says the old man, voice rising, "you give off copper and so does your friend by the peanut bowl. Chemistry is destiny. Too much copper in the human system attracts the lightning bolt. Don't blame me. I'm not responsible."

There's a long silence. Conrad's heels jitter angrily up and down on the footrest.

"Do you understand?" the old man demands. "Am I making myself clear?"

The question is for Conrad, but I'm the one who answers. I feel the old man requires something quick. "Sure. Right. We get it."

He sends me a thoughtful nod as he lays the gun down at his feet. A second later he's rummaging in his pockets, tearing out handfuls of change, spilling it down on the coffee table like metal hail, talking fast. "Of course, there are always exceptions to the rule. Me, for one. I'm immune to the thunderbolt. I could walk clear through a mob of assassins with a pound of copper in my belly and no harm, no harm. Untouchable." His fingers jerk through the coins, shoving the pennies to one side. Suddenly his neck goes rigid; a grey, furry tongue slowly, very slowly pushes out from between his lips. The old man picks up a penny and shows it to each of us in turn, like a magician getting ready to perform a trick. Presses the penny carefully down on his tongue like he's sticking a stamp on an envelope. Squeezes his eyes tightly shut. Draws the penny slowly back into his mouth and swallows. We watch him standing there, swaying back and forth, a pulse beating in his eyelids.

Conrad has had enough of this. "Hey, you!" he shouts. "Hey, you, I'm talking to you!"

The old man's eyes flutter open. It's like watching a baby wake up.

"We don't give a shit how many pennies you can swallow," Conrad says. "We're here about the album. The famous album."

"Right, the album. Of course," says the old man, springing to an ottoman, flipping up the lid.

"And another thing," Conrad warns him, winking at me. "Don't try and pass any golden oldies off on us. Troy here is a hippie. He's got standards. You know what a hippie is?"

"Yeah," says Finty, taking heart from Conrad. "You know what a hippie is?"

The old man drags a bulging photograph album out of the ottoman, drops it on the coffee table, sinks to his knees on the hardwood beside it. You'd think it was story time at Pooh Corner in the children's room at the library the way he turns the pages for us.

The pictures are black and white, each one a snapshot of a road under construction. All of them taken just as the sun was rising or setting, the camera aimed straight down the highway to where it disappears into a haze of pale light riding the horizon. There are no people in any of the pictures, only occasional pieces of old-fashioned earth-moving equipment parked in the ditches, looking like they were abandoned when everybody fled from the aliens, from the plague, or whatever.

Conrad grunts, "What the hell is this?"

"An example of the law of diminishing returns," the old man replies, dreamily turning the pages. "In a former life I was a highway builder. Unrecognized for my excellence."

"How come there's nobody in these pictures?" Conrad wants to know. "Pictures without people in them are a fucking waste of film."

"Oh, but there is a person," the old man corrects him. "Identify him. I think it's evident who he is, although there has been argument. If you would confirm his identity, it would certainly be very much appreciated."

Conrad and Finty peer down hard at the snapshots, as if there really might be a human being lurking in them. After about thirty seconds, Conrad gives up, irritably declares, "There's nobody in any picture here."

"He fades in and fades out. Sometimes he's there and sometimes he's not. But he's very definitely there now. You'll recognize him," the old man assures us.

By now Conrad suspects the old man is pulling a fast one, some senior citizen variation on the Jimi Hendrix experience. "Oh yeah, I see him now. Jimi Hendrix peeking around that big machine in the ditch. That's him, isn't it, Finty? Old Jimi Jimbo." He jabs Finty in the ribs with his elbow, hard enough to make him squeak.

"Wrong. The person in question is definitely in the middle of the road. Walking towards us. Look again."

This only pisses Conrad off. "Right. I ain't stupid. Don't try and pull this crap on me."

"Please describe him," the old man says calmly, patiently.

"Here's a description for you. An empty road. Get a pair of fucking glasses, you blind old prick."

"So that's your line." The old man's voice has started to tremble; it sounds a little like Finty's when he talks about his sister in the wheelchair, only genuine. "Just a road. Just a road, the boy says." He stabs his finger down on the photograph so hard it crinkles, turns to Finty. "You, young man. Describe him."

"Huh?" Finty glances over to Conrad for help.

"Knock, knock. Who's there?" The old man's finger taps the photograph urgently, bounces with blinding speed. "Who's there? Who's there? Knock, knock. *Knock, knock!*"

Conrad juts his jaw at Finty, a warning. "Don't you say nothing. Don't you give him nothing."

The old man slaps his knee, face alive with joy. "Not thinking, were you?" he shouts. "Telling him not to give me anything, why that's an admission there's something to give away. What a slip! Cat out of the bag!"

He snatches up the album, shoves it into my hands. Tiny points of sweat break out on his forehead. Somehow I think of them as icy. They put me in mind of liquefying Freon, or whatever gas they pump into refrigerators to keep them cold. The chemical smell is industrial-strength. It's coming from him.

"The truth now," he whispers to me. "Tell me what you see."

I feel Conrad staring at me, hear him say, "Nothing there, Troy. Nothing."

I gaze down at an empty road, scraped raw by grader blades, patches of earth seeping a greasy dampness. A burr of murky light bristles on the horizon.

"Just a road," I say. My own voice sounds weird to me, like it's coming from a ventriloquist's dummy.

"But roads don't just happen," coaxes the old man gently.

"No."

"So tell me, who else is in the photograph?"

It's no different from staring into the blank television screen. The snow shifting, forming faces of famous people locked in the circuitry from old programs. The hiss of static turning into favourite songs, guitar chords whining and dying.

"He's playing head games with us, Troy," Conrad warns. "Fuck him. Fucking lunatic. Fucking crazy old coot."

The old man leans in very close to me; I feel his alpaca sweater brushing the hairs on my bare arm. It's like static electricity. "Tell the truth," he murmurs. "Who do you see?"

I hold my breath, and then I say it. "You."

"Yes," says the old man. When he does, I sense Conrad rising to his feet, sense his shadow staggering between the two of us.

"And my head. What do you see above my head?"

"Enough of this shit, Troy," Conrad says.

I look at the picture, the old man's shaky finger guiding me to the pale grey froth on the horizon. He rests it there, the phantom light crowning his nail.

"Light."

"The aura."

"The aura," I repeat numbly after him.

Conrad boots the album out of my hand, sends it flying across the room, pages flapping. The old man and I dare not lift our heads. We just sit there, listening to the ragged sound of Conrad's breathing. It goes on a long time before he says, "You think I don't know what you're up to, Troy? Just don't try to fuck with my head. Just don't."

The old man and I sit with bowed heads, listening to Conrad and Finty pass through the house, their voices getting louder, more confident the closer they get to the back door. Then it slams, and the old man's head jerks up as if it were attached to the door by a wire. Conrad and Finty hoot outside. I listen to their voices fade away, and then I realize the old man is talking to me.

"I knew you were the one to tell me the truth. I knew it at the back door when I saw all that generous light coming . . ." He pauses, touches my head. "Coming from here."

And I'm up and running through the house, colliding with a lamp, moving so fast the sound of breaking glass seems to have nothing to do with me. Out the screen door, hurdling my stolen bike, clearing the broken spokes, the twisted wheel rims that Finty and Conrad have stomped. I'm running, my scalp prickling with tiny flames, I feel them, the flames creeping down the nape of my neck, licking at my collar, breathing hotly into my ears.

And Jimi, two months from being dead, is out there in front of me, stage lights snared in his hair, a burning, beckoning bush. And a young road builder is standing on a blank, unfinished road, his head blooming pale grey fire.

And here I am, running through the late-afternoon stillness of an empty suburban street, sucked down it faster than my legs can carry me, this hollow, throaty roar of fire in my head, that tiny point on the horizon drawing me to where the sun is either coming up or going down. Which, I have no idea.

Tick Tock

CHARLEY BREWSTER'S HANDS hadn't given him a moment's grief for nearly forty years, had behaved themselves, and then, after the young couple moved into the apartment next door, they began to torment him relentlessly.

His first encounter with his new neighbours occurred during a pillow-ripper of a blizzard, the air thick with fluffy flakes that stuck to everything they touched, tarring and feathering Brewster from head to toe as he trudged home. In a brief pause in the wind, the heavy snowfall thinned, and he caught a glimpse of a moving van parked in front of The Marlborough. A comically mismatched pair, one resembling an elf in a ski jacket, the other a gorilla in a parka, was struggling to wrestle some large, unwieldy article into the lobby of the building. A strong gust set the snow seething again and the duo vanished, swallowed up in a white whirlwind. Brewster lowered his head into his collar and plodded on.

When he reached his building, he saw the movers were a

young couple unloading a U-Haul. A waif-like bit of a girl, grimly latched on to one end of a mattress, threw him a despairing, hopeless look, enormous brown eyes swimming with tears. Her partner, furiously shoving and jerking the other end of the mattress, had his back to him, and all he could make out of the man was a grotesquely swollen torso and a massive column of neck that tapered into a shaved head shaped like the nose cone of a missile.

Bodybuilder, Brewster thought. Then added *and prick* to his snap assessment when a ferocious, eggplant-purple face swung round on him, shot him a hostile glare before swivelling back to the wife, girlfriend, whoever she might be. "How many times do I have to say it?" the man hissed at her. "*Back straight, lift with your goddamn legs!*"

She strained unsuccessfully. Brewster asked if he could lend a hand. The man muttered something that he didn't catch, but the tone made his meaning clear. *Piss off. Mind your own business.*

With a shrug, Brewster sidled past the two, took the elevator, his toe tapping the floor with annoyance. He had no doubt about where those two were headed, the suite adjacent to his, a one-bedroom that had been standing empty ever since old Mrs. Carpenter had keeled over mixing pancakes on a cold, bright Sunday morning six weeks before. The gossipy super had reported that he had found her with a wooden spoon clenched in her hand, her face freckled with dried batter.

Brewster suddenly found himself deeply regretting the old lady's demise.

He let himself into his apartment, stowed his dripping boots and coat, poured a Scotch, and wandered over to the balcony doors. Across the river, the lights of the Arts Tower burned wistfully in the midst of the falling snow, feeble sparks nestled in a bed of white ash.

He was doing his best not to let the young fellow's rudeness get to him, doing his best not to obsess on what sharp-tongued comebacks he might have unleashed. He recognized his tendency to brood and was trying to keep things in perspective by reminding himself how little a sullen neighbour really counted when weighed against all the advantages living in The Marlborough offered.

One, his apartment was within easy walking distance of campus, a big bonus since he didn't own a car. Two, its rents were high enough to keep out university students and their party-hearty habits, but not so pricey as to be beyond the means of someone who, after thirty years, was still stuck at the rank of assistant professor. Three, the majority of the residents were sedate retirees who lent the building an atmosphere that Brewster appreciated, gave it the air of a waiting room in a sleepy train station in some black and white movie of the 1940s, a place where people spoke in polite, hushed voices, where everyone minded his own business as they patiently awaited their moment of departure.

There had been a time when he had avoided acknowledging that, above all, it was the sleepy train station ambience that had decided him The Marlborough was the place to hang his hat. What he told people was that he believed that living downtown near restaurants, galleries, delis, and cinemas would keep a man in late middle age a little fresher, extend his shelf life. But the truth was he seldom stuck his nose into any of these places. Most of his evenings were lullingly the same. He had a few drinks, ate a microwave dinner off his coffee table, marked papers, fiddled with the next day's lectures, then watched sports on TV or listlessly skimmed a novel. The only books he cracked nowadays were ones he had read before. Knowing what was going to happen, how things were going to grope their way to their inevitable end, gave him a gratifying sense of omniscience.

But that night it proved difficult for Brewster to slide into his usual groove. No sooner had he finished dinner than a series of jarring hoots coming from the hallway prompted him to picture a crew of no-neck, slope-shouldered gym apes arriving on the scene to help their iron-pumping buddy set up house. A leaden-footed clumping to and from the elevator, a series of hollow booms, and loud clunks from next door put him further on edge. Next, the telltale heart of a boom box's bass began an aggressive thumping, a beat to get the movers' blood up, to whip them into even more energetic feats of furniture tossing.

It wasn't until midnight that the noise subsided and the last boisterous goodbyes echoed the length of the fourth floor. Peace descended and Brewster took himself off to bed.

He woke to a high-pitched yelping, the hysterical yap of a puppy entangled in its leash. His first bewildered, wandering thought was, *But The Marlborough is a pet-free building.* He flopped over on his side and peered into the radiant face of the alarm clock. Three a.m.

The frantic cries abruptly ended. Or maybe he had only dreamed them. But then a hoarse bellowing started next door. Brewster sprang out of bed and padded into the living room, where an enraged bawling set his heart anxiously chugging in his chest. The sort of noise that a bull on the killing floor of a slaughterhouse might make, it definitely qualified as a 9-1-1-category din.

Brewster flicked on the living room light, picked up the phone, and was on the point of dialing emergency when everything suddenly went silent in his neighbours' apartment. He pressed his ear to the wall. Faint sounds of movement could be detected over there, a series of sub-aquatic, muffled bumps of the kind that you heard swimming underwater in a pool.

He waited, minutes ticking by. Nothing. He unstuck his ear from the wall, perched himself on the edge of the sofa in uncertain vigilance. So what now? What's the drill, the etiquette of reporting a disturbance after the disturbance has ended? Officer, those two were carrying on like crazed beasts over there. Sure, the zoo's gone quiet now, but I think you ought to roust them out of bed, issue a stern warning that any more disturbances of that sort won't be tolerated.

How would that fly with the cops? Well, he was pretty sure it wouldn't, as you might say, *soar*. He would be written off as a pesky wing nut, a busybody prosecuting a feud with his neighbours.

Maybe he'd got it all wrong. Maybe what he'd heard was a housewarming fuck. The date of possession carnally celebrated. But no, that yipping had had a fearful, pleading note to it, had sounded just the way that girl's face had looked when her partner had been chewing her out for her lack of oomph with the mattress.

There was a time when Brewster would have shot over there to confront the situation head-on, but now he was a little more cautious, prudent. Besides, the current wisdom seemed to be that even though people had an obligation to report domestic disputes, they had no business trying to intervene in them. That was irresponsible and inflammatory, that was pouring gas on a conflagration. These days even the cops tiptoed onto the family battlefield with extreme caution, wary of getting blown off some wife-beater's doorstep. So after considerable mental hemming and hawing, Brewster finally slunk back to bed, only to pass the rest of the night wide awake, alert for sounds of trouble.

Locking his door the next morning, he spotted the young couple entering the elevator. They were holding hands like honeymooners, a sight that lightened Brewster's good-citizen's conscience, but his relief was almost instantly replaced by a surge of annoyance at the loss of a good night's sleep. "Hey," he called out, "hold that elevator!" But just two steps short of the elevator, the doors slid shut on the smirking face of Mr. Muscles. The fucker had deliberately punched the button on him. Brewster was convinced of it. What was the message there?

Waiting for the elevator to clank back up to the fourth floor, Brewster wondered if Eva, who during the year he'd been seeing her had increasingly claimed the right to direct the improvement of his character, behaviour, and demean-our, wasn't right when she claimed that his face was an open book, that whatever he was thinking was written all over it. One glance at his mug might have been enough to alert the button-puncher he was about to catch some blowback for creating all that racket the night before.

Down in the lobby he ran his eyes over the bank of mail-boxes. The super loved his label gun and had already replaced Mrs. Carpenter's name with the names of the new occupants: Dina and Melvyn Janacek. At least if there was any more uproar *chez* Janacek, he wouldn't have to risk challenging steroid-charged Melvyn face to face. He would be able to get his number from information, call him up, and read him the riot act. That is, if the Janaceks were listed. Maybe they didn't even have a landline. A lot of people their age didn't.

Bleary-eyed, he spent the morning plowing through first-year English essays. After several hours of scrawling exten-sive suggestions to his students on how to improve their essay-writing skills, tips that would be inevitably and blithely ignored, Brewster began to experience something akin to writer's cramp, twinges of discomfort that went scurrying up and down the tendons of his right hand. Soon he was feeling discomfort in his left hand too, as if some instrument like a darning hook was plucking at the nerves. This defied explanation since he was not using that hand at all; it simply lay quietly at rest on his desktop.

His first class was at eleven o'clock. As he lectured, the joints of his fingers grew noticeably more painful, began to involuntarily, spasmodically clench and unclench. The students had spotted this bizarre tic and were obviously fascinated by it in a way they had never been fascinated by anything he had had to say about American literature.

At noon, the weight of the lunch on his cafeteria tray made him wince when he lifted it. By early afternoon, a dull, unremitting background ache had lodged in the bones of his hand, broken by sudden bursts of acute, electric pain, as if a file was sawing on them. The intensity of these symptoms worried Brewster; he began to wonder if maybe some sort of esoteric virus wasn't running amok in his body. Deciding that he needed to see a doctor, he rang up the university hospital's clinic. Somebody had cancelled an appointment and there was an opening at three o'clock.

After manipulating and probing his hands, the doctor asked a few impatient questions, wrote out an order for X-rays and a prescription for Tylenol 3, and told him to book another appointment. The receptionist was able to squeeze him in on the upcoming Friday. Brewster had the X-rays taken and the prescription filled in the hospital pharmacy, went directly home, swallowed two Tylenols, stretched out on the sofa, and watched his hands do a spastic dance on his sternum.

He had always prided himself on his high pain threshold, but that threshold seemed to have shrunk to a pitiful nothing. The medication was giving him no relief; the agony kept looping in his hands like some gruesome CD track programmed to endlessly repeat itself.

Turning on the TV, Brewster muted the sound and stared blankly at the screen. The local news was just concluding when he heard the Janaceks out in the corridor shrilly arguing over which one of them had been responsible for paying a bill. Their door clapped shut with a gunshot-like crack.

He lay there urging himself to get a grip, get his ass off the sofa, and hustle up something to eat, but anything besides lying there and riding out the pain felt beyond him.

Next door the dispute was escalating, the volume rising.

"Please, Melvyn. Please, Dina, not tonight, kids," Brewster murmured. "Give it a rest."

Melvyn was telling Dina how he was going to fuck her up but good if she didn't shut her mouth. Dina was daring him to *Go ahead, big man. Do it, just do it.*

Melvyn did it. Something collided with the wall that separated the two apartments with enough impact to send Brewster's print of Scafell Pike, a souvenir of a walking tour he had taken in the Lake District thirty years ago, crashing to the floor.

He snatched up the phone, dialed information. They had no listing for any Janacek at that address. He called the building superintendent but got no answer, only his voicemail. All avenues of redress blocked, he staggered to his feet and roared, "What in the name of Christ is going on over there!"

And received Melvyn Janacek's prompt reply: "Mind your own business! Fuck off!"

He called 9-1-1. Ten minutes later the police arrived, a male corporal and a burly female constable. Brewster explained to the officers that he suspected Melvyn Janacek of bouncing his wife off walls. With each bit of incriminating evidence he provided, the policewoman fondled the nightstick slung in her belt a little more eagerly. *God bless you*, thought Brewster, *you're itching to use that billy club, aren't you? Here's hoping he tells you to fuck off too. Here's hoping one thing leads to another and that he finds himself on the receiving end of a righteous smackdown.*

The cops left to question the Janaceks. Twenty minutes later they were back. The corporal informed Brewster that Dina Janacek had assured them that everything was just fine; she couldn't guess what their neighbour had thought he had heard. Her husband hadn't touched her.

"Well, I'm no expert on the psychology of this, but isn't that typical of a victim of abuse? Isn't that what women often do? I mean, protect the abuser?"

"I saw no indications of physical harm. Constable Ramage here took Ms. Janacek aside and questioned her privately and she repeated her claim that she had not been subjected to violence."

"Okay, what about that?" Brewster was now appealing directly to Constable Ramage, hoping to get a more sympathetic hearing from a female ear. Stabbing his finger at poor Scafell Pike, forlorn on the floor and surrounded by splintered glass, he said, "If he didn't toss her into the wall, what knocked that down?"

Constable Ramage hooked her thumbs in her belt. Brewster suddenly realized that now she was annoyed with *him*. "I have no idea. But there's something else that came up when we were interviewing Mr. Janacek. He said somebody keyed his car. Said to ask you about that."

"Jesus," Brewster barked, astonished. "Why the hell would I key his car?"

"He said that you two had had a misunderstanding. Something to do with an incident concerning the elevator one morning."

"The business with the elevator wasn't *one morning*, it was *this* morning. Which means I had no time to key his car. How am I supposed to key his car after he drives off to work in it? Besides, I don't even know what his goddamn car looks like."

"Mr. Janacek said he didn't take his car to work today. Ms. Janacek dropped him off at his place of employment in her vehicle. His vehicle sat here in the underground parking all day." Constable Ramage paused. "You don't need to know what his car looks like. He says the parking stalls are identified by apartment number."

He saw he'd made a tactical mistake. Conceding that Janacek and he had had a problem over the elevator could be taken as an admission that they had a feud going. Brewster began to flex his fingers in time with the pain darting in them, wondered if it wasn't impairing his thinking. Then he caught the corporal staring down at his hands and he realized those convulsive movements might be mistaken as a psychotic acting out his desire to get his fingers wrapped around Melvyn's tree-trunk neck.

The corporal carefully cleared his throat. "We asked some of the other residents on this floor if they had heard a disturbance." He paused. "Nobody had."

"Well, what do you expect? Did you happen to notice how ancient they all are? Every one of them, deaf as a post."

"They had no problem hearing me," the corporal noted. "I believe I came in just fine."

"Okay, forget it," Brewster mumbled. "No skin off my ass. As far as I'm concerned, if this Ms. Janacek has a death wish, let her dream come true."

"Sir," said Constable Ramage, "don't get huffy with us. We're just doing our job. I advise you to lose the attitude."

Her partner had another bit of advice. "And learn to cut your neighbours some slack. The world would be a better place if we all just rolled with the punches now and then."

"Roll with the punches like that young woman next door rolls with them? Is that what you advise?" Brewster snapped.

"Here's what I advise," said Constable Ramage, thrusting her considerable bust aggressively forward. "I advise you to button it."

"Fine," he said. "It's buttoned. Firmly and forever. I don't give a shit if it turns into Baghdad central over there. Bombs can go off and you won't hear another peep out of me."

"You have a *good night*, sir," said the corporal. It wasn't goodbye; it was a warning.

"You too. Have a *great* night. It's been lovely getting to know you." *Good job, buddy*, thought Brewster. *Way to burn your bridges. The police will be hustling right over here next time there's a problem.*

After the cops had left, he sank down on the sofa and gazed at his aching hands in disgust. They were too slender, too delicately made for a man his size. Entirely out of proportion to the rest of him. Over six feet tall, more than two hundred pounds, and yet here he was with a concert pianist's hands dangling from the end of his arms. They weren't hands built to withstand much and he had repeatedly punished them in his youth. Now he appeared to be paying the price for that.

The hurt was burrowing deeper and deeper into the bones, flaring hotly in the marrow. Desperate, Brewster ran the kitchen sink full of cold water, emptied all the ice cube trays into it, and plunged his hands into the frigid bath. That numbed them momentarily, the briefest of reprieves, but slowly, bit by bit, the pounding resumed, wringing sweat from his forehead.

Now they were shrieking at him from the bottom of the sink.

He lifted his head. No, the shrieks were coming from the Janaceks' apartment. Hands dribbling water over the floor, Brewster crossed the living room, squared up in front of the wall, and stared at it. One of those blind rages he hadn't felt for forty years surged up in him with such overwhelming force that black specks streamed in his eyes.

Very deliberately he drew back his fist and struck the wall. Hit it again. Then again and again and again. Faster and faster, harder and harder, a frenzy of blows. Janacek was hollering something, but the rapid-fire thud of Brewster's fists obscured whatever Melvyn was saying. He slammed his knuckles into the wall until he could slam them no longer. The Marlborough was an older building and the lathe-and-plaster construction of the wall stood up to his assault admirably. Nothing more than a chip or dent here and there.

Chest heaving, he looked down at his hands, running slickly pink with mingled water and blood. There were smears of it all over the wall. Melvyn was yelling at the top of his lungs; Brewster could hear him now, threatening to report him to the superintendent.

He wasn't interested in anything Janacek had to say. A miracle had occurred. The torment in his hands had vanished. It appeared he had beaten it clean out of them.

Next morning the pain and the spasms were back with a vengeance. The rest of the week Brewster spent counting down the days until he could see the doctor again and make the case for a stronger painkiller. He was aware that the recent damage that he had done to his hands would put him in an awkward position if he didn't manage to keep them tucked away out of sight during his visit to the doctor's office. They were badly swollen and the skin over several of his knuckles was split. Charley Brewster, Munchausen case.

The only upside to his completely losing control of himself was that Melvyn appeared to have received the message loud and clear. For the last two days it had been all quiet on the Janacek front.

Friday afternoon, the doctor held up Brewster's X-rays to the light and pointed to five old fractures, three in the right hand and two in the left. "You didn't mention you had had injuries to your hands," he said, a hint of chiding disappointment in his voice.

Brewster had prepared himself for a cross-examination. "Frankly, I'd sort of forgotten about it. It was such a long time ago. And they've never given me a moment's trouble until now. Then out of nowhere, just like that my hands started to hurt like hell."

"What was it? Some sort of an industrial accident? Did you get them crushed in machinery or something?"

He had his answer ready. "No, a car wreck. Back in the days before compulsory seat belt use," he said with a wry smile. "I was a teenager, went into the windshield hands first. Trying to protect myself."

"Any other injuries?"

Now Brewster had to improvise, mentally skip from one clumsy foot to the other. "Not really. I may have sprained my shoulder. Got a few cuts. That was about it."

"You were lucky then," observed the doctor. "Very lucky." Fingering the X-ray film, he pursed his lips. "There's a bit of a mystery here. I can't see any evidence of osteo-arthritis, any inflammation around the old injury sites. Did your former physician ever treat you for pain?"

"I've never really had a family doctor," said Brewster, trying his best to look sheepish about his irresponsibility. "I've gone to walk-in clinics on a few occasions. Anyway, speaking of pain," he added quickly, maybe a bit too quickly, "that Tylenol 3 doesn't seem to be doing the job. I was wondering what else you might prescribe."

"I couldn't justify prescribing anything stronger at the moment," said the doctor. "Not until I know what was causing your pain. I could send you to a rheumatologist, I suppose," he said. It was clear he was thinking out loud. "It's possible I missed something, but I don't think so," he added, casting his eyes upward to the ceiling as if expecting confirmation of his infallibility from on high.

"I just want something to get me over the hump. Something temporary. The pain is interfering with my ability to work. I can't concentrate."

"As I say, I'm reluctant to change your prescription. The Tylenol 3 should be adequate."

"Well, it isn't," said Brewster. "I can testify to that."

"You know," the doctor replied, "sometimes – I don't know quite how to put this – people experience physical symptoms that are a proxy for other worries and anxieties. Now, don't get me wrong, I'm not saying this is true of you, I don't know you personally or your circumstances, but I wonder if you're not undergoing stress in other areas of your life: difficulties at work, relationship problems, anything of that kind?"

All of the above and more, thought Brewster. What he said was, "Nothing beyond the usual small day-to-day discontents."

"I could refer you to our pain management clinic. Cognitive behavioural therapy sometimes produces good results. The clinic takes a holistic approach. They even offer kundalini yoga classes."

"Thanks but no thanks," said Brewster rising abruptly from his chair. "I'm not a kundalini kind of guy. I guess I'll just bite the bullet and soldier on."

———

Because of Eva's busy academic life, Friday night was the one night a week that she would consent to spend at Brewster's apartment. Although they both taught at the university, they had only met a year ago, when the faculty club hosted a touring jazz trio. Eva arrived late and, finding all the tables occupied, she had approached Brewster because he was, as usual, flying solo. Looking charmingly flustered, she had asked if he had any objections to her joining him. He hadn't and so they had passed a few pleasant hours, chatting between sets, Eva talking enthusiastically and glowingly about the great work being done by The Centre for Interdisciplinary Studies, where she had recently been appointed director.

Brewster was more guarded about his own work, volunteering scarcely anything about his projects or professional interests. When the evening came to an end and he fished his cellphone out to call a taxi, Eva quickly offered to give him a ride home. She said it was a case of quid pro quo; after all, he had surrendered a seat at his table to a stranger. When they had pulled up outside The Marlborough in Eva's Mini Cooper, Brewster asked if she would care for a nightcap. She accepted the invitation, one thing led to another, and now twelve months later they found themselves peevishly staggering to the end of something that should never have started in the first place.

Eva and Brewster both knew it was over, but hadn't yet taken steps to initiate the mercy killing. They were too different for it ever to have worked. Eva was forty-seven, fifteen years younger than Brewster, and she was confidently, optimistically convinced that she was just hitting her stride as an academic. Like Gatsby, Brewster was staring longingly at the green light beckoning at the end of the dock, which was, in his case, imminent retirement from a career that had proved to be less than stellar.

Eva prided herself on being cutting-edge. Recently, her students, affronted by the way women were sexualized in advertising, had made a video that portrayed males as sexual objects. Brewster had checked this video out, a morality play that involved overweight, hairy young men in cocksock underwear licking their lips, batting their eyelashes, and provocatively plumping their ripe-for-a-training-bra pectorals for the camera. Eva assured him that this had gone viral on YouTube.

Brewster knew he was definitely not cutting-edge; he wasn't even sure that he qualified for blunted-edge designation. The opinion of his colleagues and certainly his students was that he belonged in some professorial Jurassic Park. The comments he received on Rate My Professor were dismissive. *Definately do not take a class from this guy. Only his opinion matters. I interpreted a poem and he trashed all my ideas because of punctuation. Maybe he should get a life.*

Of course, he had made the mistake of taking a peek at Eva's online evaluations, which were uniformly laudatory and enthusiastic. *The best prof ever, I learned so much I can't even say!!!!* Or *Everyday in her class is fun. If she gave a thousand classes I would take everyone. I would major in Professor Eva. She rocks my world!!!!*

Right now, Eva was at work on her laptop preparing a class. For the past few hours she had been playing and replaying two performances of Henry Purcell's "Cold Song" that she had tracked down on YouTube, one by Klaus Nomi, the other by Sting. They would be the departure point for a class discussion on representations of masculinities. The Nomi version showed Klaus arrayed in what looked to be transparent rain gear designed for the consumer determined to get wet and stay wet. From the shoulders of the cape-like garment a fan-shaped contraption rose to a towering height, a backdrop for Klaus's chalk-white face, his lips gleaming with a shockingly intense scarlet lipstick. Nomi's singing was an unearthly, piercing castrato-warble.

In contrast, a deeper-voiced, bearded Sting sang lounging on a stool in a tweedy sports coat, a long scarf of the kind worn by British football fans draped casually around his neck. The chorus of attractive women who accompanied Sting periodically panted a refrain that was either meant to illustrate the effect of frigid weather on the respiratory system or to demonstrate what effect such close proximity to Sting had on the female libido.

Hearing Klaus and Sting trill the same song for the seventh or eighth time, coupled with the incessant pounding in his hands, was slowly driving Brewster out of his mind, but he knew better than to ask Eva to desist or even to turn down the volume, especially when she was so completely absorbed in frantically scribbling notes about the meaning these enactments of masculinities indicated.

Eva no longer needed to ponder or make notes on the sort of masculinity Charley Brewster enacted. It hadn't taken her long to conclude that he was a poster boy for the bad hegemonic variety since he was white, heterosexual, and a member of a privileged profession. Once that was settled, her homophobia and misogyny sensors had gone on full alert.

They beeped a lot in his company. No matter how he combed his conscience, Brewster couldn't help feeling her sensors were prone to giving a lot of false readings.

Three weeks ago, in the middle of one of their increasingly frequent and rancorous spats, Eva had said, "You know what, Charley? Whenever any of your assumptions are questioned, you start talking like a thug, acting like a thug."

"What's that supposed to mean?"

"Every second word is a curse word. It's the way people with no ideas try to intimidate others."

"My father was a working man. It's the way he talked when something pissed him off. The gosling walks in the gander's footsteps. I got imprinted. If it walks like a goose, talks like a goose, I guess it's a goose. Don't blame me, I'm a social construct."

"I suppose *social construct* is a dig at my work. Don't belittle me because I'm passionate about what I do. Unlike you, your department's sleepwalker."

"Not passionate about what I do? I'll have you know I ferret out comma splices with great fervour."

Coming in the door tonight Eva had taken one look at him and said, "So what's wrong in Brewster's Horizonless World now?"

"I feel like shit. I've got these terrible pains in my hands."

"Pains from what?"

"I don't know. Maybe arthritis. The doctor wasn't sure."

"Did you take something?"

"I've been taking something all day. The something doesn't do squat."

"I guess that means you didn't make dinner."

"I thought maybe we could order some Chinese."

"No thanks. I'll pass on the monosodium glutamate. But please yourself. I've got work to do."

Sitting slumped on the sofa, Brewster was struck by the appropriateness of the music, how well Purcell's "Cold Song" suited the frosty atmosphere reigning in his apartment. Of course, the ice jam could be broken, the relationship ended with a single stroke. All he needed to do was to tell Eva what was the matter with his hands. *Remember when you accused me of being an intellectual thug? Add physical thug to the indictment. There was a time when I bashed a lot of people. Broke my hands three times doing it. Who knows how many times I'd have broken them if I wasn't convicted of assault causing bodily harm and sentenced to two years less a day.* Leave it at that. Make no mention of how getting skipped two grades in elementary school had caught up with the prepubescent, scrawny, brainy runt in high school where he provided easy pickings for the vultures, became everybody's favourite punching bag. No need to mention boys like Ronnie Peel, who one day at the town's swimming pool had hooked a finger in his bathing trunks and dropped a lighted cigarette butt down the front of them, forcing him to haul down his bathing suit in a panic, right in front of everybody because the cigarette stub was scorching his cock. And Ronnie's girlfriend had sent all her female posse into a snorting giggling fit when she said, "Well, that little-bitty butt is the biggest thing that's ever been in Charley Brewster's pants."

But he had had a sudden welcome growth spurt in the last few months of grade ten, suddenly sprouted tall and weedy. Over the summer holidays he ate everything in sight, tried to pack on as many pounds as he could, bought a weight set, and lifted three times a day. When he went back to school in September he was still skinny but sinewy with new muscle. Learn by doing, his father had always said, and that's what he did. He fought back, at first without much success, but with a lot of berserk determination. It scared people, even those with hard-boy reputations, that he didn't respect the unwritten code of combat. Everybody understood that if you were taking a bad licking, you gave up. But Charley Brewster didn't give up; he kept coming. And it was also understood that if you were giving somebody else a licking, you stopped at some point, or made a show of being reluctantly dragged off your opponent by bystanders. That was how things played out. But Brewster *really* had to be dragged off his victims; usually three or four guys had a monumental struggle to do it. The day he revenged himself on Ronnie Peel, Peel had ended up crouched on the ground, cowering, his arms wrapped around his head, whimpering. That's the first time Brewster broke a hand, pounding Peel's skull because he couldn't get to something more vulnerable, his eyes, nose, or mouth.

Things only got worse after that. Now, so many years later, Brewster realized how much he had resented his parents for having bowed to the school's advice to accelerate him through the elementary grades. Back then it had seemed to him that he had been grinding along with a nose in a book, playing catch-up his entire short life. He felt that something had been stolen from him, that his humiliations had cheated him out of some share of childhood innocence and freedom.

Somehow he had identified his anger with freedom, blowing off steam by drinking and brawling, by hanging out with a tough crowd that looked for trouble at a dance hall at a nearby lake. One night as he and his buddies were leaning up against a Dodge Charger in the Danceland parking lot, passing around a bottle of rye, the owner of the car, a guy easily ten years older than any of them, came storming over to shoo them off his precious vehicle. Brewster hadn't moved quickly enough for the man and he took a kick in the ass to hurry him along. That night he fractured both hands on the face of the owner of the Charger and finished high school wearing casts signed by all his new best friends.

After graduation, he got a job on a railway extra-gang. His marks had plummeted during his last two years of high school and he had barely earned his diploma. The railway crew worked six days a week, Sundays off. One of those Sunday afternoons Brewster hitchhiked into a nearby city, took in a matinee, and then dropped into a pizza house to get something to eat before heading back to camp. In the booth across from him, two couples whom he took to be university students were talking loudly and self-importantly about their classes, blah blah Psych 213, blah blah Poly Sci 333, blah blah Socio 211. They were pointedly ignoring the waitress who had come to take their order, an exhausted-looking middle-aged woman with sagging, laddered nylon stockings and a pencil tucked behind her ear. Finally she interrupted them by saying, "Have youse guys decided yet?"

One of the young men answered, "Plurally, us guys have decided on all-dressed." His friends broke up, laughed even harder when a bewildered look skimmed over her face. When she had gone, the jokester took a pen out of his shirt pocket, slipped it behind his ear, and said, "I keep my writing implement close to my deep thoughts." More hilarity.

The waitress reminded Brewster of his wan Aunt June, who had served tables for forty years of her life. "Hey," he said in a loud voice, "so in Psych 213, what did they teach you?"

"What's that?" the comedian said.

"They teach you how to be the biggest asshole you can be? You must have got full fucking marks in that course."

"What's your problem?"

"I don't have a problem. You do."

"And what's that?"

"Me," said Brewster. "I'm your problem."

"I don't think so," said the funny man's buddy. "Maybe you're the one who has the problem and doesn't know it. For your information, Johnny here is on the varsity wrestling team."

Brewster smiled, got up, and started to walk towards the door, leaving his pizza half eaten on the table. Johnny said, "I guess somebody suddenly got second thoughts."

"You're right," he said. "On second thought, I'm terrified of tangling with you. Of getting dry-humped by a rubber-mat-fucking *varsity wrestler*."

The two young men followed him out of the restaurant. When he shattered Johnny's orbital socket that was the third and last time Brewster fractured a hand. Bad luck for him, it turned out he had done damage to the wrong guy, the son of a prominent doctor, an honours student, a young man of promise who would suffer visual impairment in his right eye for the rest of his life. During the trial, Brewster refused to cooperate with the court-appointed lawyer in his defence because he sensed that he had come to a place where if somebody didn't stop him, he wouldn't be able to stop himself. The judge could barely contain his outrage, took great pains to point out how lenient he was in giving him two years less a day, a sentence that would put him in a provincial facility rather than the federal pen. Where he so richly deserved to be incarcerated.

Through a pilot program at the jail, Brewster took several university-level classes, kept his nose cleaner than clean, and earned time off for good behaviour. On his parents' regular visits his mother encouraged him to pursue his studies, his father simply sat beside her, silent and withdrawn.

Brewster's parole officer urged him to continue his education, which he did. In fact, now it seemed to him that he hadn't known when to stop going to school any more than he had known when to stop smacking people. On the curriculum vitae he submitted for his first teaching job he put down a sixteen-month backpacking tour of Europe to cover his prison stay. What he was about to confess to Eva he had never divulged to anyone before.

The doorbell rang before he got around to that. Eva said, "There's your Chinese food. Let's hope an MSG high cheers you up."

"No," he said, hauling himself off the sofa. "I never placed an order."

He opened the door to tiny Dina Janacek, her face rubbery and swollen from weeping. A little gold stud in one nostril was surrounded with a rosy aureole of inflammation. "I'm sorry," she said in a rush. "The superintendent isn't in. And I don't have my apartment key so I can't get into our place. Melvyn got mad at me and took off with my purse in the car. So I don't have my car keys, my apartment keys, my phone, my money. Nothing. I don't know what to do."

"Do you want to use my phone? Call a friend?"

"What is it?" Eva called out.

"One of my neighbours. She's in some sort of trouble."

Dina Janacek started to sob, noisy heaving gasps. Eva hurried to the door and took charge.

Dina Janacek's story wasn't very concise or coherent. Melvyn and she had gone to a club. One of his friends had asked her to dance; Melvyn had got pissed when she danced with this other guy because Melvyn was such a no-good, crazy, jealous bastard. Even though he never danced with her, she wasn't supposed to have any fun. They had had an argument and he had pulled her hair, twisted it like. When she had told him she had had enough of his shit and was done with him, he jumped in the car and drove off with her purse. She had no friends, didn't know anybody in town because she had just moved here from Calgary to be with Melvyn. They had met on an Internet dating site, where he had seemed like an extremely sweet and good person, and before she knew it she had married him in a beautiful wedding back home. But Melvyn was definitely not the extremely sweet and good person she had thought he was and he was getting meaner day by day. She was terrified of what he might do to her now that she had told him she was tail lights. So she had thought her best bet to keep safe was to go to the neighbour who had called the cops on Melvyn because he seemed to be a really responsible and caring person.

Eva was in her element, magnificently decisive. "Okay, here's what we do. I'll drive you to the women's shelter. If there isn't a bed available there you can stay with me tonight.

In the morning, we'll get hold of the superintendent and arrange for the police to escort you back to your apartment so you can collect your belongings in safety. And if I were you, I'd file an assault charge against your husband. It'll make the police more cooperative if they know you mean business."

"Well," said Dina, "Melvyn really only pulled my hair."

"That's assault. He has no business laying hands on you in anger. Don't forget it." Eva gave Dina a moment to weigh that. "So what do you think? Does that sound like a plan?"

"Yes," said Dina, but she looked doubtful.

Eva grabbed her laptop and began to hustle Dina towards the door. "Obviously, I won't be back tonight," she said to Brewster.

"No," was all Brewster said.

When Dina and Eva had departed, he fell back down on the sofa. An eventful evening in some ways, but still nothing resolved between Eva and him.

For the next two hours, he channel-surfed and drank Scotch. Around midnight the phone rang. It was Eva.

"Well," she said, "there was a bed available at the women's shelter. I've got her settled."

"That's good."

"But there's something I think you should know."

"Yes?"

"I had to use the restroom. And when I was gone, Dina grabbed the chance to use the shelter's phone to call her husband. He didn't pick up so she left him a message."

"And?"

"The message she left asked him to drop her purse off at your place. She told him she'd get it from you in the morning."

"Ouch. Double ouch."

"Okay, so she showed a lack of judgment."

"A spectacular fucking lack of judgment. Superlatives cannot do it justice. So now I might have to deal with the irate husband."

"She's young and very upset. Put yourself in her shoes."

"Better hers than mine."

There was a long pause. "If you're so worried, you can spend the night with me at my condo."

Brewster pondered this amazing concession. It was the first time Eva had ever invited him over to stay. She had often told him that she thought of her living space as personal, sacrosanct, her "room of one's own." "No," he said. "It's fine."

"You sure?"

"Absolutely."

"If anything happens, call the police. That's what they're there for."

"Yes," said Brewster, "to protect and serve. Right."

"I'm exhausted. I've got to get some rest," Eva said. She was back to normal, abrupt and tart.

"Okay," he said, but Eva was already gone.

Anticipating the likelihood of a late-night visitor, Brewster saw no point in going to bed. He stretched out on the sofa and stared at his throbbing hands. The hours ticked by, one o'clock, two. Some time around three he fell into a restless doze from which an ominous hammering woke him. When he went to the door, an incensed Melvyn, shaved head gleaming malignantly under the hallway tube lighting, fired questions at him. "Where's Dina? Where's my fucking wife?"

Melvyn was a lot shorter than Brewster had realized, stocky and wide, as if he were the offspring of two cigarette machines that had somehow mated and reproduced themselves. Drawing himself up to stand as tall and imposing as possible, Brewster said, "I have no idea where your wife is."

Melvyn was bobbing his bald head from side to side, trying to peer around Brewster into the apartment. "Dina!" he shouted. "If you're in there, you better get your ass out here right now!"

"She's not here. I'll say it again. *She's not here.*"

"People can say a lot of things," Melvyn said, squinting up at him menacingly. "People who stick their noses in other people's business should maybe think twice before they get themselves a new asshole ripped."

"I have no interest in sticking my nose in your business. The only interest I have is that you take what you call your business off my doorstep. And do it right now."

"What did you say to Dina? What ideas did you put in that bitch's head?"

"None." He produced an ominous pause before intoning, "Mr. Janacek, we are often the architects of our own misfortunes."

"And what the fuck is that supposed to mean?"

"It means go away."

Suddenly Melvyn's face crumpled, his eyes gleamed with tears. "This isn't over, you fucking old shit," he choked out.

"By no means. That slut is going to get what's coming to her, and get it fast."

"Maybe not. Because I don't believe she's available at the moment," Brewster said.

"Yeah, well," said Melvyn, "there's more than one way to tune her in. Believe it." His composure had returned, or rather his viciousness. He swung around and stalked off down the hallway. Brewster stood in the doorway watching him go. To duck back into his apartment would seem like a cowardly retreat.

Janacek didn't stop at his apartment but carried on to the elevator. His parting shot, shouted to Brewster was, "There's more than one way to fuck somebody up! Like in their head! Leave them something to think about!" The elevator's doors opened, Janacek stepped in, and down it creaked.

So what did that mean? Brewster asked himself. *What's he up to?*

Then he remembered how Janacek had accused him of vandalizing his car. Had Melvyn projected one of his own hobbies onto him? Did the man's mind run to themes? Was he about to do a little bodywork on Dina's vehicle? *Remember what you told him*, Brewster reminded himself. *I have no interest in sticking my nose in your business. Words to live by. Still.*

He took the stairwell to the underground garage, slippers slapping on the concrete steps. *There's footwear designed to strike terror in the heart of Melvyn, overawe him with your avuncular, cozy Je ne sais quoi,* he thought ruefully. Easing open the door to the underground parking, he stepped into the exhaust-fumes-saturated belly of The Marlborough.

The buzzing, snapping fluorescent lighting cast a sickly, yellowish-green pall over everything.

He spotted Melvyn hunkered down beside a Toyota Camry, industriously scratching away at the driver-side door panel, completely unaware he was being observed. Brewster took his cellphone out of his pocket and aimed it at Janacek. "Say cheese," he said loudly, and as a startled Melvyn jerked around, he snapped his picture.

Janacek clambered to his feet. "Give me that fucking phone."

Brewster studied the photo to make sure it had turned out. It had. "You take a lovely picture, Melvyn," he said and popped the cell back in his pocket.

Melvyn was swelling up, bloating with wrath; even at a distance he could see the tendons bulging on his neck. "Just who the fuck do you think you are?" Janacek roared at him.

"Me? I guess I'm a rusty time bomb. Either that or an old clock running down. Tick tock, tick tock, tick tock," Brewster said, gently swinging his head from side to side.

Melvyn gaped at him. "You are one crazy cocksucker," he said.

"That too."

"You better fucking give me that phone and give it to me *now* so I can lose that picture."

"I think not," said Brewster. "This is the first time in a long time that I can't guess how things are going turn out. It's an interesting feeling."

"You want me to come over there and take it? Is that what you're asking for?"

"Maybe." He and Janacek stared at each other as if they

found themselves stranded in a stupefying dream. Then Melvyn began to lumber forward. *Okay*, thought Brewster, *at least one thing will get settled tonight. Eva will be appalled. Finished with me.* He could hear her saying, "Are you insane? Do you think that's the way to deal with problems? Physical violence? At your age?"

His hands were balled tightly at his sides, every drop of hurt squeezed out of them. They were wrung clean of pain.

His eyes fell on an oil slick on the garage floor. Iridescent under the fluorescent lighting, it shimmered a palette of queasy, vividly unnatural colours, a petroleum-based aurora borealis that was a perfect reflection of the fear coiling in his gut. It was the most beautiful thing Brewster had seen in a long time. He couldn't take his eyes off it even as he listened to the footsteps drawing nearer and nearer.

Inexplicably, he felt his hands relax, slowly rise to cover his face, preparing himself for Janacek to strike. And that was the moment he understood how it was going to turn out, realized how happy it was going to make him to cower in just the way Ronnie Peel, the boy who had once shamed and humiliated him, who had used his swimwear as an ashtray, had cowered and whimpered as Charley Brewster rained blows down on him.

And then Melvyn Janacek's fist painted Brewster's brain with the same weird colours of the northern lights that he had seen trembling on the concrete floor, that grey, unyielding, punishing surface that now rushed up to meet him as he dropped gratefully to it on his knees.

Koenig & Company

I WAS FIFTEEN THE SUMMER my mother had her third nervous breakdown in four years. My father, John Dowd, was working on a crew that constructed bridges all over the province – rinky-dink affairs thrown across muddy creeks, piddling streams, and trivial rivers. His job kept him away from home for two-week stretches, so he wasn't there to apply the brakes the day Mother got it into her veering, hectic head to phone just about everybody in Groveland and list the sins, scandals, and missteps they had been involved in. I tried to stop her, but as my father used to say, "She had the fight on." She couldn't be stopped, not by me. A lot of people got their feelings hurt in the wild, wide swath she cut. Mother reminded them of what they believed had been long forgotten, dragged their dirty little secrets kicking and screaming into the light of day, said what had gone discreetly unsaid for years. By the time I got in touch with Father, the damage had been done.

When he walked in the door, still in his work-soiled clothes, face grey and flabby with exhaustion, and said to her, "Marjorie, what you need is a good long rest," Mother bared her teeth in a scathing smile and replied, "Well, Johnny, if you say it's time for another tune-up, I guess it's time for another tune-up."

What with all the urgent business at hand – calling in the family doctor to sign the papers and make the phone call to the mental hospital in Weyburn to have Mother admitted, stuffing a few clothes and toiletries into a suitcase, and hastily bundling her into the truck for the two-hundred-and-fifty-mile road race to deliver her for treatment – Father didn't have a lot of time to consider what he was going to do with me. On the three previous occasions that Mother had been hospitalized, he had packed me off to my grandparents in Manitoba, but several episodes of bad health had left them very frail and unwilling to take responsibility for a teenaged boy.

The long drive home must have given Father time to sort through the problem. When he got back I was informed that, although I was old enough to stay alone in the house now, he was afraid that a boy who had never so much as boiled him-self an egg could not be trusted to eat properly when left to his own devices. I would need at least one good, substantial meal a day, preferably a hot supper. A working man, my father put great faith in meat, potatoes, and gravy.

So he contacted Groveland's only landlady, Mrs. Burke, a sour-faced woman who provided room and board for three or four bachelors, to see if she would agree to feed his boy. Unfortunately, Mrs. Burke had been one of those on the receiving end of Mother's truth-telling spree, been told that none of her four children had even a passing likeness to Mr. Burke, but that they certainly bore a strong resemblance to several of her former tenants. Mrs. Burke made it clear that she wanted nothing whatsoever to do with any child of my mother's, although she did acidly mention that Delphine Koenig was looking for boarders. *If he was desperate enough, he just might try her.* Father was desperate enough, and soon he and Delphine had settled on terms. Before he headed back to work, Father gave me a cheque for Mrs. Koenig and ten measly bucks that he grandly referred to as my "emergency fund," laid an awkwardly consoling hand on my shoulder, and murmured, "Just hang in there. Your mother will come home right as rain. Everything's going to be fine."

Watching him drive away in his clapped-out half-ton, I knew in my bones everything wasn't going to be fine. Far fucking from it. If Mother's good neighbour policy towards her fellow citizens hadn't already made me a leper, my clueless father had sealed the deal. But being able to convince him of that was as likely as his shitbox truck rocketing him into the next galaxy. My father always insisted on walking the sunny side of the street, refused to face facts. If I had pointed out what was obvious, that associating in any way whatsoever with the Koenigs was social suicide, Father would have behaved just as he did whenever I dropped a hint that maybe things were going amiss with Mother. He would have said, *Wherever do you get these funny ideas, Billy?*

He would have deserved it if I had screamed at him, *Don't tell me you have no idea why the Koenig twins are nicknamed Stinky and Smelly! And do you really think Jennifer Koenig is called Jenny Likes to Play the Squeezebox because she plays the accordion and wails "They Call the Wind Mariah" off-key at talent shows at the Legion Hall, you fucking dope? Not likely.*

Because the Koenigs, right down to the youngest, grimiest, scruffiest little shoplifter and vandal in training, were the town's number-one pariahs. Everyone knew the Koenig twins were nothing but mean, lying, conniving, cowardly snot-gobblers. Like a pair of foraging jackals, they slunk about Groveland High sniffing for anything they could five-finger discount, and if they happened to get caught helping themselves to somebody else's property – a transistor radio, money left in an unsecured locker – they cringed and crybabied for mercy before getting a taste of teenager justice, a punch in the chops or a swift boot up their skinny asses. Their home-barbered white-wall haircuts, old coot's fire-engine red braces, broad-checked polyester pants, and brown oxfords contributed to making them even greater objects of disdain. It was only human nature to assume that Stinky and Smelly, in fact all the Koenig brood, had been put on earth for one reason and one reason only, to make the rest of us feel better about ourselves.

Except maybe for Sabrina Koenig, who was two grades ahead of me. She was cut some slack and given some sympathy because a bout with polio had left her with a withered leg and a painful-looking limp. Sabrina was also rumoured to be smart, which was regarded as one of nature's mysteries since the rest of the Koenig crew were a universally dim-wattage crew.

To tell the truth, I wasn't going to win any popularity contests myself, but at least I had avoided attracting persecution by keeping a low profile. Association with the Koenigs would end that, so it's little wonder that for the first three days after Father headed north I stayed well away from them. I had had enough of bad situations. I needed a recess from having to deal with my mother's recent bizarre, sometimes downright scary behaviour. I could finally get some sleep, could get a break from listening to the bathtub taps gushing on and off all night, from hearing her yell at the overworked hot water tank when it ran cold. Mother imagined the hot water heater to be part of a vast malignant conspiracy to deny her any solace and comfort in her black despair. Nor would I have to swear that I would forever be on call to push the wheelchair she believed was in her future, to pledge that I would never, ever desert her. Every time Mother lost her grip on reality, she became convinced she had multiple sclerosis and was going to end up just like her best friend, Janet Kasper, had. That she would be a woman abandoned by her husband and left to moulder away in a care home.

School was out, nothing had any claims on my time, and I was able to take it easy, do exactly as I pleased. In his rush to get Mother on her way to the hospital, Father had overlooked to pack a carton of her cigarettes. That and the forty-ouncer of Canadian Club, which Father kept stashed in the linen closet in reserve for *special occasions*, was all I needed to celebrate in style. If this wasn't a special occasion, I didn't know what was. I figured both parents owed me.

For the next several nights I sat up watching television into the early morning, chain-smoking cigarettes, guzzling rye and Coke, stroking and petting my self-pity. I staggered off to bed drunk, slept until noon, idled away afternoons reading James Bond boner-popping novels until five o'clock rolled around and I headed for The Hot Spot, a café haunted by hairy-eared retirees, a place no self-respecting teenager would be caught dead in. It seemed to me the safest location to gobble a couple of hamburgers and chug a milkshake without being noticed. But even there attention proved inescapable; the coffee-row crowd either stared at me with disapproval or, worse, flinty-eyed sympathy. I was *That Dowd boy. The one with the crazy mother who called up my Myrtle and gave her what for.*

Soon enough I had done the math and realized that café dining would shortly run dry the "emergency fund" Father had left me. And I knew he was going to be seriously pissed to learn I hadn't honoured his arrangement with Mrs. Koenig. The more I thought about it, the more I came to see that eating with the Koenigs would not only free up cash for ciga-rettes and racy paperbacks, but also might even be marginally less painful than getting gawked at by the regulars of The Hot Spot. If I was very careful and had some luck, I might even be able to slip in and out of the Koenigs' house without being spotted by some kid all too eager to spread the news that Billy Dowd was consorting with untouchables.

The Thursday after Father returned to work, I took a deep breath and set off to keep my supper date with the Koenigs. I didn't give much thought to the fact that I had already missed three meals without giving notice to the cook. But I assumed some vague lie about having been "under the weather" and Father's cheque would give me a pass on that score.

I got there by a circuitous route, by skulking down alleys. It was a scorching, breathless day, the leaves of the poplars hanging on their branches like tiny washed-out rags. The sun-stunned neighbourhood dogs didn't even have the energy to bark as I went by. The Koenigs' property was unfenced; a jungle of weeds and volunteer Manchurian elms fondled my legs as I waded through them to the back step. I rapped on the screen door and Delphine Koenig suddenly loomed before me, a massive, wheezing middle-aged woman who let loose a laboured sigh and said, "Well, he's here," and cracked open the door just enough for me to scoot through and trail her swaying hams into the kitchen. Mumbling my lame alibi, I passed her the cheque. She tucked it away in a drawer without a word of thanks. I saw no evidence of supper, caught not even the faintest whiff of home cooking. Towering pyramids of dirty dishes were haphazardly stacked on the counter and the table was covered in pots encrusted with the cysts and tumours of ancient leftovers. The whole house smelled like a laundry hamper stuffed with clammy, dirty undergarments.

"It'll be a while," Mrs. Koenig said. "Go in the living room and make yourself comfy."

I acted as per instructions. A quartet of the younger family members were sitting on the floor of the living room about a foot from the TV. Their towheads swivelled as one, levelled a glazed, eight-eyed stare on me, then swept back to the screen in perfect synchronization. Neither Stinky nor Smelly were anywhere to be seen and neither was Jenny Likes to Play the Squeezebox. That was a relief. As for making myself comfy, all the furniture in the room was buried under piles of soiled clothing, the source of the smell that had penetrated as far as the kitchen. Pushing laundry to one side of the sofa, I sat down and joined the Koenig youngsters in their mute, glassy-eyed worship of the television.

A few minutes later, Sabrina Koenig hobbled into the room, a book clutched in her hand. As soon as she saw me, alarm flickered on her lips, alarm that she quickly tried to hide by ducking down to shovel a heap of clothes out of an armchair and onto the floor. She settled down and began to read, a look of utter absorption pasted on her face.

Being given the silent treatment by the smaller Koenig kids was one thing, but receiving the cold shoulder from a girl I passed almost every day in the school hallways was a bit much. I had never spoken a word to Sabrina Koenig before, but as a paying guest I felt I was owed a smidgen of courtesy. I fidgeted irritably on the sofa, trying to catch her eye. "Hey," I finally said, my voice as sharp as I could make it, "school's out if you haven't heard."

Sabrina slowly lowered her book. "Thanks for the news flash." The book went back up, but now I had a clearer view of her. Sabrina Koenig was no beauty, but her abundant strawberry-blond hair was surprisingly clean and shiny-looking. Small pale freckles lazily drifted down her cheeks, and her teeth were of a normal shape and size, unlike Stinky and Smelly's, which were huge and rat-like and looked capable of chewing clean through heavy-duty electrical wiring.

I squinted at the title of the book. It had something to do with Abraham Lincoln. "What I want to know," I said, "is why you are reading a boring book like that when it's summer vacation?"

This time she didn't look up. "I'm reading it so I don't stay a moron like everybody else in this town," was her answer.

This was something that might have come straight out of my mother's mouth, and recognizing that, I felt an arrow to the heart. It shocked me to hear somebody who wasn't certifiably nuts, like Mother was, slag the old home town. In my experience, if you couldn't say something nice about Groveland, you had better not fucking say anything at all if you knew what was good for you.

The aroma of superheated grease began to challenge the dirty-underpants odour. Cooking appeared to be underway. From the kitchen, Mrs. Koenig hollered, "Bert, go get your lazy so and so of a father up!"

None of the television watchers moved a muscle. The mystic communion with the screen continued.

"Bert, *now*! And I mean it!"

Little Bert grudgingly hoisted himself to his feet and moved out of the living room, casting regretful glances over his shoulder at the TV. Sounds of coughing, grumbling, and cursing came from somewhere off in the back of the house. Bert reappeared, sullenly sank back down on the floor, and lapsed into his former semi-comatose state.

In a bit, Mr. Koenig appeared in the doorway and shot me a vaguely hostile stare, a bald guy nearly as fat as his wife. Stinky and Smelly had clearly got their fashion sense from their father, although his windowpane polyester pants were even more crotch-baggy and severely distressed looking than his sons'. Yawning hugely, he gave a conspicuous scratch to his balls before plodding off to the kitchen, where a low-voiced, heated discussion started up between husband and wife. I presumed it had something to do with me, the stranger in his house.

I wanted to bolt. Minutes crawled by as I struggled to come up with a plausible reason to offer Mrs. Koenig for having to excuse myself. I had taken too long. Suddenly she hollered, "Come and get it!"

The TV-drugged kids sprang to life, scrambled up from the linoleum, and stampeded for the kitchen. Sabrina, however, didn't move; her nose remained buried in her book.

I got up and dragged my feet after the others, pausing beside Sabrina's chair to ask, "So what gives? I mean, aren't you going to eat?"

"I guess *not*," she snapped. "I make my own suppers."

"What do you mean you make your own suppers?"

"Just what I said. I buy my own food, make my own suppers."

"You *buy* your own food?"

"Yeah, with the money I make from babysitting. So I don't have to eat the crap they do. Any more stupid questions?"

This was both astounding and intriguing. But the best I could produce as a follow-up inquiry was, "So who do you babysit for?"

"What's it to you? You need somebody to babysit you with Daddy gone?"

The message was clear. *Get lost.* As I left the room, Sabrina flung after me, "Oh yeah and if you're *wondering*, I do my own laundry too. None of this is mine."

The family was clustered around the stove, where two cast-iron fry pans were sending up smoke signals. Mrs. Koenig was loading slabs of fried baloney and charred potatoes, as black and hard-looking as the skillets she was scraping them out of, onto the plates her brood were eagerly thrusting at her.

As soon as the food hit their dishes all the Koenigs, Mr. Koenig included, scattered for the living room at top speed. I was the last to be served, and once I had been doled out my share of charcoal and grease, the enormous Delphine immediately fell to it, forking up her supper straight from the pans.

The kids were back on the floor in front of the TV, bent double over their plates, filling their faces. Mr. Koenig had expropriated the place on the sofa I had earlier cleared. I hovered in the doorway, wondering where I was going to plant myself.

All at once, Sabrina erupted, boosted herself out of the armchair with an exasperated, "Oh for chrissakes, *here*!" and lurched out of the room. None of her family paid her explosive exit the least attention.

We all ate in silence. When I had made a polite and minimal dent in my food, I excused myself, Mr. Koenig grunted, and I carried my plate back out to the kitchen. Mrs. Koenig was nowhere to be seen; her hunger appeased, she had disappeared.

The prospect of another dining experience at the Koenigs' kept me on edge all the next afternoon. Around four o'clock I heard a knock at the door. This was surprising, my family never had visitors. I parted the curtains, looked out, and saw Sabrina Koenig on the step, visible to anyone who might be passing by, a brown paper bag clutched to her chest. I rushed to the door, wrenched it open, and barked, "*What!*" straight into her face.

She didn't flinch; she grinned. "Hello, Billy Dowd, today's your lucky day," she said.

"Get in here." The instant she crossed the threshold, I slammed the door, panicked somebody might see me and her together.

"Where's the kitchen?"

I pointed. I didn't know what else to do. She set off in her halting, wincing stride. After a few moments of bewildered indecision, I followed, found her unpacking canned goods, fresh vegetables, and a package of meat.

I asked her what she thought she was doing.

"Making a trial run."

"Trial run of what?"

Sabrina toyed with the groceries, shifting them about on the countertop as if she were trying to arrange them in a pattern that matched the logic of her thoughts. "I thought I'd cook for you tonight. You like your supper, then we can work out a deal. Maybe."

"What kind of deal?"

"Ma cashed your daddy's cheque today. Fifty bucks. Which is way, way too much money. She took him to the cleaners. What is he, stupid?"

"Yeah. Pretty much."

"I pinched the money out of her dresser, used some of it to buy these groceries."

My mind was revving frantically, but it wasn't going anywhere, was still stuck in neutral. "And what kind of shit are you in when she finds out you stole it?"

Sabrina dismissed that with a wave of the hand. "I've got a clean record as far as Ma's concerned. She won't suspect me. It'll get pinned on the twins. They deserve some payback; the creeps have been helping themselves to my babysitting money for years."

"I still don't get it."

"Okay, so here's what I was thinking," she said, adopting the bright, chirpy tone in which things get explained to very small children. "What if I make you your suppers over here? I'm a decent cook, better than Ma. We can both eat pretty well on fifty bucks, and there'll be a little cash left over for me. You know, call it wages. Plus, I get some peace and quiet for a few hours of the day. It's a madhouse over there." Sabrina faltered for a second at the comparison, probably recalling where my mother happened to be, then resolutely kept going. "And your old man has already paid for it all so he isn't out anything. Just Ma. And she was screwing him anyway."

I considered this. "Yeah, but aren't they going to miss you at home? Wonder where you are?"

"It is to laugh. Everybody comes and goes just as they like at our house. Maybe you noticed that last night? No twins, no Jenny. Nobody gets missed over there."

I had one more objection, a big one. "But someone's going to see you. I mean, going in and out of here."

Sabrina lifted her gaze to the backyard, surrounded by an eight-foot-high lilac hedge Mother never let Father trim because she said she didn't want *anyone spying on her*. A Great Wall of China to hold the snoopy barbarians at bay.

Sabrina gave me a knowing smile. "I watched you leave last night, Billy Dowd. Weaving and ducking down the alley like some cat burglar making his getaway. Just so nobody would see you'd been at our place. You think I can't do likewise? Those lilacs will give me all the cover I'll need. Don't worry, your precious reputation is safe with me."

I flushed and blurted, "You're wrong. I wasn't weaving and ducking because – "

She cut me off. "You think I was born yesterday? Hey, I'd do the same thing in your shoes. No problem."

And that was how Sabrina Koenig tangled her life up with mine. That first night she made me a tasty beef stew, a supper Father would have approved of, something suitable for a growing boy. She did the dishes, left the kitchen spotless, then went out the back door, across the yard, and out the gate like a cat burglar. Full marks there.

What surprised me was how quickly I began to look forward to Sabrina's visits. And she began to make them earlier and earlier in the day, sometimes she showed up by one o'clock. For several weeks that summer the local TV station showed matinees that alternated Abbot and Costello movies one day, Dick Powell films the next, and we fell into the habit of watching them together. Abbott and Costello killed Sabrina, their antics made her yelp with laughter, squirm on the sofa like a little kid. The other side of her loved the Dick Powell musicals, the song-and-dance routines, the moony, dreamy, fairy-tale sundaes the old-time studio soda jerks served up.

Sabrina was a lot less chippy, a lot less belligerent off her home turf. By turns she could be goofy and serious, playful and big-sisterly stern. When it came to playing big sister, it wasn't long before she started to ask me *What are you going to do with your life?* I was fifteen, my ambitions didn't extend much further than getting my driver's licence in a year and maybe, if I could summon up the guts, inviting Jenny Likes to Play the Squeezebox to go for a ride with me in my father's half-ton.

Sabrina put the big career question to me just after Dick Powell had finished singing and tripping his way through *42nd Street*. As usual, although it was only three o'clock in the afternoon, all the curtains were drawn for security reasons, to make sure that nobody out on the street spotted who was hanging out at the Dowd residence. The room was full of heat and very dim, but in a little sparse light filtering through the drapes I could see earnestness gleam on Sabrina's face.

"I don't know," I said, resorting to flippancy. "Be a fireman. Be a cowboy. Indian chief."

"I'm serious," she said. "Don't act like a bonehead. You've got to think ahead, Billy. You've got to plan. At least start treading water now or you'll sink."

"That's pretty extreme."

"No, it isn't. You think you can just float along and one day you'll just float to the top of the world? No way, Billy, you'll end up sinking like a stone. You've got to set your sights on something."

"Okay, so tell me, what have *you* set your sights on?"

"Getting out of this town. Away from *them*."

"That's not much. Boy, what a huge ambition."

"One thing at a time, Billy. One thing at a time. I'm saving money for the day I can wave goodbye to Groveland. That's the first step."

Setting your sights on something wasn't the only thing Sabrina harassed me about. She was big on me improving myself. In fact, sometimes I got to feeling I was no different than a project for a science fair. Here's this bucket of gritty sand and look what you can do with it, blast it with ambition, blow the glowing, heated mass into a very nice glass vase you can stick a flower in. Beautiful.

One afternoon she picked up the paperback copy of *Goldfinger* I was reading, started turning the pages, stopping here and there to skim a passage. When she finally put it down, she was in full big-sister mode. "Why do you waste your time reading this crap?"

I was annoyed. "Because it's entertaining. I like it. That's good enough for me."

"No, it isn't good enough for you. That's my point. It's idiotic. James Bond boinking women with names like Pussy Galore. How old is the guy who wrote it? Ten?"

In my defence, I dredged up something I had heard or read somewhere. "President Kennedy loved James Bond. If it was good enough for the leader of the Free World, it's good enough for me."

"Yeah, but he had already got to where he was going. He was entitled to do a little slumming. You, on the other hand, seem pretty much to be spinning your wheels."

That was the problem with Sabrina; she had an answer for everything.

But mostly things went smoothly between us. At her prodding, I even started to read some of her favourite books that she borrowed for me from the library because, needless to say, I had never bothered to get a card. Sometimes we talked about them. An air of quiet domesticity established itself. Sabrina even began to do a little housecleaning, occasional vacuuming, giving the bathroom a swab, putting things back in place that I left lying around.

During our supper conversations I relaxed, did start to open up, did say a few things that, when voiced out loud, took on an air of plausibility. I even volunteered that maybe going into business would be the thing for me. "I like math; my marks are all right in geometry and algebra," I said modestly. "What's business but numbers and figures?"

Sabrina pursed her lips. "I don't know. I think business is more than that. More than numbers and figures," she said. "It seems to me you've got to be a tough nut in business, be ready to use people without thinking about it too much. You need to be selfish."

I didn't say I suspected I was just that, selfish. The thought made me uncomfortable so I switched the spotlight to her. "And you? You never say anything about what you want to do once you beat it out of Groveland. What are you going to be good at?"

"I could be good at a lot of things." Sabrina could say something like that without sounding conceited. On her lips it was a statement of fact, hardly different from declaring, *I weigh 123 pounds*. "I don't know. I like to draw and paint."

I was incredulous. "You mean you want to paint pictures for a living?"

"I said I didn't know. Just something different. Not run of the mill," she said, suddenly irritable.

We left it at that.

———

I had become so attached to Sabrina that when I realized my father would soon have a few days off from work, I felt disappointed that I wouldn't be able to see or talk to her for a while. Sometimes I wonder if the failure of my two marriages didn't have something to do with the fact that dinner conversations with either of my wives never went as easily or freely as they did with Sabrina Koenig. Maybe I was spoiled early.

The Saturday morning I expected Father to show up in Groveland he phoned me from Weyburn; he had driven there overnight, straight from the job site. Father said he had bad news; the doctors thought it would be at least another month before Mother would be ready to be released. He added, "I won't be home until late Sunday. Don't let me forget to give you a cheque for your board."

I had prepared for this. Once or twice I had heard Father talk about "working off the books," the advantages of keeping the government out of the loop, from knowing everything there was to know about your income.

"Mrs. Koenig prefers cash," I said. "On account of taxes."

The line went briefly silent. "It's a little tight," he said. "I don't have all that much walking-around money on me. I can probably give you thirty bucks tomorrow and mail the rest of it to you later when I get to a bank. You think she'll go for that?"

"I can talk her into it."

"Good boy," he said. "I like to see you showing initiative."

Next day, Father arrived, coughed up the dough for Mrs. Koenig, gave me another cheapskate instalment on the "emergency fund," and made a quick inspection of the house.

"You're keeping this place pretty clean and tidy," he said. "It looks like you're growing up. Learning to be responsible."

Having given me that sticky-fingered pat on the head, he roared off.

Sabrina and I resumed our routine. Thinking about it now, I suppose we were like two little kids shutting the real world out, imagining ourselves living in an alternate universe where life was like it was in Abbott and Costello and Dick Powell movies, everything hilarious or inconsequentially light-hearted, a place where no one was saddled with a horrible, shameful family or a crazy, angry, sad mother.

Everything was fine, better than fine as far as I was concerned, until one afternoon Sabrina went quiet while we were watching *Buck Privates*. I sent her a curious *What's up?* glance, but when she didn't take the bait I chose to let her be and concentrated on Abbott and Costello's loony capers. After a few minutes, she whispered huskily, "Hey, I want to ask you something. We're friends, right?"

Her tone alerted me that this *something* was not going to be either inconsequentially light-hearted or hilarious.

"Sure we're friends."

"You know me. Always making plans, using the old forebrain?"

"Right."

"I graduate this year. I'm going to be valedictorian."

"So how do you know you're going to be valedictorian? Isn't it months before they choose somebody?"

"My marks will be the best." One eyebrow tilted wryly. "Then there's the pity factor. My leg."

I dodged saying anything about her leg. I didn't like to be reminded of it. "Okay, so you're going to be valedictorian. Congratulations."

"The valedictorian and their date lead the graduates into the school gym after the ceremony. For the dance. It's tradition."

I played stupid, just stared at her.

"So who am I supposed to march in with? Nobody's going to ask me to be their date. I'll be humiliated. It'll be the most humiliating thing in the long string of humiliations I've had to live with."

"You don't need to be valedictorian. Nobody can make you be valedictorian. You can turn it down."

"I don't want to turn it down! Goddamn it, what's the matter with you? I want to be valedictorian! And I need a date!" she shouted at me.

There was no mistaking where she was headed. "I can't dance," I said.

"So you can't dance. You think I've been spending my last three years of high school dancing up a storm? With *this*?" She struck her stick-like leg with a white-knuckled fist, hard.

I had to look away. It says a lot about me that I knew it was wrong to feel a certain way about something but that I could still keep feeling it. The sight of that leg, the jerky way she had to flop it forward with every step, her lunging, plunging gait always gave me the heebie-jeebies, made me want to look away.

"Billy," she said, "the first dance is always a slow dance. All we have to do is hold on to each other and shuffle."

"Let me think about it," I said. "There's no hurry. It's a long way off."

"We could practise," she said. "You could get comfortable with the idea, with doing it." She waited for my answer. When it didn't come she fired a strident "*Billy?*" at me.

I was sweating clean through my pants, thinking of me and Sabrina Koenig trooping the graduates into the gym, everybody looking at us, whispering, smirking.

"I said I'll see." I was stubbornly holding my eyes off her. I heard Sabrina struggle up from the sofa, the floppy, slapping sound the sandal on her bad leg made as she crossed the floor. The television clicked off and the radio sitting on top of it snapped on. She started fiddling with the dial, setting off strangled bursts of rock and pop until she hit the only station in the area, maybe the only station in the Western world, that still devoted itself twenty-four hours to geezer music. The opening strains of Tony Bennett's "I Left My Heart in San Francisco" wafted into the room.

I raised my eyes. Sabrina was standing there in the middle of the floor, waiting for me. *All right*, I said to myself. *Suck it up.* I got out of my chair and walked towards her. As I did, she slowly raised her arms to shoulder height, held them straight out before her like zombies do when they go for a stroll. I ducked under them; she laid her forearms shyly on the tops of my shoulders, I placed my hands on her hips, and we began to gingerly shift our feet about as if we were edging our way through a field of land mines. And all the while Tony was listing all his unsatisfactory experiences in

Paris and Rome and going on about how he had been terribly alone and forgotten in Manhattan.

We started to sway. Sabrina said, "See, Billy? It's not so bad."

But it was bad. I'd had nothing to do with girls, and just my hands resting on Sabrina's rounded hips, the scent of shampoo in her strawberry-blond hair mingled with some other slightly musky, ripe, and inviting smell, a smell I believed to be a distinctly female, *sexual* smell, had been enough to produce a trouser-bolt, the head of which had poked its way out of my Jockeys and was nuzzling the fabric of my jeans in a way that it was liking *far too much*. And maybe it was only my imagination, but it seemed to me that Sabrina was imperceptibly inching closer to me as Tony mournfully crooned his discontent with various world-class metropolises.

"I Left My Heart in San Francisco" is a longish song, but that afternoon it seemed to last an eternity. Finally, the tune ended; Sabrina and I drew apart, and you could have cut the awkwardness with a knife. Her eyes wandered about the room, lighting on everything but me. "That graduation dance'll be over before you know it. Relax. It'll be okay."

When she said that, Sabrina reminded me a lot of my father. I said, "We'll see."

Over the next few weeks what I was going to do about the dance caused a strain between us. Every once in a while Sabrina would make mention of something that touched upon graduation, tell me how she had money put aside for "a nice dress," talk about the likelihood of her collecting a number of bursaries and scholarships that would enable her to go away to school. I played deaf, dumb, and blind no matter what she said. She got nothing from me.

I was angry that Sabrina couldn't see that my escorting her to graduation was not only ridiculous, it was just plain wrong. A girl could get away with dating a boy as much as four years older than she was, but a girl never dated a younger boy. No teenaged female would be caught dead doing such a thing. Other girls would have branded her a *cradle-robber*, thought she was ridiculous. Our grade eight health teacher had drummed into us that girls matured far faster than boys, not only physically but above all socially and psychologically. The implication of this was that God and Groveland had a plan for the sexes, and that plan didn't include me taking Sabrina, two years older than I was, to graduation.

If we did sashay into that gym, arm in arm, she would never be able to live it down and neither would I. Of course, since graduation was in May, that meant Sabrina would only have to suffer a month of amused condescension before she waved goodbye to Groveland forever, while I would face two more years of psychic mauling. And I wasn't risking that, for anybody.

Ten days before school resumed, when the stalemate was still unbroken, I got a call from Sabrina. She said that she wasn't going to be able to make me supper that day. No explanation. But she went on to say there was a movie on TV that night that she wanted to see. Could she watch it at my place even though it started at twelve-thirty? Her hoodlum brothers always nixed anything she was interested in viewing, just on principle.

A little miffed that it didn't seem worth her while to tell me why I was being denied my usual home-cooked meal, I played hard to get, asked what was this movie? Maybe I wouldn't be interested in it.

Sabrina said it was *Lord of the Flies*. Mr. Younger, her English teacher, had lent her a copy to read last year and she wanted to see what the movie was like. The title meant nothing to me. After some dramatic hemming and hawing, I told her, Okay, it would be all right if she came over.

Being jilted put me in a bad mood and for the first time in ages I resorted to my father's bottle of Canadian Club. Shortly before midnight I was enjoying a cocktail when I heard Sabrina's timid tap at the back door.

"Come in!"

I heard some furtive movements in the kitchen, then she stepped into the living room, revealed her surprise. It was the first time I had ever seen Sabrina Koenig wearing makeup. Her sandy eyelashes were blackened with mascara, there was blue eyeshadow smeared on her eyelids, and pale pink lipstick smeared on her lips.

"It's my Julie Christie look," she said with a tight, uneasy laugh.

"Sure. If you say so."

"What's that you're drinking?"

"Rye and Coke."

"I'll have one too."

I got up and got her a glass. The forty-ouncer was still half full so I didn't begrudge her a drink, although I was a bit taken aback she had asked for one. It wasn't Sabrina's style, but then neither was the makeup, which made her a trifle weird and scary-looking. She poured for herself a shot of alarming quantity.

Knocking back her booze, she launched into the story of how she had pillaged her sister Jennifer's makeup kit, and when she told it, she laughed too much, and in a forced way that sounded nothing like the joyful yelps that Lou Costello's pratfalls provoked. It was a relief when the movie started.

For the next hour and a half, Sabrina didn't say a word, sat silent and still, a stillness only broken when her hand went stealing out for the bottle, tipped it to slop more whiskey into her glass. About the third time she went to that well, I said to her, "Hey, you better go easy on that. You're slamming it down pretty fast." But she just ignored me, eyes glued to the screen.

The British naval frigate collected the child-survivors from the island, the movie ended. "So," I said, "what did you think of that?"

She was still riveted on the TV, which was signalling the conclusion of the day's programming, a flag bravely fluttering in a brisk breeze and the national anthem playing. "I was thinking," she said in a whisper, "those kids in the movie, they're like a big family, but then the monsters in the family take control and fuck everything up for everybody else."

I had never heard her say *fuck* before, and the two or three times it had slipped out of me, she had said, "Language, mister. Language."

"Tell me about it," I said. "Every family's got monsters."

For the first time in a couple of hours she looked at me, eyes slightly unfocused, her shockingly blue eyelids hanging at half-mast. "You talking about your mother?"

I said nothing. My feelings about my mother were difficult to reconcile and even more difficult to explain. I loved her, but right now I didn't *miss* her. I was on vacation from Mother and doing my best not to think about her, about where she was, or how she was doing, because I knew that when she came home, the pattern would start all over again. The three of us, Father, Mother, and I, would have to face the same old devil, our very own leering Lord of the Flies who would be preparing another ambush for us weeks, months, maybe as much as a year down the road. Mother's mental torments would be revisited.

"I *like* your mother," said Sabrina. "I wish she was my mother." Her speech was slurred and the pitch of her sentences wavered.

"Oh Christ," I said, "you don't know what you're talking about. You don't even know my mother."

But Sabrina showed a drunk's persistence in getting a point across. "I know your mother. She's a good person. You know what she said to me one day?"

"How the hell would I know what she said to you one day?"

"I was walking down the street and she stopped me. She said, 'You're Sabrina Koenig, aren't you?' And I said I was. And she said, 'I remember you when you were just a little thing, pulling yourself along on crutches with a brace on your leg, and look at you now, how well you walk, how well you're doing. You just keep going, girl. Don't you ever let anything or anyone hold you back.'"

I saw that she was crying, and I took this to mean I was heartless, didn't appreciate my own mother. "Okay, I'm a horrible person. My mother is so much nicer, so much kinder than I am. But you don't have to live with her or live with the consequences when she goes around pissing people off."

"I don't think you're a horrible person," Sabrina said. "You think I would have come over here and helped you out if I didn't think you were a good person? Just like your mother?"

More blackmail. What I wanted to say was, *So, okay, have my mother march into that fucking gym with you. Arm in arm. Just let me off the hook, why don't you?* Instead, I said, "You know what? I think you better lay off the booze. It's making you stupid."

She gave the coffee table on which the bottle sat a petulant shove, skidding it out of reach. "Okay, deal. No more booze. But you've got to tell me why you won't take me to graduation."

"You're drunk. Nobody can talk to a drunk. Let's leave this for some other time."

"No, I need to know right now. What's it going to take?"

"What's what going to take?"

"For you to agree to be my escort. What do you want in exchange? Because I need an escort. Everything will be worthless unless I have an escort."

"Graduation's a long way off. Just lay off. I said I'd think about it."

"What's it going to take, Billy?"

"This is getting old," I said. "It's getting ancient."

Sabrina heaved herself off the sofa and tottered out of the living room as fast as her bum leg could carry her. I was expecting to hear the back door slam, but it didn't. I assumed then that the rye had caught up with her and that she had headed for the bathroom to chuck her cookies. But I heard no retching, no gagging, nothing.

I sat listening for a long time but the house remained strangely, unnervingly quiet. Maybe she had passed out in the can. I went to investigate. She wasn't in the bathroom. That left the bedrooms as possible crash sites; she might have flaked out in one of them. I headed for my parents' bedroom, worried that she might puke on their mattress, that would take some fancy explaining. No Sabrina.

I turned down the hallway to my bedroom. It was completely dark. I hesitated in the doorway. "Sabrina, are you in there?"

"Yes." Her voice was faint and shaky.

"Look, you aren't going to be sick, are you? You haven't barfed in my bed, have you? Don't barf in my bed, okay?"

"No."

"I'm going to turn on the light. Just to make sure you're okay."

"No, don't! Don't turn on the light!" she cried, but by then it was too late.

I caught a glimpse of small, white, pink-nippled breasts, a cirrus cloud of pubic hair. A hand flew to cup her privates, an arm flung itself across her breasts, crushing, flattening them. The only mildly sexual territory left exposed was her thighs, which were equally plump, but the calf below one of them was shrunken and wasted, a streak of scar from an operation ran from her knee to her ankle.

The light snapping on seemed to have locked us in place, me hanging in the doorway, Sabrina lying frozen on the bed, her eyes squeezed tightly shut. "Okay, here's the deal," she said in a lifeless voice. "You can do anything you want. Just don't stick it in me."

Those words unglued my feet from the floor. I backed away slowly, then fled to the living room. I sat there, trying to drive the images of those breasts, that wispy, vulnerable V of hair at the juncture of her thighs out of my brain. Once, she called out, "Billy?" but I didn't move, didn't answer her.

A few minutes later I heard Sabrina moving down the hallway, the back door opening and closing.

Sabrina never came back to my house. But at the end of August my mother did. She was just beginning to swim up out of the depths of a profound depression; hour after hour she sat and smoked, toying with and twisting a book of matches. The night before school started, the phone rang some time around midnight. Mother was in bed so I picked up. It was Sabrina. In a quick, urgent burst she said, "You've got to promise me one thing. That you won't say anything to anybody at school about what happened. You do that, I'll murder you. Or kill myself. I'm not kidding, Dowd. I mean it."

"I won't."

"Swear it, Billy."

Mother wailed, "Who is it? Who's on the phone? Is it your father?"

"No, it isn't! Forget it! It's a friend of mine! Go back to sleep!"

I lowered my voice. "I swear it. Okay? Now are you satisfied?"

"I thought maybe that was the thing you wanted. I thought it might make a difference to you, how you treated me. My mistake." The line went dead.

School got underway. The first time I met Sabrina Koenig in the hallway, I acknowledged her with a nervous bob of the head, but it was as if I didn't exist, she sailed by me without a glance. Several times over the next few months I considered phoning her, but I always found an excuse not to. Also, I was preoccupied with my mother. The series of shock treatments she had had in hospital had wiped out everything that had occurred over the past year, and I spent hours coaching her, rebuilding her memory. My father was still away, working on the bridge-building crew; I was responsible for Mother.

Months went by and then it felt as if it was too late to call Sabrina or to try to make another approach to her at school. She was a proud girl and I was a scared boy. Like so often happens, our friendship died a slow death because nobody intervened in time to heal it.

May rolled around and with it graduation. Sabrina wasn't the class valedictorian. Maybe she had misjudged her chances in the first place, or maybe she was offered it and turned the honour down. By July she was gone from Groveland. Where she went I never heard.

It wasn't until last year, forty years after Sabrina's departure into the wild blue yonder, that that blank got filled in. I was on a business trip to Toronto, lying on my hotel room bed turning over the pages of *The Globe and Mail*. Normally, I never read anything but the financial and political news, but this time something on the front page of the Arts section caught my eye. My Sabrina, the *celebrated* Sabrina Koenig, was having a show at a gallery that, I gathered from the reporter's knowing tone, was favoured by collectors, was very high-end. The opening was that night.

Apparently this was *big news*, apparently Sabrina was *the real thing*. The article began with a sketch of her career. Two years as a drama major at the University of Saskatchewan, then a transfer to the Ontario College of Art. After that she moved to England, where she fell in with the Art & Language group and began to make a name for herself as a conceptual artist. But as the clipping from the *Globe* that I still carry in my wallet puts it, "Koenig's gifts and interests were too varied, too protean to confine themselves to any one theory, practice, or mode of art production." She designed soundscapes that were played in abandoned grain terminals, "aural universes by turns haunting, whimsical, mordant, terrifying; gorgeous constellations of sound ranging from the lush to the stark." Her performance pieces were said to "bear comparison with those of Marina Abramovic." When the Berlin

Wall collapsed, Sabrina moved to the former East Germany, where she became the de facto leader of a group of guerrilla artists who occupied a defunct factory, turning it into an atelier of 16-millimetre film production. The group made a specialty of short films that were outrageous, slapstick parodies of the fashion and art worlds. They presented bizarre fashion shows in which they paraded their hand-sewn costumes before the camera to the accompaniment of breathless commentary, staged elaborate fake art openings where the work of various "art stars" was caricatured. Before long this pack of pranksters became known as Koenig & Company. An Abbott and Costello influence, maybe?

How all this acclaim and notoriety had escaped my notice only highlights the possibility that just like when Sabrina and I had isolated ourselves in a world of our own making, I had withdrawn into my own closet, a cubbyhole so thoroughly wallpapered from ceiling to floor with financial statements and prospectuses, divorce papers and settlements that not even a crack or a pinhole admitted light from the outside world.

It seemed the only thing that the girl who had once liked to draw had not done was paint pictures.

The photograph of Sabrina in the paper filled me with restlessness. I got off the bed and went to the window, peered down at the rush hour traffic streaming down York Street, the clamour of horns and motors gusting up to me. I thought of her photograph in the newspaper, a photograph of a woman whose face was remarkably smooth and serenely confident, her cat-eye glasses and lacquer-black beehive hairdo ironically situating her in a past more distant than the days of our adolescence, suggesting that she had escaped the limits of both time and geography. She struck me as alien and ageless.

I wanted to see her again. But that wasn't going to happen. Her picture indicated the distance that had opened up between us, a distance that could never, probably should never be attempted to be bridged. If I went to the opening at the gallery I knew that I would most likely never get a chance to speak to her and if I did, what would I be except another insignificant voice in the chorus? I had had Sabrina to myself for a summer and I preferred the recollection of that to discovering what a tiny memory I was for her. Sabrina had been right all those years ago. To be a success in business, you need a selfish streak. I admit it, I'm a selfish man. I decided I'd rather miss a chance to see her than have my time with Sabrina rationed, than to have to share her.

But I give people their due. I am happy, glad to know that Sabrina took my poor mother's advice, that she never let anything or anybody hold her back, that she is a going concern, a *thriving* concern, and that Koenig & Company is out there in the big bad world, flaunting the family name, sticking it squarely in everybody's eye, mine included.

1957 *Chevy Bel Air*

IN SEPTEMBER 1968, Reinie Ottenbreit returned to high school for his senior year. A teenager with frank blue eyes, a scallop of toffee-coloured hair artfully arranged on his forehead, and a pair of downy sideburns bracketing a ruddy, docile face, he passed down corridors waxed and buffed to so high a gloss that they swam with a flickering, watery light. As the fluorescent tubes hummed industriously overhead, rude boys who had been amusing themselves at his expense for as long as he could remember called out, "How's it hanging, Ottenbreit?" or "How's tricks?" Reinie's sheepish response was always the same. "Can't complain." This was an answer patterned on his father's style. Karl Ottenbreit had raised his two sons to take life in stride but not to tempt *fate*.

The truth was, Reinie felt pretty much on top of the world. In ten months he would be done forever with school. His feet were set on the straightest of paths. Soon he would be farming with his father. Reinie's older brother, Edgar, was in his third year of commerce up at the university in Saskatoon – he had turned his back on a career in agriculture – so Reinie had no rival for the role as his dad's right-hand man.

But what pleased him most in that year of unalloyed promise was that he finally had himself a car, and not just any car but a beautifully preserved 1957 Chevy Bel Air. Ever since he had turned twelve, Reinie had worked for his father, serious, adult jobs involving the operation of tractors and combines worth a small fortune. For this, his father paid him a small wage because Karl Ottenbreit believed children ought to learn responsibility and the value of a dollar. Year after year, Reinie's nest egg had grown and, along with it, his manly satisfaction whenever he opened his bank book.

Still, obstacles had to be overcome before his parents relented and gave him permission to buy the car. Reinie's mother, Mabel, had been the most strenuous in her opposition. Endless family discussions circled about Reinie's headstrong desire to own an automobile, but in the end he carried the day – with a caveat attached. The Chevy was *not* to be driven to school. Mabel pointed out what folly it would be to waste money on gas, tires, and oil when the Ottenbreits already paid taxes for the school bus that stopped at their gate every morning for the express purpose of transporting Reinie to Waddell High. Her son yielded to the logic of this argument, even though he dimly suspected his mother had other reasons for her objections.

What really worried Mabel Ottenbreit was that indulging Reinie might give rise to talk he was spoiled, even show-offy. A pillar of the Augustana Lutheran Church, Missouri Synod, she knew that a teenaged Martin Luther would never have been caught dead driving pointlessly here and there all over the countryside just to pass the time, as so many young people did, singing along to the horrible sort of songs you got on the car radio nowadays. Yet after much troubled reflection and soul-searching, she reluctantly waived her opposition, reminding herself that Reinie had always been a good boy. Nevertheless, second thoughts still clung to her. That is why she insisted Reinie take the bus. To keep at bay temptation, the toils, the allurements of sloth and soft living.

Three days of school had passed. Reinie was marking them off on a calendar with the singlemindedness of a jailbird counting down his sentence. That morning he sat at the back of the pumpkin-coloured school bus, as always, alone. Usually he passed the hour-long ride to and from school plowing through reading assignments in useless, bewildering subjects such as English and social studies. But so early in the year teachers were holding off assigning homework. Still, Reinie's parents had always drummed into him that an hour wasted was an hour forever lost, so with rapt concentration he was studying a Department of Agriculture bulletin. The Ottenbreits prided themselves on being progressive, up-to-date farmers. Karl Ottenbreit often observed to Reinie that the times were changing. There was nothing Bob Dylanesque in this remark, the nonsense disrupting the rest of the world only impinged on Karl when certain offensive programs appeared on the television, and when they did, he promptly switched the set off. It was the business of farming he alluded to. "I figure you got to be flexible. No sitting back on your heels waiting on the pitch. Better to take a swing and miss than just let the ball blow by." To this, Reinie would nod sagely, seconding the motion.

The bus stuttered to a halt, bucking Reinie's eyes up from the pamphlet and his happy absorption in modern tillage practices. He squinted out at a lovely fall day. Harvest had been early that year; most crops were safely stowed away in granaries. Wheat stubble bristled on nearby fields, a blond brush cut sweeping over a knobby cranium. A deep, unfathomable blue sky was wiped with a few smears of high, thin cirrus cloud.

The bus doors flapped open, turning Reinie's gaze to a girl making her way up the aisle, a girl he had never seen before. Barely five feet tall, she wore the briefest of black corduroy mini-dresses, black tights, a pink sweater. The last bit of wave had been ironed out of long chestnut hair that fell from a precise part to frame a heart-shaped face.

When he realized the strange girl was going to park herself beside him, panic bobbed in Reinie's throat. Without a word, she plopped down next to him. The impact of her bottom on the seat jolted a gust of perfume from her body. It swirled up Reinie's nostrils, jerking his head back to the window. While the bus rumbled away, gathering speed, he desperately counted cows. Then he counted grain bins.

She had to come from a rural one-room elementary school. Each year such schools passed on a handful of students to Waddell High. Fresh faces that brought an element of the unknown, of new possibilities to a student body so sunk in tedium that it felt eternal. Reinie stole a furtive glance at her. Seen up close, she was even more exotic than viewed at a distance. There was an odd feline cast to her eyes, a provoking lift to their corners. She wore an awful lot of green eyeshadow and pale, frosted lipstick. A solemn consideration arose in Reinie's mind. His mother wouldn't approve of this much face paint on a grown woman, let alone on a girl who couldn't be more than fourteen.

She was pointedly ignoring him, looking directly ahead, her face ingeniously managing to register both profound boredom and profound disgruntlement. Turning over the sticky tumblers of his mind, a burglar coaxing a combination from a safe, Reinie struggled to marshal words, string them together in arresting phrases, even interesting sentences. He was labouring to be *smooth*. The problem was he hadn't had much practice at it. Reinie Ottenbreit had always had better things to do than chat up girls.

"I haven't seen you before," he said at last.

The girl swung her head towards him, eyes slits of contempt, triangular chin tilted imperiously. He saw that the colour of her irises exactly matched the eyeshadow. Both were a dark, haunted green.

Blindly, he attempted to grope through the fog of her withering silence. "I mean, today is Thursday. School started Monday. I would've thought I'd have seen you before now. Riding the bus, I mean." His voice ebbed away.

The pale, frosted lips wrinkled, baring tiny, hostile teeth. "I don't want to go to your puking school. They made me." Her eyes slid off his face. Reinie was left to ponder who *they* were. Her parents? The school board?

Somehow, he mustered a smidgen of unexpended courage. "My name's Reinhardt . . . I mean Reinie – Reinie Ottenbreit.

I'm in grade twelve." A taint of self-importance his father would not have approved of surfaced in the last statement. He waited, hoping she would volunteer similarly pertinent information. None was forthcoming. On the heels of a deep, shuddering breath he made another attempt. "What's your name?"

"Darcy."

"Isn't that a boy's name?"

"Who're you to talk, *Reinhardt*."

For the next thirty minutes, they sat without speaking, she showing so obvious a pleasure in Reinie's discomfort that even he was capable of detecting it. At last, the bus drew into the parking lot of Waddell High and began to noisily disembark passengers. Following Darcy into school, Reinie noticed her tights had a long run down the back of one leg. In that rent, a tender, vulnerable offering of white flesh was exposed. Pressing the flimsy Department of Agriculture brochure to his crotch, Reinie did his best to cover up the boner this enticing sight had popped. He might as well have tried to hide a chair leg with a piece of Kleenex.

For the remainder of the day, he shuffled from class to class in a dreamy, drifting daze. His condition only worsened that night. Cradling his transistor to his ear on the pillow, he listened as distant radio stations from America's heartland softly whispered to him their lovesick lamentations, their hymns to heartbreak. Often as not, the songs erupted in violent explosions of static, or simply crumbled away into a tuneless, echoing void.

———

The next day, Darcy selected a new seat partner for the bus ride. Jealously, Reinie studied her demeanour and was relieved to note she treated Marvin Gaitskell with the same scorn as she had him. During lunch hour, he wandered the hallways, praying for a chance encounter. Minutes before classes resumed, he spotted her in the gym. Darcy was leaning up against a wall watching a bunch of girls play volleyball. Hesitantly, gingerly, Reinie sidled up to her and rigidly flattened his body to the wall. She seemed in an even more ferocious mood than she had the day before. Her arms were folded under her small, haughty breasts, thrusting them upward in an aggressive fashion.

Peering down at the part in her hair Reinie hoarsely declared, "I got a car. A 57 Chevy Bel Air. Maybe you want to go for a drive tomorrow."

"That's stupid," she said. Reinie felt the floor plummet beneath his feet. Then, mercifully, he heard her add, "That there is the all-time stupidest game I ever saw. And look at them *sweat*. Like pigs."

"So, you want to go?"

"I don't care."

He didn't know what she was saying. Interpretation was not his forte. It was why he hated poetry so much. The bell loosed a shrill, strident summons. Darcy heaved herself off the wall, tossing two words over her shoulder as she made for the exit. "What time?"

"Two o'clock. Two o'clock, okay?" he called after her.

"I don't care."

Suddenly he realized something. He knew where the bus collected Darcy, but at that location two farmhouses faced each other directly across the road. "Where do you live?" he shouted as the milling throng propelled her through the gym doors.

"Pushko place," she said.

Learning that Darcy was a Pushko gave Reinie a lot to think about all that long Friday afternoon. The Ottenbreits had no dealings with people of that ilk. Everybody knew the Pushkos' reputation. Darcy's father, Eugene Pushko, made frequent appearances in the "Court News" section of the local paper. Minor offences, drunk and disorderly, operating a motor vehicle without a valid driver's licence, resisting arrest. His five sons, Charles, Lincoln, Delmar, Winston, and Everett were often seen meandering up and down the streets of Waddell, crammed in a rust-ravaged vehicle trailing a haze of oily blue smoke. All five boys were as wide as a doorway across the shoulders, narrow-hipped, and bandy-legged. They had loud, booming voices that carried for blocks. They laughed a good deal but were famous for their violent, quick tempers. Amiably dangerous was an accurate description of the Pushko boys.

Most people found the brothers difficult to distinguish from one another. Charles, Lincoln, Delmar, and Winston looked like refugees from the 1950s with their elaborately sculpted hairstyles. They wore a uniform. White T-shirts, black denim pants, cowboy boots. The only one who didn't was the youngest of the brothers, Everett. The family rebel, Everett preferred cream denims and paisley shirts. Even more radically, he affected a Prince Valiant haircut that lent him a passing resemblance to Burton Cummings of The Guess Who, or perhaps a female film star of the silent era. He also smoked menthol cigarettes, much to his brothers' disgust.

None of the Pushkos had gone past grade eight because they found school highly unsatisfactory.

A cold, doughy ball of worry formed in the pit of Reinie's stomach. His parents would not be pleased by a connection with the Pushko family in any way, shape, or form. His mother and father subscribed to guilt by association.

Saturday morning Reinie was up by five and hard at work. His father left him on his own to pound posts and mend barbed wire because he was heading off to a cattle auction. When the fencing was completed, Reinie washed the Bel Air and vacuumed the interior. For a moment, he paused, hand resting on its fin, reverent before its showroom loveliness. He had bought the car from Mrs. Braun, who had wanted nothing to do with it after her husband, old Mr. Braun, had died behind the Chevy's wheel. Stricken by a heart attack, Mr. Braun had coasted the Bel Air to safety at the side of the road before expiring. He had been a finicky, fastidious man, even going so far as to have the car's engine regularly steam-cleaned. The Chevy was immaculate except for one ominous stain on the driver's seat. In the throes of a coronary, eighty-year-old Mr. Braun had lost control of his bladder.

Reinie just had time to shower, change his clothes, and gobble a baloney sandwich before meeting Darcy at two. His mother discovered him in the kitchen, eating over the sink.

"What's the hurry, Reinie?"

He looked at her blankly.

"Are you off somewhere?"

"For a drive."

"Drive where?"

"Around."

"When can I expect you home?"

He shrugged noncommittally.

"Supper is at six. Your father will be hungry when he gets back, so don't be late."

Reinie nodded, snatched the car keys from the table, and dove out the door. His mother, a neat, tidy woman of fifty whose face, lined by the steadfast exertion of willpower, still managed to retain lingering evidence of having once been pretty, stood at the window, hand plucking the cloth of her dress as the Chevy pulled out of the yard.

Another fine day, an autumnal gift. The Bel Air sped down grid roads, unfurling banners of dust that captured mellow sunshine in their shimmering, silty mesh. The poplars lining the roads had begun to turn, their yellow leaves to loosen their grip on branches. On the narrowest lanes, the Chevy's passing whirled showers of gold from the trees, spilling them in spendthrift fashion.

At five minutes to two he arrived at his destination. An ancient windbreak of dying spruce hid the Pushko house from sight. Reinie turned into the approach, cautiously nosed his car over a potholed trail that twisted among morbid, ghostly trees until the farmyard appeared.

An acre of vehicles of every age, model, and description, cracked windshields coyly glinting sunshine, roofs and hoods rusted to a rich burgundy, first seized his attention. Then the house, an old grey stucco box onto which a series of offhand additions had been tacked. All of them clad in different-coloured siding – pink, green, robin's egg blue, mustard.

The Pushko men were squatting on the front steps of the house. Their arrangement suggested a formal family portrait, faintly evoked the photograph of Reinie's christening that his mother kept proudly displayed on the piano in the living room. But the centrepiece of this composition was not an infant but a case of beer, clearly visible between Mr. Pushko's widespread, sheltering legs. Charles and Lincoln were seated on the top step; Mr. Pushko occupied the second step all by his lonesome. Delmar, Winston, and Everett hunkered at the feet of the head of the household. Mr. Pushko's striped railway engineer's cap and mirror sunglasses somehow reminded Reinie of the cat in the Dr. Seuss book that had given him nightmares as a child.

The Chevy rolled to a stop. There was no welcome from the Pushkos, who stolidly stared at the car, bottles in their hands. Could this be a barricade mounted at the front door to keep him from Darcy? Seconds ticked by and then, just as he was on the point of backing up the Chevy and fleeing, the screen door burst open, Darcy squirmed her way between her brothers' shoulders, bumped her father aside with her hip, skipped up to the Chevy, and hopped in.

"Get moving," she said.

In the rear-view mirror Reinie saw the Pushkos, still locked in place. Then Mr. Pushko lifted his beer to his lips. The boys took their cue from him and did the same, a nicely timed and executed ripple of movement.

Darcy rummaged around in a plastic purse, produced cigarettes and matches, and soon was furiously puffing away. This made Reinie a tad uneasy. If his mother smelled smoke in the car, the questions wouldn't stop until she knew who was responsible for the telltale stink – him, or somebody with nasty, filthy habits who he ought to know better than to be associating with.

Today, Darcy looked a little rundown, a little worse for wear. Her eyeshadow was smudged, as if she had slept in it. "Take me to the drugstore," she ordered, slumping down in the seat, propping her feet on the dashboard. She held that nonchalant pose, lighting one cigarette off another, until they drew up in front of the Rexall on Main Street in Waddell. Darcy flung herself from the car and dashed into the pharmacy.

Reinie found her at the cosmetics counter. It was unattended. Darcy was slapping on eyeshadow at breakneck speed. Mrs. Bernhardt, the pharmacist's wife, suddenly hove into view and accosted her. "Here, what do you think you're doing?" she demanded.

"It's a sample," said Darcy.

"It's no sample," said Mrs. Bernhardt. "I don't have any samples. Did you go behind that counter?"

"It was on top of the counter and it was *opened*. Looked like a sample to me," Darcy said, bristling.

Mrs. Bernhardt snatched the eyeshadow from her hand. "You got some gall," she said.

Reinie spoke up. "There's been a mistake, I guess. I'll pay for it."

"First, I look in her purse and see what else she helped herself to."

Darcy flicked the clasp of her handbag, defiantly upended the purse on the countertop. Out tumbled cigarettes, matches, a mound of wadded Kleenex.

Mrs. Bernhardt pursed her lips disapprovingly. "Your age and smoking."

"Who asked you? Mind your own business," snapped Darcy, scraping everything back into her purse.

"Get out. And don't you come back here again. I got enough to do without keeping an eye on the likes of you."

"Kiss my you-know-what," Darcy said, whirling around and flouncing off, leaving Mrs. Bernhardt to viciously bang the cash register keys and Reinie to pay. When he handed Darcy the eyeshadow out in the car, she was too gleeful to thank him. "Old bitch. See her face? Did you see her face?" Darcy wriggled forward, thrusting her own face at the rear-view mirror to admire the free touch-up she had helped herself to. As she did, she planted one small hand on Reinie's thigh, steadying herself. That slight pressure obliterated everything looming in his mind – that Mrs. Bernhardt, like his mother, was a notable Lutheran dragon, and likely to squeal that he had been the wheelman for a shoplifter. The warmth of Darcy's palm burned him right through the cloth.

———

For an hour and a half Darcy and Reinie sat in a booth in Wong's Café, a new experience for Reinie since he had never before had any inclination to waste his time just hanging about the way the other teenagers did. He bought Darcy two hamburgers and two vanilla milkshakes. Each booth had its own individual station for selecting tunes on the jukebox and Darcy kept demanding quarters from him to feed the machine. She sang along softly to each song with a longing look on her face that Reinie found thrilling. When she wasn't singing or eating, she was chain-smoking. Reinie felt gratified when two girls from his home room, Beverly Steckel and Marjorie Hampton, whispered and shot steely looks in his and Darcy's direction until she turned to them and said, "What you looking at, scrags? Because I sure ain't looking at much."

This time, when Reinie pulled up to the Pushko residence, it was Darcy's mother who was enthroned on the front step. The Pushko men were nowhere in sight. "I like your car," said Darcy before she left him, hustled across the sun-blasted patch of couch grass that masqueraded as a lawn, and went bounding up the steps past her mother.

Mrs. Pushko beckoned him, a directive not to be denied. Reinie climbed out of the Chevy and approached her warily.

"I'll put a extra plate on," she said. "You better come in and eat with us."

"Really," began Reinie, "I got to – "

"Ah, don't be shy. Nothing here to scare you."

She got to her feet, laid a powerful hand on his back, propelled him up the steps and into the kitchen. There, all the rest of the Pushkos were sitting around a battered Formica table set with Melmac plates. Mr. Pushko still wore his engineer's cap and mirror sunglasses indoors. White stubble dusted his face, like a skiff of snow.

"This is Darcy's friend," announced Mrs. Pushko. She turned to Reinie. "What do they call you, son?"

"Reinie."

"Whiney? Whiney?" Mr. Pushko's deep, resonant bass boomed in the hot, steamy kitchen.

"No – " Reinie started to say, but his correction was stalled by a burst of laughter from the others. Only then did he realize Mr. Pushko had perpetrated a joke.

"Eenie, meenie, Reinie moe!" bellowed Charlie. Another wave of hilarity engulfed Reinie.

"He's company," warned Mrs. Pushko, although with a long-suffering, indulgent smile for her brood.

Darcy was less forgiving. She sat, fingers sulkily twisting the ends of her long hair.

"I should phone my mother. To tell her I'll be late," explained Reinie.

"No can do," said Mr. Pushko. "Cocksuckers at the phone company cut me off." He glared at his sons. "Too much of the long distance, these assholes phoning to every wrecker's yard in the province looking for car parts." It astonished Reinie that Mr. Pushko so readily confessed his financial embarrassment without a trace of shame.

"You – Everett, Lincoln – shove over and let Reinie get his feet under the table beside Darcy," demanded Mrs. Pushko. Her two sons began to playfully jostle each other, thumping their chairs together. It reminded Reinie of bumper cars colliding on the midway. Gradually, a gap inched open into which he self-consciously squeezed himself.

"The boy looks like he could use a beer," said Mr. Pushko. Dutifully, Charles retrieved a bottle of Pilsner from a case strategically positioned on the floor near the table. Reinie was about to refuse, but before he could get a word out Charles had set the rim of the bottle cap to the edge of the table and smacked it with the heel of his palm. The cap spiralled into the air and landed with a faint clatter on the linoleum. Presented with the foaming bottle, Reinie had no choice but to clamp his lips to it to save the floor from a drenching.

Mrs. Pushko was bustling about with bowls and platters. As soon as one hit the table, somebody snatched it up. "Give over to Reinie now," she kept urging her children. "Give the boy a chance." When nobody heeded her, she took charge and served him herself, heaping his plate with thick slices of pork loin roast, perogies, cabbage rolls, cucumbers and cream, buttered carrots and dill, mashed potatoes and gravy. Everybody tucked in, making grunts of delight except for Darcy, who showed little interest in her food after all those hamburgers and milk shakes. She toyed with a single cabbage roll, aimlessly shifting it about on her plate.

Lincoln elbowed Reinie. "Hey, Darcy," he said to his sister, "if you don't eat your supper, you ain't going to grow any pinfeathers on your chicken. No pinfeathers on the chicken, you ain't old enough for a boyfriend."

"Go fuck your hat, moron," said Darcy. Then she jumped up and stormed out of the kitchen. Once again, everybody howled laughter. Reinie's eyes flitted from face to face, searching for some sign that somebody disapproved of this vulgar exchange between brother and sister. He found none.

Reinie's wristwatch showed him it was just shy of six o'clock. He was going to be late getting home. Turning to Mrs. Pushko, who was slamming plates of gingerbread and whipped cream down on the table, he said apologetically, "That was an awful good supper, Mrs. Pushko, but I better be going."

"Nobody leaves without they have dessert," Mrs. Pushko declared sternly. "Not in my house."

Darcy's family proved impossible to escape – not that Reinie really wished to. Grinning foolishly, he ate two helpings of dessert, drank two more beers. He wasn't used to the beer. It made him feel silly, giddy, light-headed, and light-hearted. He giggled at almost everything that was said. When Darcy's brothers asked to see his car, he proudly did the honours. The boys popped the hood, inspected the motor, pored over the interior, all the while murmuring enviously.

This was followed by a guided tour of the Pushko automobile graveyard. The wrecks struck Reinie as falling into two distinct categories: definitely not running and certain never, ever to run. Reinie, who had always stood apart from the common run of humanity, burdened by all the duties and responsibilities that attended being an Ottenbreit, was sure the Pushkos were *embracing* him, that he was being accepted as *family* because of Darcy. In his befuddled, tipsy state he could have flung his arms around them, hugged them to demonstrate the vast, oceanic wave of fraternal feeling he was experiencing. His emotions even began to colour his estimation of the value of the junked cars.

Finally, as utter darkness descended, Reinie and Darcy's brothers stood companionably in the chilly fall night, warmed by the limitless potential the derelict vehicles would reveal some time in the future.

"I'm a decent welder," Reinie said. "If you ever need any help."

"Fucking A," said Charlie.

"Double fucking A," said Lincoln.

"Let's have another beer," said Winston.

They did.

Reinie came home to big, big trouble. His father was off in the pickup scouring the roads for him while his mother shouldered the task of tracking all possible leads as to his whereabouts by telephone. Of course, Mrs. Bernhardt, a charter member of the Lutheran ladies' telegraph, had seen him – with the Pushko girl. Explanations were demanded of Reinie and his answers fell far short of being satisfactory. He kept his eyes on the floor, claiming the Pushko girl was simply a new friend he had made at school. On the spur of the moment, her mother had invited him to supper. Yes, he was sorry his thoughtlessness had caused his parents so much anxiety. No, it wouldn't happen again.

Then his mother smelled something suspicious on his breath. "Reinie," she said, "have you been drinking alcohol?"

"I had a beer." Reinie was not an experienced liar. He quickly added, "Just one."

"And where did you get it?"

"Mr. Pushko gave it to me. To have with supper."

"Imagine," said Mrs. Ottenbreit, shaking her head. "Unbelievable how some people live."

Mabel Ottenbreit was determined to nip this in the green bud. She pointed to the key hook on the kitchen wall and told her son to hang his car keys there and not to even *think about* touching them for two weeks. And stay away from that Mr. Pushko. If she didn't feel so sorry for that man's wife, she would call the police right this minute and report him for supplying liquor to minors.

The sullen, defiant look her son sent her before he placed the keys on the hook frightened her just a tiny bit. It was as if Reinie's personality had altered in the blink of an eye.

After he had slouched off to bed, Mabel Ottenbreit brewed some strong coffee and sat sipping it, waiting for Karl to return. Reinie had denied there was any funny business going on with this girl, but she wasn't convinced. Neither she nor Karl had ever told their boys *in so many words* that they weren't supposed to have girlfriends, but she had assumed that because of the opinions they had expressed on the foolishness of pairing up at an early age that their message had been received loud and clear. But then Reinie had always been slower, more backward than Edgar. Certainly what she had made absolutely clear, no ifs, ands, or buts about it, was that her children had one obligation at this stage in their life and that was to get their education. That was the danger with dating. Distractions from schoolwork. At worst, even pregnancies, God forbid. And there was no surer way to pregnancies than young people dosing themselves with alcohol. And here was Reinie, taken to guzzling beer.

Last year, when her son had implored her to let him quit the choir and Luther League because he was falling behind in school, she had felt torn. Reinie had suggested that all the chores he had to do on the farm were cutting into his study time. Mabel Ottenbreit was a woman of her word and since she had said school came first she couldn't backtrack. With Edgar gone off to the university, Karl had lost one pair of hands and couldn't do without Reinie. So, reluctantly, she had agreed that her son could withdraw from church activities. Pastor Schneider had been disappointed because Reinie had a lovely voice (his one talent) and he had always been a stalwart of Luther League, not a leader certainly, but a steady attender.

Now, with graduation in sight, it appeared that her youngest, steadiest son was on the verge of making a bad turn in life. She had expected trouble from Edgar but never Reinie. Mabel Ottenbreit would never forget the day she had found those magazines tucked under Edgar's mattress, the ones with women sticking their rumps out like monkeys eager to be mounted. But Edgar had come around after a good talking to. What worried her now was what Karl had always said, that it's the quiet bull that hurts you.

The next morning when she got up for church, the car keys were no longer on the hook, and her son was nowhere to be found.

Reinie drove the countryside aimlessly until eleven o'clock, then dropped by the Pushkos'. Darcy was still in bed, so he helped her brothers cut the box off a '51 International half-ton. They intended to use it as a trailer. All five Pushkos praised his handiness with an acetylene torch. By mid-afternoon they had finished the job and went into the house for coffee. Darcy was up, sitting at the kitchen table in her pyjamas, smoking cigarettes. Reinie asked her if she would like to take a spin out to the lake.

"May as well," she answered with her usual indifference.

Darcy didn't appreciate the lake much but she liked the amusement park. They played minigolf and later Reinie watched her bounce on a trampoline until all his cash was gone. After that, they sat in the car before the dark blue lake splendidly enamelled with Indian summer sunshine, watching the crisp waves roll up onto the beach. The Chevy was parked under a big cottonwood and its shade gave the place a twilight, romantic air, which encouraged Reinie to screw up his courage and ask Darcy for a kiss.

She shrugged and said, "I don't care." Her matter-of-fact tone excited him more than any expression of eagerness or ardour could have done. He liked her not caring. It allowed her to lip off Mrs. Bernhardt when she was caught red-handed committing mischief, or to tell Lincoln to go fuck his hat right in front of her parents, or to smoke like a fiend. It made her brave, mysterious, dangerous, unpredictable.

Kissing a girl for the first time was a clumsy, fumbling affair. He kept his eyes wide open so as to inscribe the moment in his mind. He wanted to stamp and hold it there for all time: the sight of Darcy's tightly closed eyes, shuttered in green; the feel of her soft mouth working against his, the smell of her – sweat and cheap drugstore perfume.

At last, she jerked away from him. "Enough's enough, eh?" was her only comment.

That momentous Sunday kiss emboldened Reinie to stand up to his parents for the first time in his life. When his mother demanded he hand over the keys to the Chevy for safekeeping, he flatly refused.

Mabel Ottenbreit could scarcely credit things could come to such a predicament in her family. Even more distressing, she saw no recourse to this unexpected defiance. What could they do? Was Karl supposed to tackle Reinie, pin him to the floor while she fished around in his pockets for the keys?

"Nothing doing," her son repeated over and over. "Nothing doing. I paid for that car with my own money. It's mine."

Eventually the standoff led Mrs. Ottenbreit to break down and weep, something no one in her family had ever witnessed before. It terrified her husband, made him anxiously wring his big-knuckled hands and blink. He forgot all about his duty to discipline Reinie when she stumbled off to the bedroom to cry her eyes out. He trailed after her, plaintively calling, "Mother? Mother? You all right?"

On Monday, Reinie had the effrontery to *drive* to school. Once again his parents were powerless to stop him. Of course, Mabel Ottenbreit blamed the influence of the Pushko girl for this. She did her best to banish thoughts of Darcy from her mind, but the girl had lodged herself there like a sick headache. To Mabel's horror, she sometimes imagined Darcy presenting her buttocks to Reinie, peeking over her shoulder at him exactly in the lewd way those women in Edgar's magazines had.

———

Darcy made no bones about letting Reinie know how much she despised being cooped up on the school bus with those dorks. So each and every day he picked her up for school and delivered her home. Often Darcy overslept or wasn't finished applying her makeup and he had to sit around the kitchen listening to her mother yell for her to shift her precious little ass, don't keep nice Reinie waiting. He was late for school any number of times and got called to the office for a good talking-to from the vice-principal, Mr. Hector.

A talking-to from Mr. Hector was a small price to pay to please Darcy. Life had fallen into a new routine. After school Darcy insisted they go straight to Wong's Café for an hour or two, where she plugged Reinie's quarters into the jukebox, sang along to the latest hits, and turned the air blue with cigarette smoke. Only then did she consent to drive to some secluded spot where she permitted Reinie to press his lips to hers, to stroke her forearm with his thumb. That was all; he required nothing more.

November rolled around and with it Darcy's fifteenth birthday. Reinie bought her a ring that he presented to her in the Chevy. To Reinie, the grey light of the wintry day lent the moment the same intimate, sheltered feeling that the shade of the cottonwood had provided for their first kiss. By the way Darcy bit her bottom lip and appraisingly waggled her finger, trying to make the tiny stone spark in the dim light, he could tell she was pleased by his gift.

"It's real nice." There was a long, considered pause. Darcy turned to him. "So, do you want a jerk?"

"Jerk?" said Reinie.

Darcy made a fist and, very business-like, pumped it briskly up and down.

Reinie was scorched by embarrassment. The blood thudded so violently in his body he felt about to faint. He couldn't face her, shifted his eyes to the odometer. It registered 83,599 miles.

"Fine," he heard her say. "You don't want to, it's no skin off my ass."

He managed to choke out two words. "Yes, please."

"Okay," said Darcy. "Fish it out."

Troubles in the Ottenbreit household continued. His father resented the hours he spent with Darcy, the hours he spent tinkering on the Pushko brothers' decrepit vehicles. He harped about the slipshod fashion that Reinie performed his chores, even going so far as to signal his displeasure by docking his pay.

Reinie was running short on spending money; girlfriends were an expensive proposition. He felt squeezed on every side. His mother never missed a chance to make scathing, unchristian remarks about the Pushkos. Once she even screeched at him, "Don't forget that your grandfathers Klinger and Ottenbreit were volksdeutsche, Reinie. They had the good sense to get out of places like Russia and Romania to get away from drunken, lazy, thieving bohunks, and now all you want to do is hang around with them!"

It never stopped. One Saturday in February, Reinie spent three hours on the tractor, buffeted by an icy wind that cut him to the bone while he plowed snow from the driveway and opened the trail to the haystacks. When he was done, his father sourly remarked, "I'd call that a sloppy job, Reinie. If you don't straighten up pretty soon, I'll have to rethink our plans."

A blackmailer's hint. A threat to break the arrangement that they would farm together next year. It was the only thing his parents had said to him that gave Reinie a fright, gave him something to think about. Because Reinie had his own plan, and that was to make Darcy Pushko his bride whatever his mother might think and say about girls that the government ought to be sterilizing before they could breed and make more of their kind.

Of course, Reinie did not mean to wed Darcy right away. She was only fifteen and Reinie wasn't sure if it was legal to marry a girl that young. Unless he got her pregnant and then nobody would try to stop them. But that wasn't going to hap- pen because Darcy wouldn't even let him touch her bubbies. The night he gave her the hair drier and the deluxe makeup kit for Christmas, she did volunteer to take off her sweater and brassiere. But he had to swear *no touching*. The sight of Darcy, her little pink nipples jiggling up and down to the maniacal tempo of the hand job she was performing, had brought him off in a flash, had slammed him back against the car seat with an ecstatic groan. Darcy had giggled and said, "Wow. Maybe you better put windshield wipers on the *inside* of this car." Learning how quickly matters were brought to a head when she was topless, Darcy did it all the time now.

During the months of March, April, and May, Reinie Ottenbreit wore the look of a long-married, middle-aged man oppressed by the responsibilities owed to a wife and children. All this was in the future, but it was nonetheless very real to him. After his father's warning, he grew more diligent. There was plenty to be diligent about. Spring was a busy time on the farm. First came calving, then tune-ups to the farm machinery, tilling the fields, and finally seeding. It grew difficult for him to steal even a few spare hours on the weekends to take Darcy to a movie and, later, to see her bubbies do their merry dance in the glow of the Chevy's interior light.

May brought a more pressing worry. The graduation ceremony and dance were to be held on the last weekend of the month. Darcy would be on his arm for the occasion and this meant bringing her face to face with his parents. Some sort of blow up was likely, a setback just when things were on the mend with his father. Only a week before, Karl Ottenbreit had commended his son for the hard work he had been doing lately. Reinie would have liked to drop a word or two to Darcy about being on her best behaviour when she met his parents, to be particularly polite to his mother, but that might do more damage than good. He had learned this about Darcy – if she thought anybody was trying to push her around, she could turn downright nasty. Right now she was under a two-week suspension for refusing to do calisthenics in Mr. Head's gym class. With the daily drive to school also suspended, Reinie saw even less of her.

Darcy was slated to resume classes on the third Monday of May. When Reinie arrived at the Pushkos to pick her up, Mrs. Pushko said she had left already – on the bus. Reinie drove all the way to school with the gas pedal mashed to the floor. After a frantic search of the hallways, he found her loitering outside her homeroom.

"I went to pick you up," he said. "Where were you?"

Darcy made a scornful face.

"I came by your house, your mother said you were already gone."

"Yeah. Obvious."

"I need to talk to you about the corsage for your dress. What you want and all. For graduation."

"I'm not going to no ignorant graduation," she said. "Bill Aiken's asked me to go to his sister's wedding with him. It's the same day."

"But – "

"Too late. You didn't invite me. He did. A week ago."

Reinie was desperately attempting to summon up a picture of Bill Aiken. It came to him. Bill Aiken worked for the phone company. He was twenty-five if he was a day. All Reinie could say was, "How'd you meet him?"

"Came by to hook our phone back up."

"You can't do this to me," said Reinie. "We're going steady. I won't let you."

"You and whose army won't let me?"

Darcy was squinting at him furiously, her eyes more bewitchingly cat-like than he had ever seen them. In a humble voice, he implored her, "Please, Darcy. Please." Reaching out, he took her by the shoulder. Darcy squirmed out from under his hand. "Piss off," she said, ducking inside the classroom.

———

Now that he knew the Pushkos were back on the line, Reinie made frequent calls, but Darcy wouldn't come to the phone. He waylaid her in school, but she only stuck her nose in the air and kept walking. Several times he went to her house, but she refused to come out of her room to speak to him. Mrs. Pushko was sympathetic to his plight but not optimistic that anything could be done to mend the situation. "Well, Reinie, I guess she got mad at you because you wasn't showing her enough attention lately. Darcy needs plenty of attention." It was a Sunday afternoon; the Pushko boys were occupied rehabilitating doomed automobiles out in the yard, and the man of the house was snoring on the couch in the living room. Mrs. Pushko had tactfully informed Reinie that Darcy was out. He knew with whom.

"He's too old for her," he complained to Mrs. Pushko.

"No argument there. But Darcy has always had a mind of her own. I never knew what to do with her."

"I treated her nice. I don't know why she's doing this to me."

"I guess Aiken suits her better."

Reinie had done his research. "He's got a Dodge Charger."

"Oh, I don't think it's just the car," Mrs. Pushko said with authority. "Aiken is more her personality. She can fight with him. They already had a couple big fights."

Reinie was bewildered. "Fights?"

"Darcy likes something to bump up against. Like I said, it's her personality."

———

Something was happening to him. One day while pushing the grain augur to an oat bin, he found himself watching the power line overhead come nearer and nearer with every step he took. The augur hadn't been cranked down as his father always insisted it should be before shifting it. In a trance, Reinie walked on. If the metal tube of the augur touched that wire, alive and buzzing with thousands of volts of electricity, all his problems would be over, everything taken care of. Inches short of the humming line, he halted, shuddering, sweating.

Eating was an ordeal; his mother's food stuck in his throat like chunks of gravel. His parents guessed there was trouble between him and Darcy. It made them happy, they *gloated* over the breakup. It was difficult for him to sleep and harder still to get out of bed in the morning. Two or three times he had to pull the Chevy over to the side of the road, rest his forehead on the steering wheel, and sob.

The morning of graduation day, he lay in bed, unable to move, listening to his mother and father bustle about the house. They were cheerful because his brother, Edgar, was coming down from Saskatoon for the big occasion. The photographer's studio was booked for noon. A family portrait was going to be taken of the four proud, happy Ottenbreits. Edgar was expected any minute. Reinie glanced at the clock. Eleven. It was getting late.

He heard a tap on his door. "Reinie," his mother said, "you have to get up, take a shower and dress. Edgar will want the bathroom when he gets here so he can freshen up."

He didn't reply.

"Dear, are you awake?" Reinie rolled over, turned his face to the wall. The door creaked open.

"Reinie? What's the matter? Aren't you feeling well?" His mother took him by the shoulder and gave him a shake. Getting no response, she called out, her voice stitched with panic. "Karl! Karl! Something's the matter with Reinie!"

Footsteps pounded down the hall, soon Reinie felt the mattress sag under his father's weight, a hand drag him over onto his back. Two bleak, concerned faces hovered above him.

"I'm not going to graduation," he informed them.

His mother appeared relieved. "Don't be silly. You've just got a case of nerves. Of course you're going to graduation. Your brother is driving all this way just to see you get your diploma. You can't back out now."

"Yes I can."

"I won't let you quit on this," Mabel said, falling back on her reliable, no-nonsense voice. "Not like you did choir and Luther League."

"Fuck Luther League," Reinie said in a monotone. "Fuck it right up the ass."

Mabel recoiled two steps. His father sprang off the bed and shouted, "Enough of that kind of talk in this house, mister!"

Mabel was a strong woman, capable of almost instant recovery in a crisis. "I didn't hear that," she said, mouth tight and severe. "Now get up and get dressed – *now*!"

Flinging back the bedclothes, Reinie swung his legs over the edge of the mattress, picked his blue jeans up from the floor.

Mabel's voice went shrill with exasperation. "Your suit! Pay attention, Reinie! You need your suit for the photograph!"

It was as if he had gone deaf. Reinie continued to dress himself in the clothing scattered on the floor. Then he walked by his parents as if they were invisible, as if they had melted away into the stale air of his bedroom, and dragged a duffel bag out of his closet, which he began to stuff with jeans, underwear, shirts, and socks.

"What are you doing?" cried his mother. "What do you think you're up to?"

The last shirt couldn't be jammed into the overflowing duffel bag. Reinie held it up to his parents' faces, ferociously tore it in half, and flung the two pieces at their feet. Hoisting the duffel bag over his shoulder, he walked stolidly through the house, his mother and father yapping at him, border collies trying to turn the wayward sheep back into the flock. They did not succeed. Switching tactics out in the yard, they applied sweet reason, cajolery, pleas. Reinie climbed into the Chevy, locked the doors, and started the engine. His mother began to beat on the driver's window with her palms, begging him to listen, just listen. Karl Ottenbreit planted himself directly in front of the vehicle to block his son's escape. Reinie simply reversed the Bel Air, rear wheels chewing up lawn, spitting out lumps of sod. Swinging around his distraught parents in a wide arc, he raced off, leaving them stricken under a soft spring sky piled high with bland, woolly cumulus.

All day Reinie drove west, only pausing to stop for gas. As evening drew down he found himself in the midst of the Alberta oil patch, pumpjacks somnolently nodding, refinery flares waving flames against a magenta sky, the smell of sour gas, the sulphurous odour of money everywhere. That night he slept in the Chevy and by noon was employed on an oil rig. The man who hired him stood by farm boys. They were raised around machinery, weren't afraid of work, and could stand isolation. In his experience, city kids found life intolerable without an A&W or a movie house right around the corner. They were apt to quit on him.

Reinie didn't disappoint. He worked without stint, didn't flinch at the prospect of any dirty job. He took all the overtime he could get. What's more, unlike many oil workers, he didn't drink, didn't get thrown in jail, and was the very definition of dependable. Learning the business fast, he got promoted fast. In six years, what with overtime and bonuses, he was making more money per annum than a surgeon, and banking most of it. His only friend was a Mennonite boy with similar habits. In 1975, the two pooled their savings, got a loan from the bank, and started a company that contracted to service oil wells. Three years later they had thirty men on the payroll and were still expanding. By then the Bel Air was a dead article, punch-drunk from the hammering it had taken on primitive roads. Reinie junked it without a second's thought, or the slightest misgiving.

That year he married Melanie Cooper, a loans officer at the bank he dealt with. By then he had legally changed his name to Randy Bright, junking Reinie Ottenbreit the way he had the Chevy. It was Melanie who talked him into finally contacting his parents and inviting them to the wedding. He was surprised they came, surprised to see how much they had changed during the intervening years of silence. He wasn't surprised to see how much they approved of Melanie, or how much they still disapproved of him. They took the name change hard.

Melanie resigned from the bank to help him manage the business. Their first child, Tommy, was born two years later, followed by Ryan, and then Brendan, the afterthought.

Randy Bright is in his fifties now, his bushy, toffee-coloured hair thinned to a sandy grey. He is still in the oil business, but now his holdings include three motels, a cattle feed lot, a Toyota dealership, and a tool rental business.

Surfing the Internet two years ago, he discovered a 1957 Chevy Bel Air advertised by a car restorer operating out of San Bernardino, California. Without hesitation, or his usual hard-headed dickering, he paid the asking price, $160,000 American, and had it shipped to him. It's an improved, updated version of his former vehicle, with features such as a ZZ4 355 horse-power, aluminium head, roller cam engine; weld racing wheels; Positraction; the whole nine yards. It's even equipped with an analogue-faced digital radio and CD changer.

Randy Bright rarely drives the Chevy; most of the time it simply sits in his four-car garage next to the rest of the Bright family automobiles, all of them Toyotas. When business associates ask him, "How's it going, Randy?" he always answers the same way, "Can't complain." But this isn't exactly true. He worries day and night over his youngest son, Brendan. Tommy and Ryan are both married, both working in the business, both happy as far as their father can judge, but Brendan is a different story.

Brendan, who is seventeen, is a loner. Not the type of loner his father had been as a boy, but a moody, brooding, withdrawn teenager who spends most of his time in his room on the computer, listening to CDs, reading fantasy novels. His father knows the other kids give him a hard time. When his mother asks Brendan how things are at school, he always answers with a bitter smile and a grudging shrug of his stooped shoulders.

Some nights when he can't sleep, Randy quietly leaves Melanie dead to the world in their double bed and takes the Chevy Bel Air out for a spin. After a few miles listening to the wind howl by his open window, he finds a secluded spot and parks.

There was not a trace of nostalgia in his purchase of the Chevy. He bought it to confirm to himself that no one can ever again deny him what he wants. But confronted by the stars, he admits that what he most wants now is for Brendan to be a boy like his brothers are, cheerful, outgoing like their mother.

Six months ago, he walked into the garage and found Brendan with a tool in his hand, a power nail gun. It was plugged into the outlet. A look passed between them, the recognition of a fact by two minds. His father had stumbled over, yanked the cord from the wall before the boy could act. Now Brendan is seeing a therapist, who keeps telling his parents that Brendan is improving and that they should think about sending him to a wilderness camp for troubled youths in Utah for the summer. His father is doubtful about the psychologist's optimistic assessment, sees no evidence of this so-called improvement.

Lately, Randy Bright has caught himself on the point of signing cheques *Reinie Ottenbreit*. He believes this might be a sign. Changing his name was a mean thing to do. His parents are both dead, and he wonders if he isn't being punished from beyond the grave for his vindictiveness.

He doesn't trust wilderness camps in Utah, or therapists. What he would like to do is hand the keys to the 1957 Chevy Bel Air to Brendan in the hope the boy would drive away as fast as he can. On nights when the hard little stars beat against the windshield like brilliant hail and the prairie wind moans its insinuations, he can imagine Brendan speeding down some road, the CD blaring the strange music that thumps night after night from his bedroom, the wind ruffling his blond hair, each mile bringing him closer to where he needs to be.

In his mind's eye, Randy Bright hungrily watches his son until a final twist in the highway pavement whips Brendan out of sight, the Chevy Bel Air carrying him on to a waiting refuge, safety, a haven of happiness. He knows it is not going to happen, but he wishes it would, wishes that Brendan could be lucky as he has been. Thirty-five years of contentment is something, even if now the bill for it seems to have come due.

Live Large

BILLY CONSTABLE HADN'T BEEN SLEEPING soundly for weeks, and at four o'clock one June morning he found himself prowling his living room with a cup of coffee clutched in an unsteady hand. His wife, Marva, and their teenaged twin boys, Troy and Jess, had gone up to the cottage so he had no one to disturb when he flung open the drapes, switched the CD player on, and set one track repeating over and over, Richie Havens singing "Here Comes the Sun," at such thunderous volume that Billy could almost trick himself into believing that the sound waves battering him were responsible for the nagging tremor in his right hand.

The sun finally did come up, flushed by Richie from below the horizon, a burst of extravagant light that torched a strange, bird-shaped cloud, fiery wings uplifted. Somehow it reminded Billy of the cover of a book assigned in his first-year university English course more than thirty years ago. A novel by some famous writer. Stubbornly, he tried to recover the name to forestall thinking about how bad business was. It didn't work. Worry about Jenkins's upcoming phone call had raised a tender blister on his brain.

Business was so shitty that even clueless Marva seemed to sense trouble was pressing in. Why else had she suggested they resign from the Fairview Golf and Country Club? Ordinarily, Billy, who adored golf, would have protested, but feeling he deserved this punishment for his sins he acquiesced. With the club's approval he had sold his membership to Herb Froese, bolstering a cash flow that lately had dwindled to a feeble trickle.

What Marva hadn't learned yet was that Billy was looking for a buyer for the cottage. The dock, altar of his wife's tanning sessions, the sleek powerboat with its triumphal roar, the quaint log cabin, all appeared doomed. Even the house he stood in now, his gut slumping forlornly over the waistband of his Jockey shorts, was in jeopardy.

He needed a nicotine jolt. That was something else Marva didn't know, that hubby was back on the booze and the cigarettes. Two years ago Billy had awakened to an elephant squatting on his chest, a crushing coronary. In the hospital, a teary Marva had begged him to mend his ways and, contritely, he had promised he would. But in the last desperate months he had turned into a sneaky, slinking backslider.

Billy killed the music, put on his tartan housecoat, stepped into the garage, collected a pack of du Mauriers he had cached in the glove compartment of the Lexus, and circled around behind the house. Only by keeping to the great outdoors could he prevent Marva from sniffing out the stale stench of his fall from grace. There the towering blue spruces also provided shelter from the prying eyes of any early rising neighbour. Lately Billy sensed friends and acquaintances were checking him for signs of failure and finding them.

He lit up, greedily tugging smoke into his lungs as he roamed the property. He was a big man of fifty-three, with the fleshy, corroded body of the former athlete, but his bare feet still moved with nimble assurance through the dew-drenched grass. Slanting rays of sunshine strafed the back-yard. The evergreens flung spiny swatches of black shadow across the lawn. A mob of sparrows scattered from the bird-bath at his approach, flecking the sky with their panicked flight. The jay in the neighbour's tree jeered at him, mocking his disgrace.

Still, Billy began to take heart. After all, summer was his element, a season as hot-blooded, aggressive, and optimistic as he had always been. Summer fit his nature like a glove. Things were going to be all right. He would survive this. Jenkins had promised to phone by five p.m., and whatever else might be said about the flinty-hearted prick, he was a man of his word. If Billy could land the contract to install plumbing in the condos Jenkins was building, the bank could be held at bay. With mortgage rates at an all-time low, con-struction was booming and there would be more work to nab if he could make it through this bad patch. He just had to think positive, correct past errors of judgment, and everything would be fine. The trouble was waiting for the goddamn phone call. Jenkins was certain to keep him hanging by his fingernails until the last second. A power trip, as Billy used to say in the misty, faraway days of the 1960s. But, he told him-self, maybe this was all to the good. Maybe this situation was

a lesson for him, a reminder of where impatience and reck-
lessness could land you. Hugging this comforting thought
close, he headed back to the house.

At seven-thirty the phone rang and Billy's unstable ticker gave
an anxious lurch. It couldn't be Jenkins, not at this hour. Had
the boys flipped the powerboat? Wrapped Marva's Volvo
around a power pole? To his relief it was Herb Froese calling.
Herb apologized for the early morning call, explaining he had
a tee time for eleven-thirty, but one of the original foursome
had ducked out. Did Billy want to play? As his guest, he
added tactfully. At first Billy was inclined to refuse outright,
feeling this invitation to his old haunt was a humiliation, but
as he listened to Froese ramble on, he relaxed. Herb was a
hacker so apologetic about his game that playing with anyone he didn't know well gave him fits. On a busy Sunday,
there was a chance some hopeful single might attach to the
threesome and Froese would run the risk of an afternoon
spoiled by some stranger's scarcely veiled condescension
about his laughable play. Once Billy understood *he* was being
asked to do Herb a favour, he graciously accepted. At least
now he had something to occupy his mind until five o'clock,
something to help turn the dial down on his fretting. Maybe
his luck was turning.

———

Billy arrived at Fairview early. So far this year he had only squeezed in three rounds on public courses: his game was rusty, and hitting a bucket of balls might work the kinks out. As he lugged his bag towards the driving range, he felt his heart soar. It was a beautiful, warm, brilliant day. Fairview looked in great shape: add a flock of woolly lambs to all that rich green pasture and it would be a shepherd's wet dream. Then something halted Billy dead in his tracks. He spotted Malcolm Forsythe, the King of the Car Dealers, on the driving range, "working on his game." The evil little turd was always spouting hackneyed golfing clichés that sent Billy around the bend. "Keep it in the short grass," "It's not how you drive, it's how you arrive," "I don't have my A-game today." Everything about the man irked him. That abbreviated, granny backswing mechanically dinking out ball after ball as straight as a plumb line, that stupid tweed cap Forsythe had brought back from a trip to St. Andrews sitting on his head like a dried-out, weathered cow pie.

Billy had a bigger grievance against him. He couldn't forget how Forsythe's deliberately implying that he couldn't afford to buy a luxury car had driven him to lose his head, to throw caution to the wind, to make the big, extravagant gesture and impulsively order a Lexus LS460. He could see now that Forsythe had been egging him on, seeing just how far he could push him. "If a fellow has to tighten his belt, he has to tighten his belt. No shame in that. A Corolla is great value. Very economical. You can't imagine how many of them I sell to female schoolteachers," is what Forsythe had said to him and Billy hadn't been able to swallow that. And then, once he had taken the plunge, he had had to liquidate his measly fund of RRSPs so he could pay cash and avoid the credit check Forsythe would have to run to see if he qualified for dealer financing.

The very sight of the man sent Billy fleeing to the club-house. There he received the awful news from Herb Froese and his buddy Skip Jacobs that Forsythe would be part of their foursome.

As usual, Forsythe rudely kept them all waiting until seconds before their start time. On the first tee, the car peddler said, "So, boys, who wants to lay some loose change on the game and make this interesting?" Forsythe, a seven-handicapper, was always trying to milk somebody who was half the player he was. Herb Froese had paid for Forsythe's after-round drinks so many times that he flatly refused, and Skip frugally followed suit. Forsythe turned to Billy. "It's just you and me, sport. How's about it? What do you say? Stroke or match play?"

Billy took his time lighting a cigarette. "How about we play skins. Carry the money forward when we tie a hole. Forget the chickenshit stuff."

"How much a hole?"

"Hundred. That's a nice round number." The look on Forsythe's face, the awed silence that overwhelmed Skip and Herb delighted Billy.

"Jesus," said Forsythe. "So much for a friendly outing."

"Money talks, bullshit walks," said Billy, flamboyantly yanking his driver from the bag. He could sense the shrewd cogs turning in his opponent's mind. After a bit, Forsythe nodded. Apparently, the calculations had been weighed and been judged favourable. Forsythe had green-lit the project. Billy was gleeful. Now he had returned the favour, backed Forsythe into a corner.

Billy, a big hitter, always found the first hole, a 545-yard par five, extremely tasty. As he addressed the ball with his Big Bertha, he heard Forsythe snidely remark, "That driver looks like a toaster on a stick."

Billy lifted his head. "It's legal."

"I didn't say it wasn't."

The exchange gave Billy pause. "Course management" was one of Forsythe's mantras. Play it safe, weigh risk and reward like a bean counter. If Billy pulled the ball left, he was out of bounds. The story of his life. Five hours ago, he had been telling himself to correct his mistakes. It was time to listen to his own advice. Trading the driver for a three iron, he split the fairway. Forsythe went with a driver, but as their carts rolled down the fairway Billy noted with satisfaction that Forsythe had gained fewer than ten yards on him. This old dog can learn new things, he told himself. Sure he can.

His cautious attitude paid dividends for two holes; he stayed even with Forsythe. But on the third, he shamefully four-putted. For Billy, putting was like a visit to the dentist; he just wanted to get the pain over with as quickly as possible. The double bogey cost him three hundred bucks.

With all the Sunday traffic the next hole, a par three, had backed up. There were two foursomes ahead of them on the tee, giving Billy time to regroup and calm down. Also, sexy Joanne arrived on her refreshment cart. Nobody else wanted anything, they were keeping a Presbyterian Sunday, but Billy sauntered over to her.

"Where you been, Mr. C.? Haven't seen you in ages." Joanne was always glad to see him. Knowing that she was a single mother he always tipped her outlandishly and made a point of asking after her little boy.

"I guess you didn't hear. I quit the club. Too much business on the go. No time for golf . . ." He faltered. "Except now and then."

"That's a crime. Otherwise, how are things?"

"They could be better. I'm down three hundred to Forsythe."

"He's so tight he squeaks when he walks. Put a little pressure on him and he'll choke." She seized her throat, crossed her eyes, and stuck her tongue out. Billy laughed like a madman. Joanne was a great girl, even if she was what Marva called a "trailer tramp." Billy happened to like saucy trailer tramps. They were the reason he had always volunteered to take the boys to the Exhibition when they were little. Marva had accused him of lusting after corn dogs, but it was the young women in high heels and ankle bracelets, little crescents of jiggly white bum peeking out from under their cut-off blue jeans, that attracted him to the midway.

"How can I do you?" asked Joanne.

"I'll take two beers. Any brand, whatever's coldest."

During the time he stood chatting with Joanne, Billy drained one beer and got another underway. When she hinted it was time for her to go, he fumbled out his wallet and pressed a twenty on her.

"Hey, Mr. C., that's mighty big of you."

"Self-interest. So you don't forget me," Billy said. "Keep them coming."

"I'll catch you at the turn." With a cheeky wink she sped off, the contents of her cart merrily rattling.

Billy hadn't eaten breakfast or lunch; his guts had been too twisted up anticipating Jenkins's phone call for him to contemplate eating. He checked his watch quickly, but reminding himself how many hours were left before his future was decided was not a good idea. The beer on an empty stomach had started to give him a nice mild buzz. The last thing he needed was to spoil that feeling, get all jangled, get his nerves stretched banjo-tight.

By the time their foursome were ready to hit to the fourth, a green surrounded with water blinking hot sunlight, Billy's arms felt relaxed, loopy, boneless. Normally, fear of sending his ball into the drink tensed him up, but the beer had eased the wrinkles out of his swing, allowing him to follow-through with an easy, relaxed finish. Textbook. Landing with a feathery hop, his ball settled four feet from the pin. Miraculously, he overcame his yips, sank the birdie putt, and won a hundred back from Forsythe.

This easy, contented feeling carried over to the next hole and he won it too. Joanne was right, seeing Billy creeping back on him, Forsythe started to feel fingers tightening around his throat, began to piss and moan about bad breaks and bounces; his forearms had bunched up into knots he was gripping the club so hard. By the time they made the turn to the tenth, Mr. Big Shot Car Salesman was two hundred down.

When Billy glanced at his watch again, he was shocked to

see it was already two-thirty. Where the hell had the time gone? The course was congested, but he hadn't realized they were moving so slow. Three hours to play nine holes. Could he make it home in time to catch Jenkins's phone call? He would be cutting it close. Maybe he should pack it in, hike back to his car right now. Forsythe would certainly be happy to see him go and save two hundred smackers.

That thought was enough to make Billy decide to stick in there. After all, who did Jenkins think he was, expecting him to sit around all day like some girl hoping that her big crush would ring her up for a date? And scheduling a phone call on a Sunday. Who the fuck did business that way? Better to forget about it and swear off the clock-watching. Besides, here was Joanne waiting for him just as promised, parked in the shade of a stand of poplar, flashing him a lovely, toothy grin.

"Well?" she said. "How goes the wars?"

"You were right, sweetheart. Apply a little pressure to Forsythe and he wilts. I've got him pretty much where I want him – by the short and curlies."

"Good for you. Two more?"

As Joanne dug down to the bottom of the cooler to find him the frostiest brews, Billy studied the crowns of the poplars. They ran with a liquid ripple in the faint breeze, streamed like a green brook. All at once he was filled with the loveliness of it. He thought of his father, his grey, harassed face. A journeyman plumber, Richard Constable had made the daring leap to go it on his own, to run his own business. A mom-and-pop affair where he was the only worker and his wife kept accounts on the kitchen table. Slowly, conscientiously, Billy's father had nurtured the company, step by careful step, until forty years later it had become a prosperous, moderately sized concern. As long as the old man was alive he'd kept a sharp eye on the workers, on the bottom line, and above all, on his son. But when his father died seven years ago, Billy seized the chance to turn Constable Plumbing into something truly impressive. He had believed that in ten years he could get himself and his family where they deserved to be, on easy street, enjoying the good life his pop had been too timid to seize. What had the old man ever done but work? He had died in the same boxy bungalow Billy had been raised in and his mother had chased her husband's heels to the grave only one year after his demise. When had his pop ever savoured a day like this, had a pretty young woman like Joanne wait on him hand and foot? Flirt with him? Billy's bet was never. Live large or don't live at all, he thought.

His reverie was interrupted. "You okay, Mr. C.?" Joanne was holding out his beers to him, a look of concern on her face.

Billy wiped the tears from his eyes with the back of his hand. "Goddamn allergies," he said. "June is always bad." To cover his embarrassment, he took a slug of his beer.

"Whip Forsythe's ass, Mr. C."

"Consider it whipped," said Billy.

But Forsythe was far from whipped. He kept grinding away, relying on his short game to save him. Every time Billy was sure he had him on the ropes, Forsythe scrambled off them with a crisp wedge, a deadly chip, a seeing-eye putt. Neither of them managed to win a hole outright; the pot steadily increased and, as it did, Forsythe's play grew more and more maddeningly deliberate. He pondered each shot endlessly, excruciatingly studied his putts, stalked the green back and forth, back and forth. For Billy, who liked quick, brisk play, it was torture. Agonizingly the minutes ticked by, marching towards five o'clock. Despite his promise to himself, Billy found himself checking and rechecking his watch, fuming. His thoughts wandered and circled. Maybe he should ring Jenkins up and leave his cell number with him. But wouldn't that look weak, candy ass? Like he was begging?

On the fifteenth green, he leaned over and muttered to Herb Froese, "Hello? What the hell's he up to? Christ, the weekend is officially over in another eight hours."

"Why," said Herb with that sweet innocence Billy found so endearing, "he needs that putt to halve the hole. He misses, it costs him six hundred bucks. Don't tell me you lost track?"

As a matter of fact, Billy had. He knew there was substantial loot at stake but hadn't figured it to the precise dollar. It was how he had always operated, guesstimates, ballpark figures, even when it came to placing tenders. Gritting his teeth, he said, "No way he'll make that. No way."

But Forsythe did make it, a downhill, snaky, twenty-five footer. Snatching his ball from the hole with a flourish and pretending to sheathe his putter like a rapier, à la Chi Chi Rodriguez in his cocky prime, he strode past Billy chirping, "Drive for show, putt for dough."

The standoff continued until the eighteenth, nine hundred bucks on the line at the final hole. Billy had belted down two more beers and found another one lodged under the seat of Froese's cart, God alone knew how it had got where it was, or how long it had been there. It was warm as piss but he swigged it greedily, Herb watching him out of the corner of his eye, forehead disapprovingly furrowed. All that brew was catching up with him, but luckily there was a toilet nearby, so Billy trotted over to take a slash. When he flicked the light switch in the privy nothing happened, some electrical malfunction or the bulb had burned out. So he left the door open, fishing his unit out just as a cart bounced up, one with women on it. Startled, he kicked the door shut and was cast into what would have been utter darkness except for the wan glow of his wristwatch. Looking down he read the numbers 5:05.

The heat stored in the still, confined space seemed to suddenly increase, popping sweat out all over his body. He felt dizzy and short of breath, had to brace himself on one arm above the urinal. An ominous red light was blinking in the swarming blackness, a trick of his light-deprived eyes. It rooted him to the spot while a cruel, indifferent hand squeezed his heart in time with the pulsing light, filling him with superstitious dread. "Fuck," he said. "Oh fuck."

When Billy reached the tee box, everybody was annoyed with him. Forsythe said, "We got tired of waiting for you. We all went ahead and hit."

"I needed to siphon the python."

"Little wonder, the way you've been knocking back the beer," said Forsythe.

Billy put what he imagined was a contemplative, philosophical look on his face. "Ever think what a great game golf is? The only one where you can smoke and drink while you exercise." He lit his last cigarette, crumpled the package, and tossed it in the trash. "Just for my information, you didn't happen to hit it in the bush, did you, Forsythe?"

"Dead solid perfect. Just past the dogleg. Too bad for you."

"The plot thickens then, doesn't it?" Billy sat down on Herb's cart and began removing his golf shoes and socks. Skip Jacobs, who had scarcely said a word to him all day, squawked, "Jesus, what now? You got a stone in your shoe?"

Billy didn't answer, simply strolled to the tee box in his bare feet, coolly swishing his driver back and forth in one hand.

"Showboat," said Forsythe. His voice was nasty, contemptuous.

Right now, there was nothing Forsythe could say to Billy that could touch him. He was in the *zone*. He could *feel* it. "Sam Snead used to say when he needed to find his swing, he'd hit balls in his bare feet. He wanted that connection with the earth. Me too," Billy calmly said.

"Shit."

Billy was remembering when the twins were small and just learning to walk, how he had pulled off their shoes and socks and put them down on the newly sodded lawn of their first house. He and Marva had roared with laughter as the boys capered about in a high-stepping chicken gait, squealing with delight as the soft shoots of grass tickled the soles of their feet. Billy looked down at his own feet, wiggled his toes ecstatically, then looked up and peered down the long channel of fairway bounded by trees on either side, directing his gaze to a spot on the right where a peninsula of spruce extended into the fairway, pinching it even tighter at the two-hundred-yard mark. He was doing what the great ones did, visualizing the shot.

Toughest hole on the course and Billy Constable meant to bring it to its knees by hitting a high cut that would turn the corner of the dogleg and land the ball neatly on the fairway beyond. If he couldn't shape the shot, if the ball didn't curve exactly as he wanted, it would all be over. Tits up. Billy smiled, waggled the head of the driver, and took a mighty cut.

The ball soared upward like a jet rising in a steep climb off the tarmac. Billy leaned forward, held his breath, saw it bank right on cue, a slow swoop to the right, all systems go, pilot firmly at the controls, guiding it on the correct flight path, curling it around the trees. The pressure shot of a lifetime.

Forsythe looked like somebody had put his nuts in a vise grip. "Horseshit luck," he spat out.

"Drive for dough, putt for show," said Billy, jerking his pitching wedge from his bag. He had played Fairview so often he knew exactly where his ball would lie. Striking the down slope of the fairway it would have run hot, maybe as much as three hundred yards. Without hesitation, he started off walking. Moments later he heard the whine of an electric motor. Herb pulled alongside. "Hey, Billy," he said, "hell of a shot. Hop on."

Billy shook his head. "I'm walking this one. For the pleasure of it."

"You don't look so hot," said Herb. "Kind of pale. You all right?"

Waving him on, Billy announced, "Couldn't be better." Herb zoomed off, looking back over his shoulder with a perplexed expression.

He didn't need to see Forsythe frenziedly thrashing the ground with his club after he duffed his second shot to know that the dough was as good as in his wallet. Billy had known it was a done deal on the tee box, just as he had known, leaning against the wall of the hot, reeking toilet, that the other deal with Jenkins was done, but done in a different way, cooked like a goose. That tiny red light blinking malignly at him was a sign, a warning to him that there was a message waiting for him at home, and that the message light blinking on his phone was not an announcement of glad tidings, far from it. That evil little red eye on his answering machine was giving him a mocking wink: Your last hope is gone.

For weeks he had been ducking the obvious truth. Sure Jenkins had politely listened to his sales pitches, but only out of pity. Even that famously hardhearted bastard hadn't been able to bring himself to smother Billy's optimism in the cradle. At least not face to face with the victim. But then by choosing to golf this afternoon he had gone and provided Jenkins with an easy out. Given him the chance to administer a short, quick knife thrust between the ribs, a dry, matter-of-fact communication committed to tape. Thanks but no thanks.

Billy paused and looked around him. An aeration fountain on a nearby pond was fluttering a rainbow-coloured fan in the sunshine. Massive billows of cumulus rode above the clubhouse. On the terrace, blue and white parasols beckoned with the promise of shade and ice-cold drinks. His mind opened, and he saw again the bird-like cloud on this morning's horizon, when everything seemed salvageable. The word for it was *phoenix*. The emblem claimed for himself by that English writer with sex on the brain. The professor said it was mythical, an imaginary bird that rose from its own ashes. The only bit of information that ever claimed Billy's attention in the entire boring class. Well, he was toast now. Burned to a crisp and nothing left for his creditors to do but sift through the blackened crumbs of him. There was no rising from these ashes. Not with overdue goods and services taxes owing to the government, unpaid suppliers, bills and more bills.

He started for his ball, tramping right through a fairway bunker, a terrible breach of etiquette, but he was never coming back to Fairview anyway. The powdery white sand seared his feet and then he felt the lush, cool grass caress and soothe his soles.

It was only June, but Billy Constable figured he had less than twenty minutes of summer left to him. He intended to make the most of it.

Where the Boys Were

WHY THE PEEL BROTHERS? Let's say I'm a retiree who likes to reconstruct, to restore things. While whatever I write here concerns *them*, Donny and Bob Peel, supply and demand is always part of the story. Memory is an old whore eager to turn tricks with the body of the past to satisfy the customer. Think of me as the customer. Which means I'm always right. I need to see it this way.

Not all of this is speculation, my years of being the confidant and friend of Donny's wife, Anne, has given me a chance to hear a lot of Peel family history. But some of it I witnessed for myself, as a somewhat distant but extremely interested observer. Of course, there are many gaps in the story, but where's the pleasure in reconstruction if you can't tart things up a bit? The vintage car boys put a little extra car wax on those 1950s fins to bring the shine out.

A little background first. Donny was three years younger than Bob, who was both father and mother to him. That doesn't mean their parents were actually dead, just that they were dead from the neck up; two mean, stupid drunks. It was Bob who kept Donny's nose above water in the early years, towing him through the choppy waters of his youth until Donny's toes scrabbled bottom, took hold, and he was able to wade ashore under his own power, into life.

Which he eventually did. Donny has been on solid, happy ground with Anne for thirty-five years now. Most couples of their acquaintance envy them because all the Peels' disagreements are fondly trivial, minor. I know, for example, that whether or not to answer the phone when they are otherwise occupied ranks as a Big Issue in their marriage. Donny frequently reminds his wife that dodging annoying phone calls is one of the reasons he pays for voicemail. But if the telephone rings, Anne can't help herself. Her mouth gets twitchy, her eyes turn skittish and desperate, and she has to rush to answer it, just the way she once had to rush to her toddlers whenever she heard their squawks and cries.

This is how I picture it. Not too long ago, as they are settling down to eat dinner, the phone begins to peal. On the third ring Anne spooks up out of her chair and flies out of the room, Donny bellowing after her, "It's a goddamn telemarketer! And if it's somebody looking for me, just remember, I'm not home!"

But his wife's hushed voice, the tense intervals of silence radiating ominously from the kitchen, prompt Donny to lay down his fork and strain his ears. After a few minutes, Anne returns to the dining room white-faced, trembling, and announces, "It's about Bob. Oh, honey, it's bad."

It was bad, although hardly unexpected. Donny had been

waiting for that call for twenty years. A voice caressed him with official sympathy and informed him that an *individual* had been found frozen to death in an alley in Edmonton. In this individual's wallet, a piece of paper had been discovered, contact information for one Donald Peel. Was he the gentleman in question, was he Robert Peel's next of kin? And when Donny confirmed that he was, the caller asked if he would be prepared to come to Edmonton to identify the body. And Donny said, "I'll be there tomorrow."

Early next morning Donny drove off, alone. Anne wanted to accompany him but her husband said no, a long, quiet drive would give him a chance to wrap his head around this. Besides, an autopsy would need to be performed, arrangements would have to be made for dealing with the body. Everything concerning death is a long, tedious affair tricked out in streamers of government red tape, and Donny saw no reason that both he and his wife should have to endure all that paper signing and shuffling. It would be better if Anne stayed put while he settled matters.

Three days later, Donny was back home, a brass urn full of Bob's ashes cradled to his chest. Placing all that was left of his brother on the kitchen table, Donny collapsed in a chair, dropped his head in his hands, shoulders shaken by an earthquake of grief. Anne confessed to me she had never seen her husband in such a state. Donny had always locked his sorrows in a vise of self-control that verged on the unnatural. When their little boy, precursor to the two girls, had arrived blue and lifeless at birth, Donny had never shed a tear, had walked through that terrible time granite-faced.

"But now, Mr. Fenton . . ." Anne said to me, her voice fading away to nothing. Referring to me as Mr. Fenton is one of Anne's "tells," a signal to me that she's feeling very blue. Otherwise, she just calls me Joey. Sometimes Pal Joey.

Everyone who heard Anne compare Donny's reaction to the death of their baby to the death of his brother, something she repeated often to friends, detected a thread of resentment running through it that I must say is not the least bit typical of her.

I find it strange that Anne isn't able to realize that Donny's guilt and grief have reached such a pitch because he feels he failed his brother. After all, Bob had never failed *him*. It was Bob who made Donny's boyhood bearable, made him his school lunches, who brushed his mop of unruly hair into submission each morning, who let him crawl into his bed whenever his little brother woke howling in the grip of yet another nightmare. Donny had no one else to lean on. His useless mother spent mornings in front of a blaring TV, a bottle of beer in her lap, graduating to gin in the afternoons. Her husband was nearly as feckless. True, he managed to stay sober during his eight-hour shift at the mine, but when he got home he made up ground fast; after an hour or two of hard, committed drinking he was as stupefied and blotto as his wife.

The Peel family lived in a forlorn trailer court sprawled on the edge of town, their mobile home little more than a tin shoebox that banged and teetered even in the mildest wind. Mr. Peel's wages would have been sufficient to support a family, but most of his paycheque was spent on booze, although occasionally Bob succeeded in shaming a few dollars out of him to buy Donny shoes or a winter coat.

By the time Bob was ten he was delivering newspapers to earn a little cash. Because Donny couldn't bear to let his security blanket out of sight, he tagged along with Bob while he made his rounds. In those days, it seemed to the town that the Peel boys lived on the streets; if they weren't lugging newspapers up and down them, they were aimlessly, endlessly tramping them. When it got nasty at home, when their parents began to shriek and shout accusations at each other, Donny would start to unravel. Then it fell to Bob to take steps, to shove his brother out the door, to walk away his tears by wandering the dark, echoing streets. On the hottest nights of summer, they sometimes bunked down under the caragana bushes that lined the perimeters of our one park, hidden from the sight of police patrol cars.

This was how the Peel boys grew up. Within a few years, Donny had inherited Bob's paper route and Bob had moved on to other jobs, mowing lawns, digging gardens, shovelling walks, painting fences. By the time the boys were teenagers they had become self-sufficient, pooling their cash to buy clothes, school supplies, even groceries. The summer the girl from Chicago strolled into their lives, Bob was working as a groundskeeper at the local golf course and Donny, fifteen, had been hired to man the concession stand at the town's swimming pool.

Close as they were, the brothers were very different. Donny was a boy bristling with grievances; without Bob's calm, steadying influence he might easily have gone badly wrong. But whenever he was near his brother, Donny's manner changed; his usual bleak, sulky face glowed, suffused by the heat of a transfiguring love. He was far from being a good-looking boy; his mouth was too full-lipped; his nose was big and beaky. And he was small for his age, a scrawny runt, tautly wired in an unsettling, high-voltage way. But when he was in Bob's presence, you scarcely noticed any of that.

Bob, on the other hand, was a tall, lithe, honey-blond boy, the sort of Ricky Nelsonish dreamboat who made teenaged girls swoon. He was a *vessel of grace*. Donny would certainly be displeased to hear Bob spoken of in that way, but Donny is a blunt bulldozer of a man who is incapable of recognizing that *vessel of grace* captures exactly how he thought of Bob, that these words describe precisely the awe his brother's presence inspired in him.

Bob, unlike Donny, was completely comfortable in his own skin, an example of that rare bird whose self-possession is not even distantly related to arrogance. Bob Peel never wanted or asked to be admired; it just happened, like any natural phenomenon, like the weather. It was hopeless for people to believe that flattering him would win them a chance to stake some sort of claim on him. Only Donny ever had that right – except, of course, until the girl from Chicago came along.

There were plenty of people who believed they were entitled to a piece of Bob. All the local sports teams thought he had an obligation to play for them. The manager of the senior men's baseball team, who had once played Triple-A ball, declared Bob a *natural*, said that he had a bushel of talent, with a little coaching who knew how far he might go? To see young Bob Peel throw, catch, or hit a ball gave you the feeling that he hadn't *acted* on it but that he had *flowed* into it and *with* it. A thing of beauty. But Bob couldn't be persuaded to join the team, he declined every appeal to do so with a humble, polite no. Because how could he hold down a job, go to school, play baseball, and still have time to spend with Donny?

The girls had their eye on Bob too. But their flirtatious advances were always stymied, just like the overtures of the beer-bellied, rock-jawed old jocks; except Bob let the young ladies down to earth so gently on a silk parachute of shy courtesy that it was impossible for them to feel that they had been snubbed or had suffered a humiliation.

Nobody could help but adore Bob, except, of course, Mr. DiPietro, the father of the girl from Chicago. Somehow the recently installed mine manager thought *that boy* wasn't good enough for his daughter. An absolutely preposterous notion since Bob Peel was such a one-of-a-kind, deliciously *sweet* boy.

The first time Donny and Bob encountered Carol DiPietro was at the golf club's driving range. Bob had found a dog-eared copy of *Ben Hogan's Five Lessons: The Modern Fundamentals of Golf* kicking around the clubhouse, and over his lunch break he had taken to hitting balls. Bob had never played a game of golf in his life and probably never would, but he found learning golf fundamentals from Hogan's tips a pleasant way to pass his noon hours.

In my mind's eye I can see Donny sitting on the grass, eating a peanut butter sandwich, admiring his brother's smooth swing, the crisp, clean click of the balls leaving the club face, the way they rise, seem to kick into another gear, effortlessly soar into the cloudless, heat-shimmering sky. A car door slams in the parking lot, turning Donny's head. The vehicle is one he has never seen before, a Volkswagen Beetle plastered with flower-power decals, and he doesn't recognize the girl getting out of it either.

A few minutes later she walks to the driving range, toting a bucket of balls, an obviously new set of shiny golf clubs slung over her shoulder. Bob, completely focused on what he's doing, isn't even aware she's there. When she spots Bob, the girl softly sets down her golf bag, sets it down almost reverently. She is exotically pretty, olive-skinned, sloe-eyed, and sleepy-lidded. Her hair is cut in a stylish wedge bob, and she wears knee-length Madras plaid shorts, leather sandals, and a freshly pressed white cotton blouse. Donny stares at her staring at Bob until she glances his way, winks one of her sleepy eyes, and says, "My old man wants me to learn to play golf. I need lessons. Is your friend available?"

"He isn't my friend. He's my brother."

"So is your brother available?"

Bob had heard them talking and is now leaning on a three-iron like it was a cane, like he needs support. "Hey," the girl says, walking towards him, "I'm Carol DiPietro from Chicago." She sticks her hand out; Bob takes it, gives it a few pumps, says nothing.

"You got a name? That's the point of introductions, exchanging names. I say I'm Carol DiPietro and you say, 'I'm . . .'"

"Bob Peel." Pointing, Bob adds, "He's my brother, Donny."

She gives two quick nods, brisk acknowledgements that

they exist. "I'm new here," she declares. "I need to find some-one who knows what's doing. You know what's doing, Bob?"

"Know what's doing how?"

"You got your finger on the pulse? I just finished the two-minute tour of the town. Left me breathless. Where does a person locate the excitement? Everybody make their own homemade fun here? That it?"

"I guess," says Bob.

Carol grins at Donny, a flash of perfect enamel except for one front tooth, a tad darker than its partner, endearingly so. "Just like that he's got an answer. What about you, man about town? Any suggestions?"

Donny begins to rip up handfuls of grass. They fairly fly, a green shower. "I don't know. There's a drive-in theatre."

"Okay, there's a start. You boys game? Want to see a picture tonight?"

After a brief hesitation, Donny answers, sounding a bit belligerent. "Sure, we're game."

"So I'll pick you up. How do I find your house?"

"No. Not there." Donny tears grass even more furiously and aggressively.

"Okay, not there. So what's the plan? Where then? When then?"

Donny looks over at Bob. His brother is gazing off to the horizon as if he expects a possible solution lurking just below the earth's rim to rise up like a trial balloon and float into view. "In front of the post office," Bob says at last. "Nine-thirty."

"We have a date then. Double date," Carol quickly qualifies. "Double your pleasure, double your fun, two brothers are better than one."

Bob glances down at his watch. "I got to get back to work," he says.

Donny heaves himself off the ground. "Me too."

"You do your little things, boys," she replies, yanking a club from her bag. "Just don't stand me up now. Carol won't stand for standing up."

They leave her flailing away, whacking dirt with great determination.

As darkness gathered, Carol DiPietro pulled up in her floral-spattered Volkswagen Bug and hit the horn, blasting the Peels off the post office steps. Donny wedged himself into the back of the car; Bob folded himself into the seat beside Carol with his usual, fluid, careless grace.

"Punctual," she said. "Who doesn't appreciate punctual?"

The drive-in was located three miles out of town, the last mile a washboard, gravel nightmare that Carol took at top speed, the Beetle bucking, fishtailing, making heart-stopping feints towards ditches and telephone poles, the headlights of the car sparring with the darkness. "Here we are," she muttered through clenched teeth, wrestling the wheel, "having the time of our lives in Dogpatch, Canada."

Once they had paid admission and parked, Carol sprang the glove compartment and dug out half a bottle of rum she said she had pinched from her father's liquor cabinet. They cut the booze with Cokes from the drive-in's concession stand, settled in to watch a triple bill: two horror flicks and a beach party movie. At two o'clock in the morning, mid-point in Annette Funicello and Frankie Avalon's sticky romantic complications, Carol abruptly unhooked the speaker from the car window and heaved it as hard as she could, as if she had discovered a bomb somebody had planted in her car.

"They call this *Muscle Beach Party*? No sign of Frankie's love muscle in those trunks. Dee Dee must have taken it and bronzed it for her high school art project." She flipped the car keys to Bob. "I'm buzzed and tired. Home, James."

All the way back to town, Carol sat slumped in her seat, picking at a ragged cuticle and yawning. Outside the DiPietro's ranch-style, Bob handed her the keys, and the three of them climbed out of the vehicle. In turn, Carol kissed both Peel boys on the cheek. "You're sweet guys," she said, weaving from side to side, dazed by rum and fatigue. "What say we hook up again tomorrow night. Same time, same place?"

The Peels bobbed their heads, watched her enter the house, then set off for the golf course. Bob had a key to the clubhouse. Sometimes the boys crashed there when things were too awkward at home.

I imagine them turning restlessly on the sofas that face the clubhouse's big picture window, which offers a panoramic view of the snug little valley that contains the golf course, its fairways grey under a canopy of rapidly paling stars.

There's licence taken here, embellishments perpetrated. There will be more. But it's clear that something like that must have happened because soon the Peel boys and Carol were inseparable, causing her father a sleepless night or two because she was hanging out with low-life trailer trash.

Carol hadn't come with her parents when they had made the move to our town from the States. She had been left behind in the Windy City to attend a boarding school run by nuns. Carol was only a temporary visitor for the summer vacation. I suppose that no matter how much Mr. DiPietro hated her spending time with the likes of the Peels, he assumed that his daughter's returning to Chicago would put a stop to that nonsense.

In those days most of the upper echelon of the mine was American, and many of their teenaged sons and daughters went to private schools in the U.S.A. Their parents were parents who thought ahead, who calculated. A transcript from an American school would carry more weight than one from Canada, ease admission into good colleges stateside. Every summer their offspring migrated north, birds of a startlingly different feather from the native species, the boys in particular. Many of them were enrolled in military academies, had savagely shorn heads, square-shouldered parade square gaits, and addressed anyone over the age of thirty as ma'am or sir. A far cry from the cigarette-smoking, spitting, slouching town boys.

The girls too seemed a breed apart. They went to private schools that prepared them to be ladies who would be suitable wives for the crewcut, manly, preternaturally polite boys. Unlike our local low-rent femmes fatales, the American girls did not go out in public in hair curlers, or in skin-tight stretch pants that made their asses look like they had been vacuum-sealed for freshness. Even in skimpy two pieces at the pool, the girls from the U.S. remained unimpeachably demure, even when they were slathering their lovely limbs with cocoa butter.

All but Carol DiPietro. She was far from demure. She was foul-mouthed. She dabbled in danger. One weekend she talked the Peel boys into driving into the city with her to try to score some grass; if they were lucky maybe even a couple of tabs of acid. Dope of any kind hadn't yet made its way to Dogpatch, but she had high hopes it would be available in a more worldly centre. She, Donny, and Bob spent an afternoon trawling suburban strip malls and accosting likely looking teenagers who went tight-lipped when Carol asked them to hook her up. Back then, weed could land you in serious trouble with the law, and kids were wary around strangers trying to pump dealer information out of them. The trio returned home empty-handed except for a bottle of vodka that Carol had paid a rummy outside a liquor store to buy for them and that they drank rocketing down the highway in Carol's Bug.

Then there was the incident with her father's pistol, which had travelled to Canada hidden away amid the household goods in the back of a United Van Lines truck. After six months, Mr. DiPietro hadn't yet gotten around to unpacking the revolver. Carol discovered it, along with a supply of ammunition, when she was rummaging through storage boxes in search of her collection of *Seventeen* magazines. Not long after that, as she and the Peel boys sat outside the A&W in her Volkswagen, she dramatically popped the clasp on her purse and triumphantly waved the pistol in their faces. "Check this out," she said with a dangerous grin.

Bob said coolly, "Put that away. Somebody might see." Nothing much ever ruffled him.

Donny was vibrating with excitement. "Where the hell did you get that? Is it real?"

"Yeah, it's real. It's Poppy's. It's what he calls nigger-protection insurance," Carol said. "He hasn't needed it here because there's a shortage of them in Dogpatch. I thought we'd warm it up a little. Let it know it's still loved."

And warm it up they did, on a stretch of deserted country road, Bob the wheel man while Carol hung out the passenger window, doing a Bonnie Parker, snapping off volley after volley into the wall of brush flashing by, screaming death and destruction at the top of her lungs. Carol saw no irony in discharging a firearm from a flower-power vehicle since the gun belonged to her father and she was not at peace with Poppy. Poppy she detested.

By then the Peels and Carol had exchanged a certain amount of information about their respective families. Donny, who has never been a subtle fellow, once suggested to Carol she didn't have it so bad. After all, her father had bought her a car.

"Who dropped you on your head? That's his way of saying sorry for locking me up with a bunch of loony lesbo nuns and their sick pet of a priest," she said. "That creep Father Doyle, the only thing he's interested in having me confess is unclean thoughts. In finding out if they 'trouble me.' I tell him, 'Hey, no trouble at all. I just finger them away.' Jesus, no matter how hard I try, I can't get myself kicked out of Sacred Heart Academy."

Probably it was because Carol was imagining that she was peppering Poppy that she fired off nearly all the cartridges in a frenzy before Donny's insistent pleading to *Let him have a go* stopped her. Bob pulled the car up at a played-out gravel pit, the sides of which Donny pocked with the last handful of bullets, little puffs of sand and pebbles spraying like dusty blood.

Bob declined to touch the gun.

After Donny had had his fun, the question arose as to what to do with Poppy's firearm. Carol had finally understood that if she put it back *without the bullets*, her father would know that she had been meddling with it. Maybe it would be better if the pistol simply disappeared, leading Poppy to believe that it had somehow gone missing during the move.

Bob suggested pitching it in a slough. But Carol had a better idea, one that flushed her face with thoughts of sowing future mischief. "Why not bury it here?" she said. "Somebody finds it years from now, they think it's a murder weapon maybe. Just imagine that."

So that's what they did, scraped out a hole in the gravel, dropped the pistol in, and covered it up. Laid it to rest.

None of this scared Donny, not the dope-foraging expedition, nor Carol's crazy spree with the pistol. He never got truly frightened until the three of them saw *Where the Boys Are*. The movie was already old news by them, but almost all of the teenaged fare shown at the drive-in consisted of stale reruns. It didn't much matter what was up there on the silver screen because most of the action was taking place in the cars anyhow.

Where the Boys Are is a cousin to the beach party movies that Carol delighted mocking, but despite a family resemblance, it is a very queer, misfit relation. The way I remember it, a group of college girls go to Fort Lauderdale for spring break to pursue boys, but unlike Annette Funicello in the beach movies, some of these girls actually contemplate losing their virginity. They have even read *The Kinsey Report*.

Donny had never heard of *The Kinsey Report*, and it had never crossed his mind that the co-eds depicted in *Where the Boys Are*, decent, wholesome girls from good, solid, middle-class American families just like Carol DiPietro's, could have *desires*. He had never dreamed Carol might have a similar itch, despite her wildness. He had always thought her smutty talk was just an act, her way of saying, *Hey, I'm one of the guys too. We're all buddies here.* Now he began to wonder if her dirty talk wasn't her way of dropping a hint that she wouldn't say no to a little action.

Donny has always been a slow boat to China, not that swift on the uptake, but when he seizes on a notion he doesn't let it go. As Anne once said to me in a moment of disloyal candour, "Donny's dogged. It's his best quality and his worst."

He began to look for signs that he might be right about Carol, and he found them. Not long after they had seen *Where the Boys Are*, Carol invited Donny and Bob to drop by her house. Her father wouldn't have stood for entertaining the pond-scum Peels under his roof, but he and his wife were off attending a company barbecue. The boys sat in the living room with its fieldstone fireplace and rich broadloom carpeting while Carol, in a rage, paced back and forth slicing and dicing dear old daddy. Father and daughter had fought that morning and she was out for blood. She said you'd think he didn't know which country he had been born in, he was so old-fashioned, "such a wop." In his books, Frank Sinatra was the top actor and singer in the world. Joe DiMaggio the best ball player who had ever lived. Rocky Marciano the greatest heavyweight. For christ's sake, he even got misty-eyed listening to Connie Francis, and she had taken a white-bread name to hide the fact that she came from a family of macaroni-eaters.

It was at this point that Carol dug up the 45 of "Where the Boys Are" from Poppy's record collection, set the platter spinning on the hi-fi, and stood in the lush meadow of DiPietro carpet, singing along to it, pretending that she and Connie were performing a sappy duet. Carol's performance definitely began as tongue-in-cheek. She made Connie's mating call to the boy waiting somewhere around the corner *just for her* as ridiculously and romantically dopey as she could, but as she sang that began to change. By the end of the song what she was doing was evident to Donny. He saw she was really serenading Bob, and Bob was lapping it up in his serene, collected way, a slight smile hovering on his lips. Carol DiPietro was announcing that Bob was the boy for her.

Several nights later when Carol pulled up outside the trailer court to drop the Peel boys off, Bob eased himself out of the car, yanked the passenger seat forward, and let Donny exit from the back. But then Bob dipped his lanky frame and slid back in the Beetle. "See you later," was all he said, not bothering to glance Donny's way, avoiding his brother's abject eyes.

Donny watched them drive away. After they were gone, he did what he and Bob had done so many desolate nights in the past; he returned to town to grimly walk the vacant streets. He hoped to cross paths with the Volkswagen, hoped that it would stop, hoped to hear Carol chirp, "What's the trouble, Bubble? Can't sleep? Jump in." But it never happened that night, or any of the nights that followed, which he spent trudging the brotherless hours away. He never once glimpsed Carol's car. *So where were they?*

He knew now that he was a third wheel. It wasn't that Bob and Carol shut him out totally, but the time always rolled around when Carol evicted him from the car as if he were a stowaway. Worse, she started to treat him like a mascot, a good-luck charm. "If you hadn't jumped at the chance to go to the pictures that day at the driving range, everything might have been different. Because Mr. Shy Guy here would never have made a move, right?" she'd say, giving Bob a knowing, complicit nudge with her elbow.

In August, as summer was winding down, Carol launched her campaign not to go back to Chicago, to enrol in the local high school here. There were no-holds-barred fights with Poppy. "He puts it all on your head," she reported to Bob. "He says you're ruining my future."

And sweet-natured, reasonable Bob said, "Just take it slow. Ease him into the idea."

"Wake up and smell the coffee, Bob!" she yelled. "School starts in two weeks! There is no time for slow!"

Carol was right. Shortly, she got packed off back to Chicago. The day she left, she clung to Bob, buried her head in his shoulder for a long time before suddenly, fiercely turning on Donny.

"You better keep all the other skirts away from your big brother. He's mine. You got that? When Christmas rolls around I'll be back to check what kind of job you've done."

Donny was happy to see her go.

For the next few months letters flew between Bob and Carol. A minimum of one a day, sometimes two. Then in November, a calamity occurred. One of Bob's letters was returned to him marked *Not Here. Address Unknown.*

It was the first time Donny had ever seen his brother panic. Bob settled into a phone booth with a fistful of quarters and finally got connected with Sacred Heart Academy in Chicago. The voice on the other end of the line informed him that Carol DiPietro was no longer a student there and that the school could not, under any circumstances, divulge her current address. Bob waited another ten days for Carol to get in touch with him, but no word came.

That's when he went to John DiPietro's house and demanded to know where Carol was, stubbornly holding his ground even when Poppy ordered him off the property, threatened to call the cops and have him charged with trespassing and a lot more.

Then Bob sprang the question that had been troubling him ever since he had learned that Carol had left Sacred Heart. Had she been taken out of school because she was pregnant? Because if she was, he would marry her. He would quit school tomorrow, get a job, make a home for Carol and the baby. Please, just tell him where she was.

DiPietro lost it entirely. He raved that he'd rather see his daughter dead, would kill her with his own two hands rather than see her marry some shit-bucket bottom-feeder like Bob Peel.

That was enough for Bob; it convinced him his guess had been correct. He took his father's car and drove out to the gravel pit. It was November and very cold, a light skiff of snow whitened the ground. It took him a long time scrabbling about in the frosty sand and pebbles with his fingernails to recover Poppy's pistol.

Bob had got it into his head that brandishing a revolver in Mr. DiPietro's face would scare him into admitting the truth and into telling Bob where Carol was. It didn't. Poppy was a hard-ass veteran of World War II and he wasn't going to buckle to somebody who, in his books, was nothing but a cheap, greasy, little punk. While his wife wailed and twisted her hair in her fists, Mr. DiPietro raced down to the basement, came back with the double-barrel he used for trap shooting, jammed it in Bob's face, and told him that he was going to count to ten and if Bob wasn't gone by then, he was going to blow his brains all over the wall. Bob calmly laid the revolver on the coffee table, said goodnight, and walked out of the house, Mrs. DiPietro's screams reverberating in his ears.

Mr. DiPietro didn't report Bob to the police. Likely when his rage ebbed, he realized that explaining an unlicensed handgun to Canadian cops, a firearm as good as smuggled over the border, might be a tough sell. Mr. DiPietro had a position in the community to maintain.

———

Bob left town that night in his father's Pontiac with whatever money he and Donny had stashed under their mattresses. It took him eighteen hours to reach Chicago, driving non-stop, and another two hours of scooting up the wrong exit ramps and surfing big-city traffic to make his way to Sacred Heart. Unlike Mr. DiPietro, the sisters had no hesitation about calling the cops when they saw he didn't intend to leave until he got answers to his questions. Bob spent three nights and two days in the county jail before he was shipped back to Canada, no wiser about Carol's whereabouts. Mr. Peel's Pontiac remained in the Windy City, held in an impound lot.

Bob didn't return home. He phoned Donny from the Canadian side of the border and told him he was going to catch a bus back to Chicago and renew his search for Carol. Donny begged him not to do it, but Bob's mind was made up.

It was another year and a half before Donny heard from his brother again. Bob wanted to know whether there had been any messages for him from Carol. Had she visited her family maybe? Donny said there had been no letters and that the DiPietros had gone to Chile, where Poppy had been sent by the company's head office to solve some sticky problems in a copper mine there, or so he had heard.

It turned out Bob was in Wisconsin shovelling shit on a dairy farm and saving all he could of his measly wages to hire a private investigator to track down his missing girlfriend. When Donny asked him where he had been for the last eighteen months and what he had been up to, Bob was vague. He said, *There were some things that some people thought needed taking care of.*

Then the subject reverted to the DiPietros' move to Chile. Bob said, "That's a good tip, Donny. I'll have a private investigator look into it, once I get some cash. Maybe that's why I haven't heard from Carol. I think her father kidnapped her, made her go to Chile."

Donny said a person could mail a letter from Chile. They had a postal service there. It wasn't Antarctica. From the way Bob was talking, he thought his brother might be drunk, especially when he began to ramble on about "finding his family."

"You don't need to find us. We're where we always were. We're here," snapped Donny. "Where do you think we got to?"

But by family Bob didn't mean the Peels. He meant Carol and the baby who most likely didn't even exist.

Donny said, "If there's a baby – and I don't believe there is – it's been adopted by now. And if Carol wanted to get hold of you, she would have."

But Bob was sure Carol's lunatic father was keeping her away from him, and he clung to the bizarre idea that she would never have agreed to let their baby be adopted, that the toddler was waiting in some orphanage for the day when he and Carol would be reunited as a couple and they could take their child home with them.

Donny did his best to persuade him he wasn't thinking straight, but Bob wouldn't listen. That was that, he *knew*.

Another period of silence descended, one that lasted a year. By then Donny had finished school, had got hired at the mine, and had rented a two-bedroom apartment so that when Bob finally returned to our town, his brother could move in with him. Late one night Bob called. He was back in Canada, living in British Columbia, picking fruit for the summer. He admitted that he had never managed to save enough money to hire somebody reliable to investigate Carol's case. He wanted to know if Donny could lend him what he needed? When Donny asked how much that would be, Bob named a preposterous, astronomical figure. So, playing for time, Donny urged him to come home and get a job at the mine. Then they could pool their money like they had in the old days, for a common cause, and when they had enough to hire a private detective, the search for Carol and the child could well and truly start from a solid foundation.

Before he hung up, Bob said he'd give it some thought.

But Donny never found out what Bob thought. Once again contact between them was broken. It was ages before Bob confessed that his long silences were the result of frequent hospitalizations. An idea had taken hold of Bob, not in the way ideas took hold of Donny, by taking root in his mind, but by invading Bob's whole being, his brain, his blood, his gut, his nerves, his very sinews. Somewhere out there, Bob was certain, Carol and the child were waiting for him to rescue them. This was a fact as incontestable as the force of gravity. End of discussion.

At first this obsession didn't interfere very much with Bob's ability to hold some kind of menial, low-paying job, to get by in the world, but over time he drifted further from reality in the pursuit of his ghostly family. Where once he had had one person to save – Donny – now he had two.

Donny did everything he could to stay in touch with his brother. For several years, he used up all his vacation time paying visits to Bob, trying to talk sense into him, trying to get him some help. But if he pushed too hard on that front, Bob was prone to head for the hills, to vanish.

When Donny married Anne, he was determined that his older brother be there to stand up with him as his best man. That meant driving all the way to Thunder Bay to collect Bob and then driving him halfway across the country after the wedding to get him back to Ontario. Anne accompanied them, although she says it wasn't her idea of a dream honeymoon.

During the next three decades Bob became an ever more distant and shadowy figure in Anne and Donny's lives. He neglected to come to either his mother's or father's funeral. Only one thing gave Donny hope: Bob had stopped mentioning his lost family to him.

But surely this was because Bob wanted to protect his younger brother, believing it upset Donny too much to be reminded of the tragedy that had befallen him. He knew that despite what Donny said about it all being in his head, deep down his brother recognized the truth of things, understood, and was suffering his terrible loss right along with him.

It was only when Donny's oldest daughter, Janet, got married that Bob forgot himself and made a slip of the tongue. He was sitting at the head table in the new suit Donny had bought him when he leaned over and whispered to Anne, "I wonder if my little girl's married now too." Bob confessed to his sister-in-law that he always thought of his lost child as a girl, and that he always saw her as the spitting image of her mother.

It wasn't long after that Bob pulled his last vanishing act. Donny had no idea where he was until Bob was found on that snowy street in Edmonton, a frozen corpse, nothing in his pockets but a wallet that held a carefully printed note identifying Donny as his next of kin.

Donny put his heart and soul into organizing his brother's memorial service, but you could see how deeply disappointed he was by the sparse turnout. But Donny clearly wasn't thinking straight. Most of those who once knew Bob have long gone. That's the nature of a mining town. The price of ore falls and rises. When it goes down, people get laid off and strike out to find work elsewhere. They don't return. There's almost no one here who remembers Bob. Those who came to the funeral came out of respect for Donny.

When I speak about no one coming back here once they've left, I'm a contradiction to my own statement, an exception. Fifteen years ago when my father died, I returned to take over his law practice and escape a relationship that had gone terribly wonky and dramatic. I found out that with a minimum of stress you could earn a good living here doing property transfers, wills, the odd divorce and child custody case, this and that. But it was also mind-numbing, tedious work so three years ago I sold Fenton Law. I pass my summers here. The attitude of the town towards men like me isn't what it once was. I am extended a grudging, cool tolerance. It's all I can expect, but it's not quite enough so I spend my winters in Thailand.

Donny himself conducted the memorial service, surrounded by gaudy banks of flowers and old snapshots of Bob that had been blown up so large that they suffered an ominous, disturbing distortion. Believe me, Donny is no public speaker, and it was painful to hear him dully sing his brother's praises, dab a muddled picture for eyes that had never seen Bob in the flesh, in his splendid prime. Of course, the service ended with Connie Francis singing "Where the Boys Are." Donny had got Anne, who is far more tech-savvy than he is, to download it for him. It was a ghastly greeting card moment, but I wept, recalling where the boys were, Donny and Bob, so long ago. And me too, I suppose.

Afterwards, Anne and Donny had a few people over to their house for snacks and drinks. When the place cleared, Anne and I sat in the kitchen talking quietly and drinking margaritas. I'm her ear to whisper into. She went on about how traumatic all this had been for Donny, how she feared he might never get over it. "He's so depressed," she said. "He loved his brother so much."

"Bob was easy to love," I said. "Years ago I had the most tremendous crush on him." The words took me as much by surprise as they did her.

Immediately, Anne looked startled. She gave a glance over her shoulder to make sure we were alone. I knew what she was thinking. How dreadful it would be if Donny ever heard me say such a thing. But having confirmed her husband was nowhere in the vicinity, she relaxed. "Why, Pal Joey," she said, grinning with mischievous delight, "the things you say. Just make sure Donny never hears you talk like that. You'd never get in this door again if he knew you had once had designs on his brother."

I was mildly offended that Anne had misunderstood what

I was saying. "It wasn't *lust*," I told her. "It was just that Bob was so kind. When the other boys started picking on me, he would say a few quiet words and it would end. It wasn't that they were afraid of him; he had *presence*. And Bob liked being needed. Bob liked taking care of people."

She gave me a puckish look. It was as if she hadn't heard a word I'd said. "So now I know why you've been pumping me for stories about Bob and Donny for all these years. You are still lovelorn."

Who could resist Bob Peel's beauty and kindness? I couldn't. Even though I always knew that he was up a blind alley in my heart, unreachable.

This was nothing I wanted to talk to her about. So I said, "Lovelorn? Maybe for July of 1967. A month is my expiry date for carrying a torch."

Disguising my pain and grief with flippancy worked. Anne laughed and I smiled, poured myself another splash of tequila, and thought of the two of us, Donny and me, keepers of the memory of Bob Peel, the boy who had never wanted or asked to be admired, only loved.

Anything

WHEN TONY JAPP ARRIVED without an appointment at his agent's office to announce he was finished with the business, Probert squirmed uneasily in his high-back-mesh-executive ergonomic chair until an opportunity came for him to break in and ask, "So is this about Betty?" Betty, Tony's wife of thirty-five years, had died three months before. The question was not unreasonable, given how cut up his client had been by his loss.

All Japp said was, "No," sounding as if he meant it. But then he was an actor.

They talked for a few minutes more, Probert looking understanding and empathetic, Japp stoic and resolute – like Brutus before he threw himself on his sword. Tony had once played that role at Stratford to good notices. At last, his agent sighed and murmured, "I know you, Tony. Six months, twelve at the outside, and you'll be asking about jobs, audition calls. Acting's in your blood."

"It was," said Japp. With that they shook hands and Tony left, feeling only a little disappointed that Probert hadn't tried harder to dissuade him from laying to rest his old life.

Probert's prediction was wrong. It took almost a year and a half before Tony Japp, in a way neither of them could have foreseen, climbed back on the acting horse. By then he was living on the Qu'Appelle Valley property that had been bequeathed to Betty by her parents, frugal, industrious people who had left her pretty well off when they died. Nine months after Tony gave Probert the news that he was kicking the acting-can down the road, he made another decision that left his friends and colleagues in Toronto wagging their heads in disbelief. He moved to Saskatchewan. *The guy's unmoored by grief* pretty much summed up their reaction.

Tony suspected *unmanned by guilt* came closer to hitting the mark. After all, he had never grasped Betty's sentimental attachment to her family's cottage in the Qu'Appelle Valley. His wife had always claimed to have been happiest there – although Tony had trouble believing anything even remotely pleasant could have taken place in that godforsaken setting. By July, the lake floated leprous-looking archipelagos of blue algae; the barren, parched hills surrounding this toxic puddle left Tony feeling as if he were residing on the site of some nuclear disaster that had blasted every living thing with a lethal dose of radioactivity. He thought of the place as "Chernobyl," a nickname he was careful never to let escape his lips when his wife was within earshot. She would have gone ballistic.

As soon as Betty got her hands on the property, she began a relentless renovation and expansion of the cottage. The work dragged on for five summers and Tony was luckily absent for most of the construction since he had gigs at various summer drama festivals. When he chanced a few discreet remarks about the expense and practicality of Betty's home improvement frenzy, he got a tart rebuttal: "God isn't making any more lakes. The value of recreation property will only go up with time. It's an investment."

Tony knew that his wife was not really intent on upping the value of the property; what she was busy doing was feathering them a nest for their golden years. Winterizing it so it could be occupied year-round was what tipped her hand. Betty's plan was for them to retire there when Tony finally came to his senses and agreed to give up acting.

Telling Probert that his forsaking stage and screen had had nothing to do with Betty had been a bald-faced lie. Before she had fallen ill, Betty had been able to talk about little else. "You've had a good run, Tony. Take it easy now, enjoy life. What Mom and Dad left us put our money worries to rest. Face it, you're never going to top *Aid* or get back to where you once were. It's just not in the cards," she would say, giving him a little tough-love, truth-telling lecture that always sent him into a three-day sulk.

Aid had been the highlight of Tony's career, a CBC series in which he had starred as Bobby Casgrain, a legal aid lawyer whose dyslexia had pinned the *stupid* label on him as a boy, the child of an unmarried welfare mother whose drug habit had landed him in the care of stern foster parents. These psychic scars had turned Bobby into a social crusader, a righteous defender of down-and-outers, a rule-flouting lawyer often cited by judges for contempt, a legal bad boy affectionately supervised by his wise, matronly boss, Alice Dawe, the supportive, nurturing Mommy he had never known. Casgrain was the quintessential Canadian Perry Mason, a defender of the marginalized, the scourge of heartless Crown prosecutors and prejudiced cops.

The moderate success of *Aid* during the early 1990s had earned Tony tepid Canadian fame, although that had now cooled to the point where only occasionally, very occasionally, did somebody passing him on the street throw him a puzzled glance as if to say, *You look familiar. Didn't we go to school together?*

But Betty's death had left him with concerns other than giving a boost to his sagging star. He was nagged by feelings of guilt, feelings that he had an obligation to appreciate what his wife had loved, to take a stab at accepting what Betty had spent so long preparing for them. A retirement home in the valley.

But before he could do his duty by Betty, the condo in Toronto needed to be sold, loose ends tidied up, and arrangements made to ship his belongings halfway across the continent. All of this took much longer than he expected, the result of which was that he had arrived in the Qu'Appelle Valley in late autumn, winter ready to pounce. Which it did shortly, with a vengeance. Soon howling blizzard followed on the heels of howling blizzard. On the days when the sky didn't blanket everything in sight with a pall of snow, the wind came shrieking down from the hills to thud against his doors, to lament in his roof vents, to groan in the throat of his chimney.

Suddenly Chernobyl had gotten much worse. Chernobyl had frozen solid. Yet as relentlessly white and empty as the landscape had become, it was nothing compared to the void within him. After his wife's death, Tony's friends had talked him into seeing a therapist. But he had given up on counselling because, as far as he could see, it wasn't doing him any good. Now he wondered if maybe his therapist, a very pleasant, sympathetic, capable young woman, hadn't been able to get through to him because there had been nothing for her to reach, that his core was a blank, had always been a blank.

Perhaps that had been the root of his bewilderment on those occasions when other actors talked about recognizing some part of themselves in a character, of using that bit to begin to flesh out a role, to add layers to the onion. They had been talking about working from the *inside* out, which had always seemed strange to him. A notion he distrusted. Because Tony Japp had always been an *outside-in* actor. He began with the words on the page, although they had never been all he needed. He had always required something more, something tangible, something real and solid, something he could touch and handle. He had needed to hold the onion, and for Tony Japp the onion had always been the right costume, the right prop.

In *Aid* the onion had been Bobby Casgrain's lawyer's robe spattered with "two all-beef patties, special sauce . . ." and Tim Hortons doughnut-glaze stains. Bobby's grubby appearance had been a recurring joke worked and reworked by the showrunner. But for Tony that greasy rag wasn't a joke; it *was* Casgrain, not just camouflage that lulled prosecutors and judges into underrating him, taking him for an incompetent mook. The robe was Casgrain's history, a messy life made visible.

If he had had to rely on locating that squalor inside himself, Tony would have come up empty-handed. His life had always been a neat and tidy affair. Sometimes he would recall, with a twinge, overhearing two young actors talking about him. One of them had said, "The only part Japp ever got exactly right is the one in his hair." At the time he had been able to dismiss that remark as simple envy. Because with the right costume, he had always been right for *any* role. Tony Japp had never suffered from typecasting, had never lacked for work.

Yet when the odd spell of unemployment came, Betty had complained he was impossible to live with, a moody pain in the ass. Now Tony asked himself if those infrequent stretches of joblessness hadn't provided him with a troubling glimpse of what he faced now each and every morning in Chernobyl: his profound, essential emptiness.

His therapist had encouraged him to express his anger over the loss of his wife, which she assured him was a normal response. But Tony wasn't sure he felt angry. He could *simulate* anger for the counsellor, which he did convincingly on any number of occasions. But the line between what he felt and what was just acting was never clear. He *did* feel a terrible grief over his wife's death, of that he had no doubt, but he couldn't be sure that the tears he shed in the therapist's office weren't simply squeezed out of him to fulfill her expectations of how he ought to be behaving. It was easy enough to do. For years he had wept on cue for cameras and audiences.

Spring came in torturous increments. On the lake the ice began to rot, forming tiny puddles that glinted maniacally in the strengthening sun. Japp's eaves gargled meltwater and the sand on the beach shyly crept out from beneath the snow. The worst winter in a decade was ending. Then one morning as Tony stood on his front steps drinking his morning coffee in a weak shimmer of sunshine, a whitetail doe staggered on to his lot and crumpled to the ground, lay there panting, stark ribs heaving under its mangy hide. Tony ransacked his fridge for anything a deer might eat, but the doe was too weak to take a carrot or even a leaf of lettuce from his hand.

In a panic, he called the cell of the local handyman, a fellow he had often seen riding around in a half-ton with a 30.30 in a gun rack in his back window, and implored him to come put the animal out of its misery. But Bits Bodnarski didn't view this as an emergency; besides, he was busy pumping out a septic tank and estimated he couldn't make it to Tony's place in less than four or five hours. Given Tony's description of the deer's condition, Bits thought the doe would be long gone before he got there but if Tony wanted him to haul the body to the dump he was willing to do that.

A city boy and a newcomer to the area, Tony had no idea who else to turn to, what else to do in the unnerving situation he found himself in. The thought of watching the deer slowly expire before his very eyes threw him into a panic.

Suddenly, he became determined to put distance between himself and the deer, between himself and Chernobyl. He booked a room in The Bessborough in Saskatoon, jumped into his car, and beat it, leaving Bodnarski to deal with the mess.

Next morning Tony decided to go for a walk in downtown Saskatoon, hoping a little air might dispel the previous night's morbid dream about the doe. A nightmare garishly embroidered with vivid, gruesome details that he couldn't remember actually having witnessed while kneeling beside the dying animal: a swollen tongue lolling in a blue-grey mouth, an eye scummed with a thick, yellowish mucus; a pungent, scorched-coffee-bean stench rising from the hide.

On his stroll, Tony stumbled on a vintage menswear store that piqued his interest. Thirty minutes later he left the shop with a leather hat box under his arm. According to the owner, the woman who had left the hat with him on consignment had told him it had never been worn. Her grandfather had ordered the hat, a homburg, from Europe in 1950, but before it arrived the old man had died from a massive coronary. For sixty years the homburg had been shuttling from one of his descendants to another until it had finally passed to her. But as she had said, "What use is a stupid-looking hat to me?"

Tony had fallen in love with the hat at first sight.

———

Back at the hotel, he unsnapped the brass clasps of the hat box and reverently laid the hat, a dove-grey felt with Prussian blue velvet band, on his bed. The leather sweatband was in immaculate condition, not the slightest discolouration. As the woman had claimed, the homburg had clearly never touched anyone's head. It was virgin.

The hat was merely a taste, an *amuse-bouche*, just enough to make Tony aware how ravenous he was, how starved he was for the full-meal-costume deal. The *Yellow Pages* yielded only one tailor who offered custom-made suits. Within the hour, he found himself in a seedy section of town in a small shop run by an Iranian immigrant. When Tony showed the man a picture of the 1930s-era suit he had located on a website and had printed off in the hotel's business centre, the tailor assured him he could have it ready for him in forty-eight hours, no problem, "Same as Hong Kong. Better than Hong Kong." Tony selected a charcoal wool pinstripe and patiently submitted to having his measurements meticulously taken.

By the end of the day he had visited several other men's clothing stores and completed his costume: a trench coat with a leather collar, a couple of dress shirts with French cuffs, a pair of distinctly foreign-looking Italian shoes, a set of abalone cufflinks. He was excited, just as he used to be when a role started to come together, when he sensed himself getting a handle on a part. Best of all, he felt himself filling up, not feeling quite so hollow anymore.

———

The suit was ready on time, just as promised. And Tony had been able to extend his reservation at the hotel. Location was every bit as important to him as the costume. The Bessborough, built in 1928, had a marble-floored lobby, crystal chandeliers, and well-worn Bergère chairs in the hallways, the proper stage setting for the man he was envisioning. Maybe not quite *Grand Hotel*, but then he wasn't John Barrymore's Baron Felix von Geigern, except for the Homburg. Even more important than the physical setting The Bessborough provided was the hotel's reputation for sheltering ghosts.

Tony had learned that from the teenaged bellhop who had shown him up to his room when he had checked in. The kid was obsessed with "the Bez's ghosts." The soul of the suicide who had thrown himself over an upper-floor railing and cracked the marble floor of the lobby when he landed there. The man in a grey suit and fedora who wandered the hallways late at night, but, hey, nothing to worry about from him, he always gave everyone a nice smile, that was it.

When Tony had spotted the hat he had immediately thought, *What better way to banish the ghost he had become than to* play *a ghost.*

Tony came down from his room a little before six and seated himself in one of the Bergère chairs near the entrance to the restaurant. In his hand he held his final prop, a copy of Georges Bernanos's *Sous le soleil de Satan*, a book he had picked up that afternoon in a second-hand bookstore. Tony had thought that the reference to Satan on the cover had a nice atmospherish touch to it and that a French novel wasn't really at odds with his conception of the character he was playing: a pre–World War II gentleman of Mitteleuropa, cosmopolitan, slightly jaded, and frayed by history, a man who by now would have been in his grave for nearly fifty years. But that was the point, wasn't it? A ghost was supposed to be dead.

He sat there for an hour without anybody giving him a second glance. Not the harried-looking business travellers who bustled by him into the restaurant, nor the families from rural Saskatchewan visiting the city on shopping safaris. Tony felt underappreciated, a little like he had when Probert hadn't more forcefully protested his decision to quit acting. Which led him to hunt up excuses for why he wasn't attracting more attention. First of all, it wasn't exactly the hour people expected to encounter spectres. Second, matinees were always a tougher sell, audiences less responsive and appreciative.

Tony decided to fuck it, find some place outside the hotel to eat.

His mood lightened a little as he walked over the Broadway bridge. Spring was becoming a reality. The air was milder, softer; sunshine flashed on the scales of the river and the trees bore pale green parasols of budding leaves. It wasn't a stretch to imagine yourself in Budapest, sauntering over the Danube.

And, even more encouraging, he was drawing looks from

those he met on the bridge, most of them hipper young people than the sort you ran into at The Bessborough. One
young Johnny Depp wannabe in a trilby even gave him a
grin and a thumbs-up, one wearer of hats saluting another.
Tony asked himself when was the last time he'd seen an actor
in a homburg? Al Pacino in *The Godfather II*? David Suchet in
Agatha Christie's Poirot? At any rate, it put him in distinguished company.

He chose to take a light supper in a French-style bistro.
Gratifyingly, one or two heads turned when he made his
aloof and self-possessed entrance and was seated at a table
beside a window where he could watch people strolling
about, enjoying one of the first truly warm evenings. Placing
his homburg and *Sous le soleil de Satan* conspicuously on
the table, he asked for a glass of red wine and a plate of
charcuterie in the faintly Germanic-sounding accent he had
been working on all afternoon, nothing Colonel Klinkish,
just the slightest shading of pronunciation and intonation.
When the food and wine arrived, Tony shot his French cuffs
and tucked in with more appetite than he'd had in ages. He
even indulged in dessert: a vínarterta, a double espresso,
and an Armagnac.

Tony could feel himself growing more confident, owning
the part, so much so that he opened the Bernanos, propped
it against the vase on his table, and began to pretend to
read. His French was almost non-existent, but he felt it was
a crime not to take advantage of a prop.

———

Someone was talking to him. Tony looked up in surprise and discovered a very attractive woman standing by his table, smiling down at him. He couldn't catch a word of what she was saying and then he realized that that was because she was speaking French. For an instant, his mind blanked, but then he recovered, answering her in his faintly German-inflected English. A pro carried on when things took an unexpected turn, as they often did in the theatre.

"I am sorry to say, madam, that a conversation in French is beyond me," Tony said with a formal, apologetic tilt of the head. "What you see is a man attempting to recover a little of the French he had long ago – when he was a schoolboy. And failing miserably."

"If it's a recovery operation," the woman said, "I wouldn't start with Bernanos."

"No, a little modesty about one's abilities would be more correct."

The woman laughed, a bark of unrestrained pleasure, of spontaneous applause. She was fiftyish, tall and handsome, rather dark, flamboyant, and Gypsyish-looking with her large gold bangle earrings and blue silk scarf tied around her head, knotted at one temple, its ends dangling down over her left breast.

"I took you for French because of the book and because you look so European."

Tony said, "Ah, my dress, my appearance. That is my father's influence. He was very European, very correct." He paused to leave the impression he was searching for a phrase. "*Old school*, I think the young people say. And this," he explained, reaching out to give the homburg a fond pat, "was my father's. On certain days when I am very sentimental I wear it to honour the old gentleman's memory." Tony dropped his eyes to his wide-lapelled, pinstriped suit. "Responsibility for the rest is mine. My eccentric taste or calculated exhibitionism, who can say? Well, I have been thirty years in this country, but old habits die hard." Was that speech over the top? Too much? She seemed to have swallowed his line.

"I think that's charming," she said, seating herself without an invitation. Tony found her openness, her *genuineness* appealing. And he could see that she was intrigued by him. That was flattering. He hadn't intrigued anybody in a long time. She offered her hand and said, "Susan Breck."

He took it. "Tonio Japp." Where the hell had Tonio come from? He'd read *Tonio Kroger* once, long ago, maybe that was the source of it. He wasn't sure how to categorize the look that passed over her face when he said the name. Amusement? Disdain? Did she find Tonio pretentious? Hurriedly he said, "But my friends call me Tony."

"Tony it is."

He asked if she would like something.

She said she had just dropped in for a quick cup of coffee.

He suggested she take a liqueur with it.

She conceded. "All right, you only live once," she said and then began to explain to him why she had spoken to him in French. In a former life she had taught it in high school. "It's lucky for me you didn't answer in *la belle langue*," she said gaily. "If you were a native speaker I wouldn't have been able to keep up with you. Drumming French into teenagers' heads all day long doesn't do much to polish your own ability."

She mentioned that she was just back from a wonderful holiday on the Mexican Riviera. An annual event. Each year she and a girlfriend went down there to escape the last gloomy, slushy days of winter. "At least it gives me a head start on my tan." She coyly lifted the strap on her wristwatch, displaying a milk-white band of skin. Mickey Mouse stared at Tony from the face of the watch.

It was a relief that she was more intent on talking about herself than making inquiries about him. She enumerated interests: travel and movies, classes in watercolour painting and Latin dancing. Then she switched gears, turned a shrewd, appraising eye on Tony and asked him flat-out what he did.

He said he was retired.

"Retired from what?" she wanted to know.

This was tricky ground, details were likely to trip him up. "Life," he said.

"Too bad for life," Susan said. "So what brings you to Saskatoon, Tony? It can't be business if you're retired. And this place is hardly a hot tourist destination."

He had to give her something, and once Tony started talking, things came spilling out of him that he wouldn't ordinarily say, especially not to a total stranger. He thought his unusual behaviour was a consequence of the long winter, his almost complete isolation for months and months. Not another human being to talk to.

He told Susan that he was a widower. That he had recently moved from Toronto to live in the Qu'Appelle Valley. As he talked about his new home in Chernobyl, he found himself recasting it in a more favourable light for her. He painted a picturesque spot that he chosen to come to for the sole purpose of measuring and reflecting on his life. A few pensive, sober touches to the newly christened Tonio Japp.

"But," he said, "one needs an occasional break from all that. I get hungry for a little human company – even if it is the company of strangers." He looked about the bistro. "A meal eaten surrounded by other voices, even if they are unfamiliar voices, can be pleasant enough."

"Hey, I get that. I can see where you're coming from. We've all been down that road one time or another. Seize the day."

He wondered if Susan might be a divorcee. A widow would almost certainly not have been able to refrain from letting him know that she too was acquainted with grief and loneliness.

Tony ordered another round of drinks, sat back, and listened to her bright, cheery talk. Outside, the street was darkening. Cars streamed by, their headlights leading their occupants who knew where? A little after nine, Susan glanced at her watch, bent to gather her purse up from the floor. "Well, Tony," she said, "this has been a slice, but I better be on my way. I get a bit nervous walking alone at night."

"I left my car at the hotel," Tony said. "Otherwise, I would offer you a lift. But if you feel anxious, permit me to call a cab and see you safely home."

"No," she said. "A cab would be silly. I live quite near here. Just downtown. It's just that I stayed longer than I expected to." She gave him a smile that he read as implying, *And it's all your fault. You fascinating man.*

"I'm staying at The Bessborough. We could walk together."

"You don't mind?"

"Not in the least. A pleasure."

Tony paid the bill and they set off. With the sun down there was a bite to the air. Susan had turned silent and looked lost in thought, although she walked purposefully and briskly. Maybe it was to dispel some tension she felt, but perhaps it was only to keep the chill at bay. When they had crossed over the river she halted at the foot of the bridge and announced that it wasn't necessary for him to see her all the way home. It would only take her minutes to get there.

Tony wondered why her mood had changed in the course of a short walk. Did she suspect he had designs on her, was she worried that he might prove difficult to get rid of? "If you're sure . . ."

"Absolutely."

What anodyne *coup de grâce* to the evening would bring this awkwardness to an end? It was nice meeting you? I enjoyed our little talk? Tony adjusted the homburg and reminded himself that he was a gentleman from Mitteleuropa with a lifetime of sophisticated experience. "Might I invite you to join me for lunch in the next few days?" he said softly. "That is, if you are unattached." He smiled in a way that he hoped would soften that last remark, which a woman of a certain age might find indelicately phrased.

Susan Breck cocked her head as if she had discovered some new, surprising angle from which to view him. She gave a hoot of laughter. "What a way to put it! If you mean am I attached to anyone at the hip – no, I'm not."

"So," he said, "perhaps lunch tomorrow?"

"I wouldn't rule it out." She started rummaging about in her purse. "Look, can I let you know when I've figured out exactly what I've got on my plate for tomorrow? Give me your contact info and I'll be in touch." She handed a notepad to Tony, who took a few steps that brought him under the light shed by a street lamp. He wanted to make sure that whatever he printed would be perfectly legible, that Susan Breck would have no problem deciphering it.

When he returned the pad to her, he said hesitantly, "Maybe I should get your number . . ."

"No need," she said brusquely. "I'll be in touch. I promise not to keep you dangling." There was a formidable, no-nonsense quality to her voice. Tony could imagine her laying down the law to her students back in her teaching days. That settled, Susan Breck left him, walking with an assurance and confidence that dismissed any suggestion that she found dark streets intimidating.

By eleven o'clock the next morning Tony was growing more and more annoyed he hadn't heard from Susan. Her definition of what it meant to keep someone dangling wasn't the same as his. Maybe she had only asked for his contact information so that she could dodge turning him down to his face. But at eleven-thirty his laptop timidly pinged, alerting him that he had an email. It was Susan announcing she could do lunch today. She recommended that they meet at an Italian trattoria near The Bessborough for which she provided the address. Tony fired off a reply. Yes.

———

Most of the trattoria's patrons were clustered near the big front windows, basking in the spring sunshine, but Susan was seated at the very back of the restaurant in a dimly lit booth. He took her preference for a secluded nook as a promising sign. She was looking even more exotic and flashy than she had the night before: bright scarlet lipstick, mauve eyeshadow, heavy mascara, a turquoise choker and matching earrings, silver rings and bracelets worked in Mayan designs. The bracelets chimed brightly with every move she made and they chimed a lot because Susan was in high spirits. Everything she said was underlined and emphasized with reckless flourishes.

They had a leisurely lunch and killed a bottle of wine with it. Tony even coaxed her into joining him and taking a grappa with her coffee. By the time they left the trattoria, Susan's vivacity had crossed the frontier into tipsiness. "With all that booze my afternoon's shot," she said, squinting against the sun.

They began to drift down the street.

"Well, we can find something else to do. Seeing you're at loose ends."

"*Unattached*, you mean." Susan stood on tiptoe to give the crown of the homburg a sharp tap. "What's going on under that *chapeau*? Let me guess."

Tony grinned sheepishly.

They turned a corner and there was The Bessborough looming at the end of the block. Susan began to give Tony mischievous smacks to the behind with her hand-tooled Mexican purse. It was as if she were driving him towards the hotel. "What's this, *Tonio*? What're you cooking up, *Tonio*?" she demanded in a loud, challenging voice.

He had been cooking up nothing, not really. But hearing his name repeated in that taunting way made him feel ridiculous. What could be more ridiculous than a sixty-year-old man in a silly hat who somebody was swatting down the street as if he were some sulky, dawdling child? People were stopping to stare at them.

"Jesus, stop that," he muttered and realized it was the first time his carefully practised accent had slipped.

Immediately, she parroted back at him, "Stop that. Stop that. *Stop that.*"

At least when they entered the lobby of the hotel she quit paddling his buttocks. As they rode up in the elevator, Susan propped herself against the back wall in a hip-slung street-walker pose and curled her lips provocatively.

"Why are you looking at me that way?" Tony demanded. But he got no reply, except that the corners of her mouth went up a little more.

Sexual excitement and anticipation were leaving him choked and breathless. The lunchtime booze had given him a bit of a buzz. By the time he got the door of his room opened, Susan had fished a package of condoms out of her purse, which she tossed down on the bedside table like a calling card. She had come prepared. That gave a lift to Tony's self-confidence, which the playful spanking had done a lot to undermine.

Susan went to the window, drew the curtains shut, switched off the light, and began to peel off her clothes efficiently, matter-of-factly.

In the half-light of the room, the areas of her body that had been protected from the Mexican sun by a swimsuit gleamed white, breasts and abdomen and pudendum appearing to thrust themselves forward, demanding attention, her tanned face, arms, and legs receding, blending with the surrounding dimness. Naked, she appeared to be nothing but a practical assortment of sexual parts.

And that, it seemed, was what he was to Susan Breck. Tony Japp or Tonio Japp, whoever the hell he was now, clearly wasn't *there* for her except to be brusquely instructed. *Do this, do that.* When she climaxed astride him, her orgasm registered itself in a series of quick muscle contractions that swept up from her thighs to her diaphragm. She toppled off him and lay absolutely still, then after a moment of lassitude swung her legs out of bed and said, "I'm going to clean up," in the preoccupied voice of someone reminding herself that a chore needed doing.

Tony lay in bed listening to the white-noise hiss of the shower, which, combined with the wine and grappa, suddenly clutched him and dragged him down into sleep.

Tony opened his eyes, ran his hands over the sheets and his eyes around the room. He called "Susan?" several times, but there was no answer. She was gone. He would have liked it if she had stayed; her presence, any presence, would have been welcome after the dream he had just awoken from. In it, he and his wife were waiting to board a flight in a vast airport reminiscent of Heathrow. When Betty told him she was going to take a quick look around the duty-free shop, he merely nodded. She disappeared into the crowd of travellers, and as she did, he glanced at his watch and was astonished to see that they had lost track of the time. It was only a few minutes before their gate would close. He stood up to call her back, but before a word left his mouth he suddenly found himself in the Qu'Appelle Valley on a fiercely windy day, whitecaps breaking on the beach.

Each time the waves slapped the sand, he grew more and more uneasy, sure that there was something he had forgotten to do, something besides keeping an eye on their departure time, something of the utmost importance. But for the life of him he couldn't think what it was. He sensed it hovering behind him, back where Betty's beloved cottage stood. But he couldn't bring himself to turn and face it because if he did that, he would have to acknowledge the neglected presence.

Tony eased himself out of bed and went to his laptop. Staring at the screen, he tried out and tested various phrases in his mind. Then he tapped out an email.

> *Dearest Susan,*
> *I should very much like to see you again. When?*
> *Tonio*

He knew it was a very stiff and formal-sounding appeal, but he didn't want to drop out of character. For the time being.

Tony lay on the rumpled bed, one ear cocked for the ping of his email. But his laptop remained mute. He was worried that he had offended Susan.

If he could speak to her he was sure he would be able to clear things up. But none of the Brecks listed in the telephone book had heard of a Susan. Likely she didn't have a landline. So he tried to track down her cellphone number on the Internet, but the process defeated him. He wasn't very tech or online savvy.

Firing off another email was an option, but that might leave the impression he was being a pest. Worse, a stalker.

He wondered if she had been disappointed by his sexual performance. Having married young, and having always remained scrupulously faithful to Betty, his experience in that respect was rather limited. He had always been wary of getting entangled with women, even though many of his fellow actors thought nothing of an affair on the road. He remembered one who had justified his infidelities by saying, "Any port in a storm, Tony. Any port in a storm." But Tony had known that convenient harbours were often not so snug as they seemed, that shoals and rocks often lurked just below the surface. He had seen enough shipwrecks in his day.

Loyalty had always been second nature to him. Loyalty had landed him in Chernobyl.

Tony hadn't heard from Susan for almost forty-eight hours. Several times he had contemplated calling the front desk and telling them that he was checking out but he never acted on those impulses. He scarcely left his room and whenever he did, he had bursts of magical thinking on the street. That woman looks like Susan; it means I'll have a message waiting for me from her. That Mexican restaurant on the corner – that's got to be a sign. She adores Mexico. But none of his hunches delivered on their promises.

Late on the second night that she had been incommunicado the phone rang in Tony's room. It was Susan. In a fearful, urgent whisper she said, "Tony, I've got to see you. Now."

"What time is it?" He was trying to locate the face of the bedside clock. Being jerked out of sleep had left his voice as blurred as his brain.

"Two o'clock. The desk didn't want to put me through because it's so late. But I told them it was an emergency. Tony, I want to come over."

"You sound upset. What's wrong?"

"I'll tell you when I get there. Meet me in the lobby. I don't want to have to explain myself to the desk clerk. I don't need any more shit tonight. Promise me you'll be downstairs."

"Of course. I promise."

Tony threw on his clothes and hurried downstairs. Fifteen minutes later Susan arrived, looking haggard and red-eyed from weeping.

"Susan . . ." he began.

She went right by him, in a headlong rush for the elevator. "Not here," she snapped over her shoulder.

The desk clerk was doing his best not to look like an eavesdropper.

When they got to his room Susan flung herself down on the bed and said to the ceiling, "Crack me something from the minibar. Cognac if there's any."

Tony found two Hennessys in the fridge. Susan sat up, took the glass he proffered.

"What happened?" said Tony.

"Bad fight with my husband."

"Husband?"

Susan ignored that. "It was terrible. Eddy's a very abusive guy."

"Abusive? Don't tell me he hit you."

"*Verbally abusive.*" Susan paused. "Somebody he works with saw the two of us in that Italian restaurant. The schmuck said something to Eddy, likely something totally innocuous and innocent, but it set Eddy off. He gave me the third degree all night. Because I wouldn't give him your name or explain who you are, he practically threw me out of the condo. I needed somewhere to go."

"If he felt that way, he's the one that should have gone."

"Tell that to Eddy."

There was a pause in which Tony thought a thought he would sooner have avoided thinking. "You said you were unattached."

"What I said was that I wasn't attached at the hip. I'm not *attached* in any way that matters. There hasn't been any real feeling between Eddy and me for years. When it comes to me, all he has is a sense of ownership. 'Nobody gets what's Eddy's' is the way he thinks. That is, not until he decides to get rid of it. Which I guess is what he wants to do now. Well, I'm ready to go. I've had twenty-five years of his horseshit."

Soon Tony joined her on the bed.

———

Susan insisted on going back to the condo right after break-fast. Tony wanted to accompany her, but she assured him that everything would be fine. She'd have the condo to her-self because Eddy had a six o'clock flight that morning to Toronto. He was enrolled in a week-long course of some sort or other, something he wouldn't be able to duck out of or postpone. Eddy was a chartered accountant and his firm insisted that he attend seminars that would keep him up-to-date on the government's latest tax code changes.

Susan said she needed to get a move on, to clear her per-sonal possessions out before he returned, to find someplace to live. It seemed to Tony that the prospect of ditching Eddy filled her with elation.

Tony helped Susan find new quarters in an apartment build-ing that rented furnished executive suites by the week. She said that would give her some "breathing space" while she hired a lawyer and tracked down some more suitable, permanent accommodations. But after an initial burst of activity, neither of these things seemed to be pressing concerns for her. She said there was no need for them to sneak around any longer so most days they took long walks on the riverbank trails. One afternoon they went to a matinee in a multiplex in a sub-urban mall. A half an hour before the film finished, Susan took Tony's hand, slid it under her light summer dress, and as she eased his fingers into her, whispered in his ear, "That's what I like about you, Tonio. You're such an old-world, sophisticated type. You never take liberties."

When they weren't together Tony couldn't stop mentally doodling plans for a new life, a new future that might include Susan. Maybe he should move to Saskatoon so he could be closer to her. There was nothing stopping him from selling the property and buying a condo or renting an apartment here. Susan and he could spend winters in Mexico. She was crazy about Mexico; she'd likely leap at the chance.

But before any of that could happen he knew he would have to come clean about who and what he really was. The old-world gentleman façade couldn't be maintained forever. It was a dumb prank that had got out of hand. If he explained it to Susan that way, she'd understand, see that his reasons for doing what he had done were essentially innocent. Just a case of an old trouper getting carried away. He had never had any intention of deceiving anyone, not long-term.

After days spent working up as self-deprecating and humorous a confession as he could devise, Tony decided that the bistro where Susan and he had met was the place to deliver it. Its romantic associations might help her receive his apology in the proper spirit. He made a date to meet her there for lunch.

Susan was already in the bistro, seated at the table where they had had their first encounter. Tony had specifically requested it when he made the reservation. He wore what he thought of as normal, *honest* clothes, corduroys and a commando sweater, a commitment to straight-shooting in the future. He kissed Susan, sat down, and ordered a gin martini; he needed bracing. Susan asked for a crème de cassis. As soon as their drinks arrived, Tony leaned across the table and touched Susan's forearm, to bring her attention back to him, from the street outside where it had wandered.

"Susan," he said, "I have something to tell you." And he began. He had left the accent back at the hotel and he wondered what she made of his new voice, this wardrobe straight out of the L.L. Bean catalogue.

Tony had carefully rehearsed what he was going to say, but in no time he lost his way in the maze of the last eighteen months. He jumped from one thing to another without making the connections clear: his renunciation of acting, exile in Chernobyl, poor Betty, a ghost in a grey suit, the strain the endless winter had put on his nerves, the dying deer.

As confused as this leapfrogging monologue was, part of his mind remained clear, still, and focused on whether or not Susan was piecing together this patchy story. She seemed to be stitching it up, seemed to be grasping what he was telling her. She didn't look angry. Or shocked. Or hurt.

He staggered to an anticlimactic end. "I never intended any harm by it. You see that, don't you? What is it they say – sportscasters? No harm, no foul." He gave her a weak smile and waited.

Susan glanced at the window and studied the passersby for a moment. Then she turned back to him and said, "Jesus, Tony, did you think I didn't recognize you the second I spotted you? From that old show *Aid*? I used to make a point of watching it just to piss Eddy off. It drove him nuts. Bleeding-heart liberal crap, he used to say, and my taxes are paying for it. So when I came in here and saw you in that weird outfit, the first thing I thought was, Where are the cameras? I thought maybe I'd walked onto a location shoot. Location shoot, that's what you call it, isn't it?"

"Yes," said Tony, "location shoot." His lips felt numb. *He* felt numb.

"But no cameras. And I notice that you're reading that Bernanos book, and I ask myself, What's that about? So I speak to you. And you answer in that accent – what was it supposed to be? From the Balkans or something?"

"Actually, Austrian . . . I think."

"And then I wonder if maybe this guy thinks he's so famous that he has to wear a disguise. To protect himself from the public. But you used your name. So I figured it might be some sort of male sexual fantasy. Like pretending you were the Marlborough cowboy or something when you went on the prowl for women."

"Shit," said Tony despairingly.

"And, hey, that was fine with me, *Tonio*. We had fun, didn't we? We're all adults here. And you've cleared the decks for me to tell you what I have to say. I appreciate your honesty and maturity. Truly." She smiled brightly, confidently. "And now I guess it's my turn to return the favour."

"Your turn?"

"It's just that Eddy and I have been talking," said Susan. "In fact, he's been phoning me every night. Whining. Apologizing. And I've been asking myself, Do you walk away from twenty-five years of marriage over an adventure? I've had them before and Eddy got past them. He's willing to do it again. That says something, doesn't it? And divorce is a big step at any age, let alone mine and Eddy's. A person has to consider." Her tone became earnest and confiding. "What I think really pissed him off was that his co-worker saw us together. Eddy's touchy when it comes to losing face.

Take Mexico. He has a pretty good idea that I get up to things down there, but there are no embarrassing repercussions for him. So he doesn't think about it. You come right down to it, he's a sensible man."

He was expected to draw an implication from that last judgment on her husband. Be sensible like him, *Tonio*.

Slowly, he got to his feet. "Yes, I see." He left her there, stuck with the bill.

Tony set out from Saskatoon very early. Usually, he was a poster boy for defensive driving, but not that morning. He motored flat-out, pedal to the metal, 1960s rock on the sound system as loud as he could crank it, hand drumming the dashboard in time to the beat, head bobbing maniacally, eyes wildly flicking from side to side as if he expected to be blindsided any moment. None of it worked, none of it drowned out the monotonous whisper in his ear, the thought cycling and recycling in his brain, which relentlessly whined one question. *Are you real? Are you real, Tony?*

Shortly before ten o'clock he pulled up to the cottage, lurched out of the car to find a message taped to the window of his back door: *Clean up your goddamn mess. Other people live here or haven't you noticed.*

It was unsigned, but Tony knew that it had to come from his next-door neighbour, Fred Martin. Betty had had trouble with him when she was renovating the cottage: protests about the noise, about the building materials that a careless contractor had once let overflow over the property line and onto Martin's yard; a never-ending series of complaints that accelerated to threats of legal action.

Tony had no idea what might have set the guy off now and he didn't intend to investigate. Given his own sour mood, things would only escalate if he got sucked into listening to Martin piss and moan about some minor problem that anybody in his right mind wouldn't give a second thought to.

He took his suitcase into the house and left it sitting in the middle of the kitchen floor. The recent spell of warm weather had turned the air in the cottage unpleasantly stuffy. Tony cracked the window above the kitchen sink, filled the kettle, and put it on the stove to boil water for a cup of instant coffee. While he waited, he wandered into the front room to take a look at the lake. The ice was almost gone. How many days had he been away? Ten, maybe. But it felt like a lifetime. And all the while the sun had been hard at work, dissolving all memory of winter. The kettle whistled for his attention.

In the kitchen, he walked into a wall of stench so thick somebody could be excused for thinking it was solid. It was as if Death Himself had taken a shit in there. The sickening smell was invading the cottage through the window he had just opened. Tony rushed over, slammed it shut.

Standing there he identified the source of the disgusting odour.

He rang up Bits Bodnarski. Furious, he yelled, "Tony Japp here. That deer is still laying out in my yard. Stinking to high heaven. Why the fuck didn't you haul it to the dump!"

"I come by," said Bits. "Nobody was there."

"I thought we had an understanding."

"My understanding is cash on the barrelhead. I don't see cash upfront, I don't do the job. I been stiffed often enough by you summer people. All of a sudden you've packed up and gone. Money owing."

"Well, come and do it now," said Tony. "I'll have a cheque for you."

"That carcass will be falling apart by now. I try and load it in my half-ton, it'll fall apart. Besides, I'm not having my truck reeking to high heaven for the rest of the summer. I ain't breathing that every day. That deer'll have to go in the ground, but I ain't burying it. I got a buddy who's got a Bobcat, maybe he might do it. I know his number if you want to try him."

Tony took the number. He was in luck. Bits's friend said he had just finished a trenching job. He could come by some time that afternoon.

The man with the Bobcat showed up a little after lunch and went to work digging a pit for the deer. Tony stood at the kitchen window watching the machine roar and buck and chew earth like a thing possessed. Its frenzy, its urgency swept into him.

Just as the operator began to scrape the remains of the deer into the hole, Tony burst out of the house, his arms full of clothes, yelling frantically at the operator to stop. The man halted, stared in disbelief as Tony flung everything he had bought in Saskatoon down onto the bloated, maggot-seething deer: the Italian shoes, the top coat, the homburg, the suit, the shirts, even the cufflinks. All that committed to the grave, he turned and went back into the cottage.

Tony was lucky, he got through to his agent without delay. In fact, Probert answered the phone himself. Tony didn't beat around the bush; he said he was ready to go back to work.

"Jesus, Tony," Probert said, "I'd hate for you to go to all the trouble and expense of moving back to Toronto without some firm offers on the table." Tony hadn't heard that cautious, guarded tone from Probert before. Was that reluctance?

"Then get me some firm offers."

"Easier said than done. For one thing, when it comes to movies it's all blockbusters now. The Americans aren't coming up here to shoot those small indie films so much anymore. Which was your bread and butter. And theatre – half of next season is musicals."

"Okay, I know at sixty it won't be easy. But don't forget, I've got a record in television. And I'm the right age for certain bit parts. A judge. A coroner. Somebody's father. A chief of police. Five or six lines, I don't care. I've always been a character actor. So now maybe the characters I have to play are smaller than they used to be. I can accept that."

"Tony, Tony . . ."

"Listen to me," said Tony, voice teetering. "The layoff has been good for me. I'm rejuvenated. I feel I'm at the top of my game. I *know* I'm at the top of my game. The juices are flowing, Probert. Haven't I always been able to play anything?

You know it. Everybody knows it. It's my calling card. My door opener. I've proved it time and time again. Let me repeat. I can do it. You have to believe in me, Probert. I'm the man who can play anything."

The roar of the Bobcat going past his window, exiting the scene, made it impossible for him to hear Probert's response.

"Anything," he reiterated in a whisper, voice bled white of conviction. "Believe me. Tony's the man who can play *anything*."

Counsellor Sally Brings Me to the Tunnel

NEVER ONCE, NOT ONCE, did Ma ever talk about her brother, Ted, without sticking a little yellow Post-it note to her anecdote, without adding, "That man *is a holy terror*." And that bewildered the living beejeebers out of me when I was a little kid because what could I make of that? *Holy* terror? How could terror be holy? And Uncle Teddy? Was he a *terror*? Not in my books. Back when I was six, seven, eight, nine years old, I thought he was more fun than a barrel of monkeys.

Live and learn.

My shiny new therapist, Counsellor Sally, is very big on living and learning. According to her, my present behaviour is a response to what happened to me in my childhood. Sorry, *conditioned responses*. And since your perceptions of things when you are a child are frequently unreliable, I must learn to get *past all that*.

I have been ordered to see Counsellor Sally because I got

caught telling certain little white lies to my high school students. A busybody father who looked into my claim to have been an Associated Press war photographer in Vietnam reported this harmless fib of mine to Principal Drogan after his son brought the news home to his war-crazy dad that his history teacher, Mr. Molson, had been in the midst of the fray during the Battle of Hue. It seems that the guy who squealed on me is one of those military history buffs, a nut who had recently bought some encyclopedic book on the subject of AP photographers in Vietnam. Finding no reference there to yours truly, he undertook further research on the Internet, which yielded no record of a Bert Molson snapping carnage in Southeast Asia. So in a fit of outrage he hightailed it to Mr. Drogan with this news, and because Drogan hates my guts he proceeded to accuse me of being a pathological liar and immediately initiated proceedings to have me arm-twisted into retirement. No, let me get the sequence correct. It was only *after* Drogan found out that I had once told the kids in my class that in his youth their principal had been lead singer in a punk rock band called Pitchforking Dead Babies that steps to have me unceremoniously ushered out the door commenced.

But a compromise has been worked out between the Teachers' Federation and the administration, one of the conditions of which is that I have to take a six-month medical leave of absence and undergo psychological treatment, and then, well, it seems, *we'll see*.

Now Counsellor Sally, who has oodles of compassion but not much imagination, refuses to accept my explanation that I told a few untruths simply to make history live for my students. She believes my claims to having had combat experience have something to do with Uncle Ted, who, she points out, was a veteran of the Second World War. Haven't I mentioned that several times? And that my refusal to contemplate retirement is rooted in my abandonment issues.

Yadda, yadda. Everything circles back to how my father walking out on Ma and me when I was an infant naturally has had repercussions on my psychological health. But how can you feel abandoned by someone you never knew? That makes no sense. And second, I don't blame my never-laid-eyes-on Pops for making tracks, given that living with Ma would have meant a lifetime shackled to her family, that whole tribe of feckless screwballs. Because Ma would never have dreamed of *abandoning* them, even if my father had happened to invite us to tag along with him when he headed for the hills. You can take that to the bank.

Counsellor Sally actually said, "Have you never considered that your stubborn attempt to hang on to your teaching job might be related to feeling abandoned, all alone in the world now that most of your family is dead?"

"Not really. Not so much," I told her. "Ma's still kicking."

But she kept on doggedly pursuing the same line of thought. "Nevertheless, your Uncle Ted passed away quite recently."

"Six months ago."

"Now this is just something for you to think about. No judgment implied. Perhaps you are so attached to your teaching position because you feel it's the only thing left that you can count on. People depart the scene; they die. Maybe institutions appear more durable and dependable, more lasting, more reliable to you than human beings. Many people your age look forward to and anticipate retirement. Why not you?" She paused. "And retirement would permit you to make a graceful exit."

I ignored that. Fucking quisling. Who's her patient? Who is she supposed to be helping? Me or Drogan?

"You've claimed that you've never embellished your accomplishments before. Could it be that your recent losses have made you anxious that, in a manner of speaking, you will lose your students too? In a symbolic sense. Might you feel that you aren't *worthy* of their respect and, as a consequence, this leads you to inflate your status, to try to impress them with imaginary exploits, imaginary feats of bravery?" She paused. "Do you never ask yourself why this self-mythologizing started so soon after your Uncle Ted's death?"

As I say, a session with Counsellor Sally is like doing a circuit around a racetrack; you always finish just where you started.

She wouldn't leave it alone. "Maybe you believe your pupils will eventually reject you just like Uncle Ted rejected you. That they will withdraw their approval just as he did."

"He only rejected me after I put him in the hospital. I'd say he had a point."

Guess what? I've been doing some research on abandoned child syndrome, and *The Diagnostic and Statistical Manual of Mental Disorders* does not recognize it as a condition. My hack therapist is treating me for a mental disorder that does not even *officially exist*. And I would point that fact out to Counsellor Sally if I didn't have to make nice-nice and play along with her in the slim hope that I will get a clean bill of health and be reinstated. On her say-so.

Not too long ago, Counsellor Sally happened to say, "I found your description of you waiting for your Uncle Ted and Aunt Evie's annual visit to your hometown very moving. The picture of you standing outside your mother's house all day long, your eyes searching the road for his car to appear, that was very poignant. You must have adored him."

Okay, I admit that at *that* time I thought Uncle Ted was pretty much the kitty's little pink ass. In my starry eyes he was a big success, unlike all my other loser aunts and uncles who, aside from their stints in the services during the war, had never dared to peek over the horizon past the little town of Connaught. Staying put in a small town where everybody knows everybody else meant that the Aker family's reputation for being prickly, flighty, pugnacious types with king-sized chips on their shoulders meant nobody in their right minds would hire them for full-time work. The men were condemned to eke out livings as casual labourers and self-employed handymen; the women as housecleaners, washerwomen, and babysitters.

True, a few of the Akers took a stab at more ambitious entrepreneurship. Like Uncle Bob, who started a short-lived trail-riding business with a string of cadaverous horses that looked like they had been pre-owned by the Four Horsemen of the Apocalypse. And Ma herself established that unfortunate Boys and Girls Gymnastic Academy, which she somehow felt she was eminently qualified to run because she had been a physical training instructor in the Canadian Women's Army Corps during the Second World War. That stone dropped to the bottom of the money pit even faster than Uncle Bob's.

So who can blame me for gazing longingly up the road on those long-ago summer days? The thing was, I couldn't wait to lay eyes on what kind of car Uncle Ted would be driving that year, what spiffy automobile he had traded up to: a shiny new Buick, a chrome-encrusted Oldsmobile, a Caddy, once a Mercedes-Benz, a Benz years before they became the standard conveyance for realtors, lawyers, and chartered accountants. Benzes were an uncommon sight back then, so soon after the war. Who wanted to be seen driving a Kraut car? Except Ted, who always loved to stand out, to thumb his nose at the crowd.

The Benz was my favourite set of wheels of them all. In particular, I loved the straphangers that could be clutched to keep me from ricocheting from one sturdy Teutonic door panel to the other when Teddy rocketed us through the countryside, went tearing around some corner on a dirt road, then slung his marvel of German engineering, tires shrieking and spitting gravel, into the next hairpin turn. And there were also the leisurely tours about town so as to see and be seen, Aunt Evie in her muskrat coat riding shotgun beside Uncle Ted, me in the back seat, fascinated by the weird coincidence of their colour-coordinated gingery heads (they might have been brother and sister), but no, on reflection, Teddy's hair had more of a *cranberry hue*, its brightness dampened by a Wildroot Cream-Oil slick. I can see it as if it were yesterday, his big, veiny, virile hands locked on the steering wheel, the right one glinting with a huge signet ring. His shoulders squared in a camel hair car coat. Aunt Evie's perfume rolling into the back seat, wave upon scented wave.

And all this glamorous prosperity was a result of Uncle Ted having taken the path less taken by Akers, namely gainful employment. He did dangerous work in unspeakable places where you got paid good money to risk your life sinking mine shafts and blowing big holes in mountains. Ted had defied the dire predictions of all those authority figures, teachers, officers of the law, and justices of the peace who had warned him when he was an adolescent that he was headed for jail. For that, Teddy never forgave them, and he nursed a grudge against each and every one of them until his dying day.

Speaking of which, one afternoon as Uncle Ted is sedately piloting the Benz through our sleepy streets while the multi-tasking Aunt Evie smokes a Sweet Caporal and adjusts her blood-red lipstick in the rear-view mirror and little nephew Bert clings to the trusty straphanger just in case Ted decides to *goose the juice*, who does Uncle Ted spy with his beady little eye? Why none other than his old elementary school principal, P.J. Gillam, out tending the roses in his front yard. And Teddy hits the brakes, cranks down the window, looses a blast on the horn, and calls out, "Is that a fucking teacher I see? A man among boys and a boy among men? Come on over here and box my ears now, Pyjamas Gillam! Try that one on for size now, why don't you?"

P.J. scuttles into the house and Aunt Evie starts scolding Ted about holding silly grudges forever and not letting bygones be bygones and scaring old men. Ted doesn't appreciate this and he warns her to button it, zip it, and stitch it just as the chief of police, Carmen Kostash, arrives on the scene, draws up behind us in his squad car, and carefully, very carefully approaches the driver's window of the Benz. Carmen Kostash is walking on eggs because he went to school with my uncle and knows that hearing the name Teddy Aker in conjunction with a complaint call is a bit like hearing the words *blood in your stool* bandied about in the doctor's office. The chief suggests apologetically that perhaps Ted has said something that was misinterpreted or misheard by P.J., so just as a gesture of goodwill maybe he'd like to ease on down the road to put Mr. Gillam's fears to rest. You think?

Uncle Ted doesn't think. He says this being a public roadway he'll park here for as long as he pleases. It just so happens he's a big rose-fancier, and he's got as much right to sit here and admire Pyjamas's flowers as anybody else. And Aunt Evie butts in to say that his love of flowers is news to her, but he just ignores this and bores in on Kostash, asks him why the fuck did P.J. plant roses in his front yard if he didn't want people to look at them?

Kostash has no answer to that. So he goes and sets his ass down on the principal's doorstep, probably to persuade Gillam that now that he's under police protection he shouldn't demand that the chief make an arrest, which is the last thing Kostash wants to do, to provoke Teddy.

Meanwhile, Uncle Ted has turned on the radio because he's decided he's here for the long haul, no way is Pyjamas going to put the run on him. Patti Page is singing a mouldy oldie, "How Much Is that Doggie in the Window?", and Uncle Ted cranks up the volume as loud as it will go and starts woof-woofing along to the tune. At the top of his lungs. But believe you me, he doesn't sound like any cute little puppy dog in a pet shop window, but more like some bloodthirsty Rottweiler or killer pit bull ready to sink his teeth into the nut sack of anybody in a uniform.

Evie starts whining at Uncle Ted in a coaxy little-girl voice: "You better stop that, Teddy Bear snookums, because barking at a policeman is not a good idea. Remember what happened at that border crossing at Detroit when you were a smarty-pants with the American customs officer? You want to spend another night in jail when we're supposed to be having a nice, relaxing holiday?"

Which only revs Uncle Teddy up, the memory of that night in the clink, the injustice of it, and he starts to yap and yip even louder, looking every bit as rabidly foaming as Old Yeller in his final hours, and Chief Kostash hurries to his car to call for backup, and in the blink of an eye reinforcements arrive: a scrawny, pimple-blotched constable with his car light flashing and the siren wailing. The sound of which sets Teddy off howling as if the woo-woo of the alarm is too painful for his decibel-sensitive doggie ears.

Kostash and his right-hand man still don't dare approach the Benz, choosing instead to confer beside the rose bed on how to handle the animal control problem. Teddy continues with the canine ruckus, snarling, snapping his teeth, etc., all this despite the song on the radio having changed to another lichen-encrusted hit, Doris Day's "Que Sera Sera." Kostash is probably running archival film in his mind of times when somebody tried to restrain or interfere with Uncle Teddy when his blood was up and how unpleasant the consequences of that had been.

So the law decides to let sleeping dogs lie, even if the dog in question isn't sleeping but is wide awake and flouting the noise bylaw. Kostash and his sidekick just hang back, hoping that Ted's noisy woofer will poop out, which it eventually does. Teddy's voice becomes nothing but a gasping, asthmatic snarl. With his vocal cords having betrayed him, Ted throws the Benz in gear, carves a *Fuck you, Charlie!* doughnut in the street, and peels off, well satisfied *that he showed them.*

But Aunt Evie is sulking over her husband's naughty behaviour, causing Teddy to turn on the charm offensive, to whisper sweet nothings in his new husky, barking-impaired voice, to tell her she's his kewpie doll, his gunga-poochy-snuggy-bum, but none of this wipes away her pouty face, so he boots her out of the car at Grandpa Aker's, where they've bunked down for their holiday. Teddy tells her she's giving him grief and she needs *some think-about-it time, so she can get her head out of her ass and a smile on her face before he gets home for supper.* And then off go Uncle Teddy and his nephew Bert, with Uncle Ted's super-swell Remington pump-action .22 (which travels with him everywhere in the trunk of his vehicle, even on vacation) on a rat-shooting spree at the Connaught dump to celebrate having given P.J. Gillam a little something he won't soon forget.

I think it's interesting that Counsellor Sally would ask if I ever regarded Uncle Teddy as a father figure. It was just the opposite; it was he who aspired to be a father figure to me.

In fact, Teddy wanted to *adopt* me. I don't know when he first made this weird proposal to Ma; it may have come shortly after my father deserted us. But the first I heard of it was when Uncle Teddy and Aunt Evie moved back to Connaught. Ted had gotten fed up taking orders from no-nothing foremen and bone-headed contractors who had opinions about how he should go about blowing rocks and other obstacles-to-progress to smithereens. So Aunt Evie and Uncle Ted decided to strike out on their own, become their own bosses. All those years that he had worked in remote camps, Aunt Evie had been a cook for the men on these job sites and, unlike spendthrift Teddy, she had kept her fist clamped tight on every dollar she had ever made. This amounted to a nice nest egg, which they invested in our burg's motel/café/beer parlour, a notorious, stinking shitbox frequented only by the town's low-lifes and a few budget-conscious tourists passing through Connaught on their way to the Rockies. Ma said that Evie and Ted had come back home to lord it over everybody else in the family, to pass themselves off as "big business tycoons." Ma had never quite gotten over the failure of her gymnastic academy.

Evie was in charge of the café, and Ted all other guest services. Aside from being an enthusiastic, awe-inspiring bouncer who tossed troublemakers through plate-glass doors and sent them tobogganing down the concrete steps of the bar on their bellies, Ted didn't have the necessary skill set for success in the hospitality industry. Plus an occupation where a ready supply of alcohol was at his elbow did nothing to restrain his lifelong weakness for binge-drinking.

When Teddy went on a drunken tear, it was the rest of the

Akers who usually bore the brunt of it, with Ma and me most often his targets of choice. Like all the Akers, Teddy had a grievance against the world, but his biggest grudge was against Ma because she'd had a child, something Teddy couldn't do because he had caught a case of the mumps during the North African campaign that had left him, as he so often self-pityingly announced when pissed out of his tiny mind, "shooting blanks." To Teddy, it was a travesty of justice that Ma, who was a single parent and poor as a church mouse, should be raising a child when he and Evie, who could give a kid so much, didn't have a chick of their own.

Back in the days that Ted was lavishing gifts on me (a BB gun, an Alamo set, a Davy Crocket coonskin cap, comic books, hard cash for sugar orgies), I didn't comprehend that his presents were ham-handed attempts to *alienate my affections*. And to a certain extent this campaign of seduction worked pretty well until Uncle Ted's impatience got the better of him. When Ted didn't get what he wanted, his resentment built and his normally low impulse control dropped to zero, especially when he got into the sauce. It was then that he would drop in unannounced to pay Ma and me a visit.

Let me illustrate. It's one o'clock in the morning and Ted is hammering on the door, howling to be let in. Ma is screaming out a window, "Take a hike! Go home to Evie! She's the one who signed up for the life sentence with you! Not me!" and I'm rolled into a ball on my bed with a pillow mashed down over my head to block out the brouhaha. Then the door-kicking starts and Ma relents because we're renters, and explaining a splintered door to a landlord who you are already in arrears to is nobody's idea of a good time.

Teddy comes lurching into the house, bottle of rye in hand, bouncing off walls, knocking over chairs, roaring, "Where's my boy? Where's my boy!"

Ma says, "He's got school tomorrow. Let him be. Give us a break."

But there's no deflecting Teddy. I have to haul myself out of bed and stand shivering in my Jockeys in the kitchen as he unspools one of his slobbery rants.

"You want to know something? Your father was a lazy, useless, stupid bastard who married a lazy, useless, stupid bitch. Look at your underwear. It's yellow as a Chinaman's ass. I wouldn't be caught dead in underwear like that. Hasn't your mother ever heard of bleach? Evie bleaches my shorts and irons them to boot. She irons the sheets and tea towels. She irons my socks. There's a woman who knows a thing or two about housekeeping. Your Aunt Evie is a wonderful woman and would have made a wonderful mother. Don't you wish you had a mother like her, Bert? She puts your mother to shame but good."

"So go home to your precious Evie then. Go get your shorts bleached. Preferably with your famous blank-shooting pecker still in them," Ma tells him.

But thoughts of dear Evie turn Ted maudlin and sentimental. "Do you know, Bert," he says, "Evie and me offered to adopt you, to give you a decent home, decent clothes, a regular, normal upbringing. But your dippy mother put the kibosh to that idea. Because she's a selfish bitch who thinks about nobody but herself. Can you imagine how she broke Evie's heart? Have you any idea how much your aunt loves you? How much I love you?"

And then to show me how much he loves me, Ted starts singing the Patsy Cline song, the one about "I love you so much it hurts me, and there's nothing I can do." Teddy crooning, weaving from side to side, making these grandiose, lizardy lounge-singer gestures meant to convey the unspeakable pain that resides in his fond, gooey heart.

All of a sudden love gets shoved to the back burner and he's talking about trust. "You and me, Bert, we're two of a kind. In the whole goddamn Aker family you're the only one I can trust. I got eight brothers and sisters and there's not one of them I'd trust as far as I could throw them. Because they're all jealous of me, that's why. But you I trust. You want to know how much I trust you? I'd put my life in your hands. Who was that guy who shot the apple off his kid's head? I'd let you shoot a apple off my head, Bert. Right now I'll do it. I got the Remington out in the car and I'll let you shoot a apple off my head. No problem. Right now, out in the dark you can shoot a apple off my head. That's how much I trust you, Bert."

And Ma says, "I'll shoot an apple off your head if that's what you're looking for. I've got a bag of Macintoshes. Want me to get one?"

"Fuck that noise. You'd drill me between the eyes, give you half a chance."

"It could happen," Ma replies. "Seeing how unsteady you are on your feet."

"I'll show you how unsteady I am. Want to bet I can't kick a cigarette out of Bert's mouth? I can do it, that's how steady and solid I am on my feet. Like the fucking Rock of Gibraltar. Put this cigarette in your mouth, Bert. You're a truster, aren't you? Me and you are trusters, aren't we, Bert?"

"He's not putting a cigarette in his mouth so you can put a boot under his chin, weld his molars together. That's not going to happen."

"You better shut your hole. I'm not talking to you; I'm talking to my good little buddy Bert. How's about it, little buddy? Come on, you can trust your Uncle Teddy. Be a truster."

But, as Counsellor Sally knows by now, I'm not a truster. "Smoking's bad for you," I say to Uncle Teddy, desperate little weasel that I was. Am.

"Sure, smoking's bad for you, but you're not going to smoke it. You're just going to let me kick it out of your trap. Hey, nothing to worry about. You're safe in the hands of your absolutely steady Uncle Teddy."

"It's lit. There's smoke coming off it. I'll breathe it in."

"Well, yeah, it's lit, but I got plenty of unlits. A whole deck of unlits. I'll give you one of the unlits if you want. For chrissakes, this is a trust experiment. So be a truster, Bert."

"You're lit, Teddy, that's what you are. Lit up like a goddamn Christmas tree," Ma says.

And then Uncle Ted falls in a chair and starts to sob because I won't fucking trust him. Nobody trusts him.

Counsellor Sally wonders if Uncle Ted wasn't damaged by the war. She concedes that that doesn't excuse his dreadful behaviour, but, on the other hand, doesn't my mother bear some responsibility for letting me be subjected to incidents like that? Don't I have to ask myself why she didn't call the cops on Uncle Ted when he was drunk and abusive?

My answer to those questions is: first, it's likely that Uncle Ted did more damage to the war effort than the war did to him. Second, that long before "What happens in Las Vegas stays in Las Vegas" became an advertising campaign slogan, the Akers had their own version of that catchphrase. What happened in the Aker family stayed in the Aker family. An invitation to anybody to put his nose in Aker family business was viewed as the basest, lowest treachery. That's why Ma never squealed to the cops on Teddy. Because that would have been fucking unthinkable. So the home invasions continued, for years.

During all that time Uncle Teddy's popularity with me went into a slow decline; his Dow Jones Affection Index sank, his Standard and Poor's Best Uncle Rating got severely downgraded. By the time I turned fourteen, thanks to Teddy, I was a mess, very twitchy and jumpy, very spooked. When I looked in the mirror, black-ringed, sleepless lemur eyes mournfully confirmed my downward spiral. As Counsellor Sally is surely well aware, all the latest, up-to-date literature confirms that pumping the teenaged male body full of gallons of stress hormones makes for a seething toxic stew, has a detrimental effect on a growing boy's physical and mental health. I've heard it said, on the best authority, that it might even lead to rampage-killing fantasies. This was the gist of a documentary that cited many recognized authorities in the youthful-serial-killers field that I recently viewed with interest and appreciation on PBS.

A flash of headlights on my bedroom wall, the clunk of a car door out in the street, and the old fight-or-flight response would kick in, the hypothalamus would begin to fuss and bother, the hormone spigot would open full force, the adrenaline, the noradrenaline, the cortisol would gush, and I'd pop straight up in bed, thinking, *It's Teddy! It's the third degree in my underpants again!*

I freely admit I was a Molotov cocktail of unstable incendiary chemicals. One night when Teddy and Ma were having an argument about whether or not it was a sister's duty to cook a brother bacon and eggs at three in the morning, and Teddy had his arm cocked to pitch a bottle of beer at her head if she didn't and Ma was taunting him to *Let 'er rip!*, Teddy flicked the Bic to my fuse by turning to me and saying, "She's asking for it. You're my witness, Bert. She's asking for it. Nobody could blame me. The years of shit I've taken from that woman."

That was enough to flush this out of me. "You're a lunatic," I said. "A grade A lunatic."

Teddy's eyes went all squinty because they didn't trust his ears. "What?"

"I said you're a fucking lunatic." A little louder, a little more authority wedged into my cracking, quaking adolescent voice.

"Bert," Ma cautioned, "careful. He's drunk."

"I'm a lunatic? Well, you're a punk. A little pussy punk," Uncle Ted said to me, mouth contorting. "That's what you are."

"I'd rather be a little pussy punk than a lunatic like you." I rolled my eyes and stuck my tongue out of the corner of my mouth to demonstrate just how gaga he was. "You belong in a straitjacket."

Uncle Ted bucked himself off the chair. I broke for the

living room. Ma had waxed the floor that day. (She was a far better housekeeper than Ted ever gave her credit for.) Given the fact that he was pissed to the gills and in his stocking feet, Ted had difficulty negotiating the sharp turns I was making around the furniture, and he hit the deck just as I went pelting up the stairs for the attic. Which was not such a clever move since the attic was a no-exit dead end used by our landlord as a dumping ground for junk abandoned by former renters. There I took refuge behind a scarred dresser that some previous tenant had used as a tool cabinet, its drawers filled with rusty wrenches, hammers, and pliers, an assortment of nails, screws, nuts, bolts. I could hear Ted coming in loud and clear from down below, issuing threats and warnings about how I had better get my ass down those stairs, take my medicine because if he had to come up there, it'd be ten times worse. And Ma was screeching, "Lay off, he's just a kid, pick on somebody your own size!"

A slap, a yelp of pain, sobs. Until I heard that, I'd never imagined my tough nut Ma was capable of crying.

The stairs began to creak. The piece of furniture I was behind was heavy oak and stuffed with hardware, but when I put my shoulder to it and pushed with all my might it budged, started to move, groaning menacingly. Lucky for me, there were wheels mounted on the legs, otherwise I'd never have gotten it to the top of the stairs, a vantage point from where I could see Teddy stealthily creeping up on me, step by step. I caught a glimpse of Ma standing at the bottom of the stairs, hand pressed to her nose, blood trickling between her fingers.

"Ma," I called out, "get away from the landing."

She was clearly in a state of shock. Because instead of doing what Ma would normally have done, bombard me with questions and protests: *Why should I get away? Who are you to give me orders in my own house?* she just numbly stepped aside.

I saw it click in Teddy's head what was coming. The alarm bells started to jangle. He was putting two and two together and it was adding up to bad fucking news for somebody.

I gave the dresser a shove.

A series of ass-over-teakettle, dreamy dresser-bounces, the former tool cabinet gathering momentum, drawers popping open to sprinkle rusty hardware confetti all over Teddy. He was half turned to flee when it crashed into him, knocked him clean off his feet, launched him into the void, hands scrabbling at air. The whump and shudder when Ted landed and the dresser landed on him travelled all the way up to where I stood, a mini-earthquake under my feet.

A moment of silence. Ma stepped over to stare down at the legs and arms jutting out from under the chest of drawers. She glanced uncertainly up at me, then bent over and put a question to the furniture. "Ted, can you hear me?" Nothing but some lab frog twitching of the limbs. "I better call the boys," Ma said, straightening up decisively. Meaning her brothers.

My uncles Ben, Bob, and Oswald, the baby of the family, answered Ma's mayday. They pried Teddy out from under the wreckage. One of Uncle Ted's canines was poking through his upper lip; Ben suspected broken ribs and a dislocated shoulder, maybe a concussion since his brother was stumped by questions concerning his age, name, and present location.

Ben lit a cigarette and said to me, "You do this?"

I nodded.

"Good job," said Oswald. "You want to give him a few smacks while you got the chance? Got him where you want him?"

I shook my head.

"Don't you never learn, asshole?" Bob said sternly, trying to get Ted's vacant eyes to focus on his face. "Shame on you, hitting your sister. What's the matter with you?"

They hoisted him up, lugged him outside, and pitched him unceremoniously into the bed of Oswald's pickup truck. By then Uncle Ted had begun to talk – after a fashion – but his verbal stroll down memory lane didn't make much sense. "See Naples and die. What a fucking joke," he intoned to the stars above. "Naples, that pile of steaming spaghetti shit. You spend one day there and you *want* to die."

Ben reckoned Teddy was reliving the twenty-eight-day military detention in Naples he had been sentenced to for carelessly discharging a Beretta M1934 in a field kitchen mess line. "Somebody cut in front of the war hero for chow," Ben explained. "Teddy was packing a pistol – he had took it off a dead Italian officer – so he pulls it out and lets off a few rounds at the line-jumper's feet."

"Evie or the hospital?" said Oswald, who had no interest in good old days war nostalgia.

"Better be the hospital," said Ben. "We take him home, Evie might smother him in his sleep. She's going to be right pissed off."

"I vote for taking him home then," said Bob.

In the end, they hauled Teddy off to the hospital, where Ben's diagnosis was pretty much confirmed: concussion, dislocated shoulder, broken ribs. The only thing he had missed was the fractured ankle.

The night I tipped the dresser down on my Uncle Ted was the night I deserted the ranks of the Akers, mentally resigned from Ma's family. Soon I went as hippie as it was possible to go in a redneck backwater. I grew my hair long, became a Kahlil Gibran and Rod McKuen fan, and drove Ma bonkers spinning *MacArthur Park* over and over on my RCA portable record player. The Akers did not approve of the sensitive butterfly that had emerged from the chrysalis.

Contrary to what Ma and I feared, Ted never paid a revenge call on us, never arrived to settle scores. For months, we had our ears cocked for the sound of a car door slamming in the street outside, for pounding at the front door. It's hard to explain. Maybe Uncle Ted's humiliation at being bested by a kid was more than he could take. Maybe he had recognized something of himself in my eyes as I committed the dresser to the no-recall force of gravity.

Of course, during the three years I had left before I finished high school and could scram from Connaught, I occasionally ran into Uncle Ted on the streets. He looked right through me, Aunt Evie too. I might have been a pane of glass. Back then I thought Uncle Ted had closed the book on me and I on him. However, according to Counsellor Sally's reading of my situation, it's not over yet.

———

I left Connaught to go to university, the first of the Akers to take such a step, which they considered a calculated slap in the face to family values. Who the hell did I think I was? But as much as I was intent on strigilating the last vestige and particle of Aker family values off me, I couldn't get myself entirely free from them. For one thing, I had a duty to visit Ma, something that I couldn't completely dodge given the long summer breaks teachers get. And when I came home, Ma's sense of family loyalty always led her to host an Aker get-together. This included the whole smorgasbord of uncles and aunts: Ben, Bob, Oswald, Randy, Dot, Jackie, Carmen. As an added bonus, my grown-up cousins were added to the menu, all of whom seemed to have carried on the Aker tradition of bad career choices. The cousins included an ostrich/emu rancher, an instructor in a Brazilian jiu-jitsu studio, a full-time flyer deliverer, a bill collection agent. The only Aker missing at these family shindigs was Uncle Teddy. He was still nursing a grudge against Ma and holding himself imperially aloof. However, she was regularly supplied with plenty of intelligence on Uncle Ted by her other brothers and sisters, intel that Ma insisted on passing on to me whenever I visited, despite my protests that I couldn't care less about what Teddy was up to.

But over the years Ma kept the updates coming and they made it clear that time was not being kind to Uncle Teddy, that bit by bit the years were chipping away at him, that he was beginning to flake. First, his ticker began to act up and he needed a pacemaker. Next, he developed such a severe case of rheumatoid arthritis that he couldn't carry on in the hospitality industry any longer and was forced to sell the motel. Then came prostate cancer.

Things between him and Evie were slowly disintegrating too. Teddy's afflictions made him more irascible than ever. "Little wonder," Ma said, "the man is twisted up something awful. He's like a corkscrew. First, they clamped braces all over him to try to keep him from corkscrewing up even worse. That didn't do the trick so he had surgery to put metal rods in his wrists and screws in his ankles to try to straighten him out. None of it's working. Teddy's not straightening out. And Ben claims he's in terrible pain. You know what Ted is like at the best of times. I wouldn't want to be Evie now for all the tea in China."

Apparently one morning Uncle Ted took exception to some harmless remark Aunt Evie made at breakfast. He upended the table, scattering fried eggs, coffee, plates, and cutlery all over the kitchen, stormed out of the house, and beat it to a flyblown hotel in a village twenty kilometres down the road. There he settled in, hardly a place that any sensible man with a disability would choose for a permanent residence since to get to his room Teddy had to crawl painfully up the stairs on all fours.

Most of his day he passed swilling draft, munching pickled eggs, and brooding about the low class of company he had to keep in the hotel's beer parlour, where he didn't have the option of pitching anybody who offended him through plate glass like he'd so much enjoyed doing in the good old days. The inevitable finally happened. Teddy got into a dust-up with a young man with a purple Mohawk. He just couldn't forgo *telling the asshole what a fucking eyesore he was*. Things escalated between the generations. Teddy gave Mr. Mohawk a chop to the head with the metal brace on his wrist and Mr. Mohawk threw the old man over a table. The same day, Teddy got his eviction notice.

All the Akers assumed that Teddy would be moving back in with Aunt Evie, but she had different ideas. She swung into action, applied to Veteran Affairs for a disability pension on Ted's behalf, and before he knew it he had been squirrelled away into a tiny suite in a government-subsidized housing facility for senior citizens. She was not having his feet back under her table.

To everyone's surprise, Teddy didn't make as much of a fuss as they had expected about Evie's taking his living arrangements in hand. Probably he was feeling defeated and untypically listless. Only two weeks before he got kicked out of the hotel, a technician treating his prostate cancer had given him a dose of radiation that damaged his bowel. Teddy had to be fitted with a colostomy bag and that indignity must have been hard for a man like him to accept. He had always been vain, what used to be called a fine figure of a man: tall, broad-shouldered, physically powerful, and agile. Now he was a human pretzel with what Uncle Ben told Ma Ted called his "shit purse" tucked under his shirt.

Teddy must have been living in his cramped senior's suite for eight or nine years before I paid him a visit. That was entirely at Ma's instigation. Time had passed and the Akers had been dropping all around her like flies. Ben was the first to go. Bob the pony-wrangling entrepreneur next. Then Aunt Dottie. Aunt Carmen.

Against all odds, Teddy was the one who hung in there like a bad smell.

The growing Aker body count softened Ma's attitude towards her brother. On one of my visits she said to me, "A person can't help but feel sorry for Ted. What a life he leads. Sitting in that apartment day after day, never getting out, eating that Meals on Wheels slop. I've got some lasagna in the freezer that I bet he'd enjoy. You could take it over, pop it in the oven for him."

I asked her why she didn't take him the lasagna and pop it in the oven herself.

"Oh," she said, "Teddy would never take anything from me."

"And he would from me? I'm the one who tried to murder him once."

"Oh that's different," Ma said. "He would take lasagna from you. You're a man." Ma has always had a never-ending supply of non sequiturs.

So I agreed to play lasagna delivery boy. What harm could Teddy do me now? When I was going out the door, I found out. Ma said, "Make sure he gets a good look at you through his screen door. Knows who you are. Evie says Teddy's got a pellet pistol in there."

"Jesus Christ. Why's he got a pellet pistol?"

"He watches a lot of cable TV from Detroit. You know how things are down there in America. House break-ins. People killing each other left and right."

"But Connaught isn't Detroit."

"Well," said Ma, "Teddy never gets out. So what does he know about the world anymore?"

It was a fine July day. Teddy's suite faced a sunny courtyard. I rang the bell and called to him through the screen door, trying to outshout a television raving in the background. "Ted, it's your nephew Bert!"

A querulous voice answered, "Who?"

"Bert Molson. Your sister Adele's boy."

"The furniture-mover. What the fuck do you want?"

"Ma asked me to bring you some lasagna. Can I come in?"

"Suit yourself."

As I eased into the suite Teddy put the television on mute. The temperature in his apartment was Saharan. High summer and a space heater pumping out heat full bore. The place was shrouded in shadow, the blinds drawn. The television screen shed flickering light on a little old man, all aggressive nose and furious eyes, scrunched up in an enormous recliner. Holy terror slumping down into itself, a landslide of flesh.

I showed him the casserole dish. "You want me to heat it up for you now, or do you want it in the fridge?"

"Fridge."

I stowed the lasagna, went back to the living room, and settled down on a chair. As my eyes grew accustomed to the darkness, I scanned the room for evidence of a pellet pistol. Noted a suspicious lump under the afghan covering his lap. Also noted six impossibly cute, fuzzy Teddy bears sitting in a row on the chesterfield. Teddy caught me staring at them.

"I order those off the TV. Give them to the Home Care girls. The ones I like. Young women appreciate cuddly things. Cuddly things like me," he added grimly.

"You certainly have a plentiful stock of them. You must have a lot of favourite young ladies."

"Not too many lately." I got up and turned on a light. His eyes narrowed against the sudden brightness. "You ever hear of verbal abuse?" he said abruptly. I had no idea where that had come from.

"Yeah. There are notices up about it everywhere now."

"I never heard of it before until that bitch Home Care director came by. Said they got a strict no verbal abuse policy. She told me I better watch my mouth with her staff. The woman had a ass on her like a double-wide trailer. I told her to get the hell out of my place, and go out the door sideways so she didn't stick there and make me have to call for the jaws of life."

"Okay, good demonstration of the concept of verbal abuse. Well done, Ted."

"I never took shit from anybody and I'm going to take it from some fat ass that bosses a bunch of diaper-changers?"

The question was purely rhetorical, but I answered it anyway. "Highly unlikely."

He stirred in his chair, wincing with pain. "Even in the army I never let nobody push me around," he said, still riveted on explaining his long-term take-no-shit policy. "I got called up this one time before Colonel McTavish on account of a spot of trouble with some limey Red Caps outside a pub in Leatherhead. 'Gunner Aker,' he says to me, 'this is the fourth time you've been up before me in the past six months on charges. Young man, you are no credit to your King, your country, or your family.' I looked him straight in the eye and cut the cheese. Good and loud. 'Beg pardon, sir,' I says, 'it's all that rough cider I drunk last night. Same rough cider got me in trouble with the Provost Corps.' I got twenty-eight days for that fart." He looked around his apartment as if he expected to spot an eavesdropper lurking in the shadows. "And now I can't even say what I think in my own jeezly house."

"Loose lips sink ships."

He had a lot to get off his chest. Ma had said that with all the deaths in the family Ted had no one to pay calls on him anymore. Evie, who used to drop in on him now and then, no longer went to see her husband because whenever she did he threw a fit and accused her of having had him "locked up in the Black Hole of Connaught."

"You can't even flirt with the good-looking nurses," said Teddy. "Where's the harm in that? When it comes to women I'm like a dog chasing a car. What would I do with it if I caught it? I don't mean nothing by it; it's just talk. I told one of them a little story and she said it was 'inappropriate.' I think she was the one complained to the fucking double-wide." He scratched his face with the brace on his wrist and grinned hugely. "It's kind of funny what I told her. See, when I was overseas I wrote this letter back home to Rudy Demchuk. I says to him, 'Over here in England I get nothing but chicken, chicken. There isn't a night I don't go to bed without a breast in one hand and a thigh in the other.' Well, Rudy's reading that out to some of the boys in the lobby of the post office and they're splitting a gut. The United Church minister comes in and wants to know what's so funny. So Rudy, who's a character, hands the preacher the letter and winks at the boys. The minister reads it over and says, all thoughtful, 'You know we hear these stories about rationing in Great Britain, how hard things are over there, and I think it would be wonderful if I could share Mr. Aker's letter with my congregation. It would be a great relief and a terrific boost to the morale of all the parents of boys serving overseas to know their sons are being so well taken care of over there in the Old Country.' And Rudy agrees that would be an excellent idea and the fucking innocent dope takes my letter with him and reads it out in church to everybody." Teddy paused. "So you tell me, what's the harm in trying to give somebody a good laugh now and then with a story like that?"

I said nothing. Teddy sat there, eyes fixed on me. Suddenly he said, "You called me a lunatic once. You think I'm a lunatic?"

Honesty is seldom the best policy with the old. "No."

"Because the double-wide says she's sending somebody over to give me some sort of test. I told her, 'Don't bother because if they show up they're not getting in my fucking door. Sure, maybe I give those Home Care girls a little shit when they do a half-assed job around here. But it's good for them. They need toughening up. They ought to learn life's no bed of roses.'" He hesitated. "So do you think they're sending some head doctor over here because of this verbal abuse business?"

Teddy looked worried. It wasn't often anybody saw Teddy looking worried. I tried to reassure him. "Whoever comes won't be a psychologist or psychiatrist. More likely a nurse or a social worker. They do this sort of thing with seniors all the time now. Maybe she'll ask you a few questions like, What day of the week is it? Who's the prime minister? What season is it? When's your birthday? Just to see how you're managing. Don't sweat it. You'll pass with flying colours."

Teddy patted the lump under the afghan. "They send somebody over here, somebody's going to be sorry."

"You'll be the one who's sorry. So lose the pellet pistol, Uncle Ted. In fact, you better give it to me right now. For your own good."

Teddy ignored that. "I know something about head doctors," he said, "how they operate, the fuckers. In Italy an officer took me out of the line and sent me to a casualty station on account of I climbed out of a slit trench under a mortar bombardment and stood up in the open. I figured, Fuck it, if I'm going to die it's not going to be like a rat in a hole.

"This doctor come to see me, he looked about thirteen years old. For chrissakes, he had *braces*. Tin-toothed cocksucker. He said they'd given me to him to examine because when he got back home he was going to specialize in mental cases. Not them words exactly, but that's what he meant. You wouldn't believe the kind of shit he asked me. I says to him, 'One more question about my mother and I'll drive your Adam's apple out the back of your skinny neck.'" Ted fumbled for a package of cigarettes on the table beside him. It was difficult to watch the agonizing effort it took him to make the lighter work. When at last he got his cigarette going, he sucked a long, grateful breath of smoke into his lungs. "This casualty station was in some rich Italian's house, and after I threatened this doctor they strapped me down on a bench that was by the entrance. I guess it was there for the peasants to cool their heels on while they were waiting to kiss the ass of the big shot who owned the place. That bench was all marble and colder than a witch's tit. This is December I'm talking about and I could have caught pneumonia laying there on that fucking slab of ice. I probably wouldn't be here now if Colonel McTavish didn't order that quack to release me. The colonel told him my only problem was that I was a malingerer. McTavish sent a corporal to collect me, probably to make sure that the doctor didn't make a fuss about letting me go. Me and the corporal ran into him when we was leaving the casualty station. I stopped and said, 'I'd like to make an appointment, please.' 'What do you mean? Appointment?' says the doctor. 'An appointment for after the war,' I says. 'I'll look you up so's we can have a nice long chat about *your* mother.' He didn't know whether to shit or go blind."

I got up and said, "Well, I better be on my way."

Teddy put his hand under the afghan and yanked out a very realistic-looking pellet pistol. One of those replica models that get kids shot by the police when they wave them around. "Take it," he said. "In case I get an itchy trigger finger."

I did.

On reflection, maybe I shouldn't have mentioned Uncle Teddy and the psychiatrist to Counsellor Sally. I don't want her musing about a family history of mental instability. I should also have kept my mouth shut about the pellet pistol, but sometimes Counsellor Sally's sympathetic demeanour can lull me into saying things I don't mean to divulge.

She wanted to know what I did with the pellet pistol.

"I don't know. I got rid of it."

"That doesn't sound very definite. How did you get rid of it? Was it disposed of safely?"

"I smashed it to pieces and dropped it down a chimney."

"That's not very funny," said *Consigliere* Sally. "I happen to have seen *The Godfather II*."

"Oh, Christ," I said, "that was a joke. After all, it's not a real gun. It's not all that dangerous."

Counsellor Sally said, "Remember when we began our sessions? I said that everything we talk about is confidential. The two exceptions to this rule would be if you were to speak about harming yourself or someone else. That I would need to report."

"And I haven't done either of those things."

"Correct. But I would like an assurance from you that you are not contemplating doing something rash. In regard to Mr. Drogan. For my own peace of mind."

"You can sleep easy. I wouldn't dream of it. I destroyed the pellet pistol. Scout's honour."

"I'm glad to hear it." Counsellor Sally shifted in her chair. She didn't look entirely convinced by my assertion. "But let's return to your 'joke' about the pistol. You don't think that didn't contain an element of aggression? Just like the 'joke' Uncle Teddy told the Home Care nurse? That it wasn't intended to make the hearer of it ill at ease, to make her feel some discomfort?"

"No, I don't."

"Is there a possibility that telling me about your uncle's hostility to being examined for a mental or emotional problem was a way of expressing your own resentment towards me?"

I didn't bother to answer that. The two of us sat in silence for a time. Then Counsellor Sally said, "I would like to make an observation."

"Feel free."

"It strikes me that you speak about your uncle's actions with a certain ambivalence. On the one hand, you seem to think it important to leave the suggestion with me that you disapprove of his behaviour, but – how shall I put this – I can't help thinking that I detect a tone of approval, even admiration in your voice when you talk about him. Would you say that in some way you might even admire your Uncle Teddy?"

"Maybe," I said grudgingly.

"Can you elaborate?"

"He always stuck up for himself. As he would say, he refused to take shit from anybody."

"And you feel that you have failed in that regard."

"Well, I'm taking shit from Drogan now, aren't I? Truck-loads of it."

"And your Uncle Teddy's attitudes, his ways of dealing with others – do you consider them healthy?"

"Not healthy maybe. But effective."

"Would you call injuring others, alienating others, an effective approach to life problems? Look at the outcome in your uncle's case. He ended the last years of his life alone."

"Look, I'm not holding him up as the gold standard of

decorum. All I said was that he didn't let people take advantage of him."

"The picture you draw of your Uncle Ted is of a very aggressive man, often violent, certainly an intimidating presence. So how did it make you feel when you saw that power so diminished in his final years? Your uncle ill, shrunken, frightened?"

"Did I say he was frightened?"

"You left the impression with me that he was."

"Okay, maybe a little spooked because he thought he was going to get labelled a head case. I can identify with that."

"Perhaps you identify with him in a different way. See a similar fate in your future. Isolation. After all, you have no life partner. That may frighten you."

"Wife."

"If you prefer that term."

Counsellor Sally waited. I kept her dangling. Finally, she glanced at her watch. "I see that our time is up for today. But I think we've done some good work, opened up some issues. Let's revisit them next session."

The last time I saw Teddy he was still worked up over the prospect of somebody coming to "dig around in his head." It had been four months and nobody had shown up. The waiting only seemed to increase his anxiety. I told him that that was how bureaucracy worked or rather didn't work; things got lost in the shuffle. It was highly likely that the paperwork had been overlooked, a call hadn't been made – who knew? –

he should stop worrying about it and breathe a sigh of relief.

Teddy was pretty sure now that the nurse who had reported him to his nemesis the double-wide was the one he had told the chicken joke to.

"She's some kind of religious nut," Teddy said. "In the old days you knew where you stood with church-going people. Everybody was either United Church, Anglican, or Catholic. But now people belong to these screwy churches you've never heard of. You got no idea where they're coming from. It's all hellfire and Blood of the Lamb." He stared at the images on the muted TV. It was never off. "She asked me to pray with her," he said.

"That's definitely not something she's got any business doing. That's off-limits. You should complain to her boss."

"Double-wide?" said Teddy. "Not fucking likely. And it wasn't so bad."

"Don't tell me you *prayed* with her."

"I didn't pray. She did. I let her. So what?"

"So what? There's a principle involved. She's not entitled to stuff her religious opinions down her clients' throats. It's unethical."

"There was this program I seen on the TV," said Teddy evasively, his gnarled fingers beginning to pick and worry the afghan. "It was all about people who died and then come back to life."

"What was this, some evangelical program?"

"No. *Scientific*." Teddy's voice was vehement. "It's been proved. These people really died – their hearts stopped and then the doctors brought them back. And they all said they went down this long black tunnel and they saw this light shining at the end of it. And they said they'd never been so happy because they saw old friends and family waiting for them. Heard beautiful music. Shit like that.

"I asked the religious lady what she thought about that and she said there wasn't no light at the end of a tunnel for nobody unless they accepted Jesus into their heart. Otherwise, it was the Other Place. What do you make of that?"

"I told you what I think. That woman should keep her opinions to herself."

Teddy ignored my observation. "But for guys like me," he said, grinning uneasily, "I bet they got a trapdoor in the floor of that fucking tunnel. They mean to spring it under us when we're on our way to the light. Get us when we're not suspecting nothing. But me, I'm going to run down that tunnel full speed so when they spring that trapdoor I'll have a good head of steam up and then I'll be able to give one mighty leap and sail clear over the hole."

I laughed and said, "Well, Ted, if that religious lady is right and you clear the trapdoor, they'll just lock and bar the door to the light on you. If they have any admission standards at all."

The look that came over his face. I don't know how to describe it. Holy terror might come closest to what I saw there. He seemed stricken dumb, scared out of his wits. But Teddy being Teddy, he recovered soon enough. "Well then I'll pound on that door to be let in. I'll kick the son of a bitch down. Me, I don't give up."

———

The next time I saw Counsellor Sally she didn't revisit the issues that she had claimed we would return to. She threw me a curveball, a slider. She said that she had been thinking about the untruths I had told my students and that they puzzled her. Counsellor Sally said that she felt she knew me better now and had come to question her suppositions about why I had done what I did. I no longer struck her as being the kind of person who desired to inflate his importance. Quite the opposite. So why?

"Boredom, I suppose."

That surprised her. "Boredom?"

"The kids knew how preposterous my lies were. How preposterous *I* was. Crazy old Molson. My antics amused them. They were bored; I was bored. Besides, I was just putting in time until the end of the year when I would give the school notice I was retiring."

"But now you are adamant about *not* retiring. I don't follow."

"Well, I never expected Drogan to find out what I was doing. I thought it was just between the kids and me. But when he decided to force me out I got my hackles up. I thought about all those years I had sat through staff meetings listening to that self-satisfied fraud and never once objected to any of the crap he was peddling. I took it. But all that time I guess I couldn't keep what I was thinking off my face. Seeing that look year after year must have pissed him off. Then I committed the unforgivable sin, made fun of him to my students. Talked about him being lead singer in a punk rock band. That I had to pay for."

"But if you are reinstated, what then?"

"If I get my job back, I'll hand in my letter of resignation. But not until then. I should have retired years ago, but I didn't know what else I would do with my life. I was hanging on through sheer inertia. I'm not proud of that." I shrugged. "But if I win the battle, I'm gone. I'll go out in a blaze of glory."

"Well," Counsellor Sally said thoughtfully and jotted something in her notebook. She looked up at me and sent me a gentle smile. "Let's see what we can do about facilitating this outcome."

Four months after I saw holy terror written all over Uncle Teddy's face, he died. The pneumonia he had escaped that winter when he had been strapped to a cold marble bench in Italy finally claimed him. Aunt Evie asked me to give his eulogy. She said he had always had a soft spot for me. Her grief was spectacular. She had one of what she called "Teddy Bear's bears" placed in his coffin to keep him company.

When I came to write Teddy's send-off, none of the conventional plaudits could truthfully be applied. Good husband, good brother, good uncle. Definitely not. So I told the story of Teddy's plan to leap for the light. I thought it was the truest thing I could say about him.

The minister, a young woman whom Evie had enlisted to perform the funeral service and whom she had strong-armed to visit Teddy's deathbed, said to me, "Just before your uncle died his legs were going like crazy under the covers. Like a dog chasing a rabbit in its dreams. Given his condition, I couldn't see where the strength to make such an effort came from. I guess you answered that." She gave a girlish toss to her hair. "Your uncle was a charming man. On one of my visits – that is before he lost consciousness – he said to me, 'If all the ministers had been as good-looking as you, I'd never have missed church.'"

I'm sorry I told Teddy that the door to the light would be barred to him. I'm not sure why I did. Maybe it had something to do with those nights long ago when he stood hammering and kicking at *our* door, shouting like a maniac while I cowered in my bedroom. But now when I imagine the hollow thunder of an old man battering at a locked door with his arthritic fists, there at the end of the long dark tunnel of his life, I only hope that the door did give way and that he stumbled, roaring, into a great spill of light.

Daddy Lenin

THE LINEUP AT THE ATM had stalled again, leaving Jack
Corbin to wonder why, after three years of retirement, three
years as master of his own time, he hadn't figured out yet
that withdrawing cash from the bank near the university
during a Friday lunch hour was a truly bad idea. There were
eight people ahead of him, students checking their accounts,
gauging how much the kitty could be pillaged for weekend
festivities. Most were texting as they waited their turn, heads
bent in the reverential silence of parishioners shuffling
towards the communion rail.

The queue shunted forward and Jack caught sight of the
man who had just surrendered the machine. Someone who
wasn't a student, someone roughly his own age, maybe two or
three years older, a man in his mid-sixties dressed in a stained
trench coat, someone who came surging back up the line, legs
scissoring, kicking at the skirts of his coat as if in disgust, arms
savagely chopping at his sides. But oddly enough, given all

this hectic action, his face was eerily composed: high cheek-bones crimping a faraway gaze, bald head glowing with a serene lustre, lips tucked in a smile blending world-weariness and self-satisfaction.

Kurt Jorgensen, Jack thought with a jolt. *Daddy Lenin. Holy shit, it's Daddy Lenin.*

Forty years ago, Rodney Stoyko had been the one to give Jorgensen his nickname, to spot his uncanny resemblance to the lovingly preserved corpse lying in state in the Kremlin. Even in his twenties, Jorgensen had displayed a virile waxy dome that, along with the trim moustache, the clipped beard of the professional revolutionary, and the glittering eyes tucked in the perpetual squint of someone gazing long and hard into a utopian future, had made him a dead ringer for Vladimir Ilyich.

Jack could see his fellow graduate student Stoyko smirking at him, asking in a mock-conspiratorial whisper, "How are things in the inner circle? Is the fearless leader happy with the Politburo, Jackie? Any rumours of another purge to trouble the sleep of the faithful?"

But that was Stoyko's bitter-grapes joke after Jorgensen had made it clear that he was no longer welcome at his table in the Apollo Room, the seedy watering hole where the students Jorgensen had judged worthy of his company met on Fridays to drink beer and listen to him expound. Jack's wife, Linda, was frequently there too, despite the fact that she wasn't a student. She was working in a Safeway because his teaching assistantship couldn't keep their household afloat financially. Jack naturally assumed that Linda was tolerated in the Apollo Room on the strength of his special, privileged relationship with Jorgensen. After all, he was Daddy's chosen one, his right-hand man. Jorgensen was supervising his thesis, had even dictated his topic: Robert Brasillach, French fascist, anti-Semite, novelist, newspaper editor, and author of a seminal film study. Convicted of treason in Paris in 1945, executed at the age of thirty-five for "intellectual crimes" despite pleas for mercy addressed to DeGaulle from the likes of Camus, Mauriac, Cocteau, and Colette. Brasillach, the literary comet who had burned himself to a cinder in less than a decade.

Jack had been given the nod from Daddy. Poor Stoyko had not; he had been consigned to Siberia because Jorgensen had judged his mind tediously, unforgivably ordinary. That was what everyone in Daddy's circle dreaded most: banishment.

That the man Jack had glimpsed was his old mentor was scarcely likely, but he *needed* to know. He scrambled out of the bank after him.

The sidewalk was packed with twenty-somethings dawdling in the autumn sunshine. The bright, acidic light spilling from a cloudless sky flooded Jack's eyes, dissolving the crowd of students in a swarm of colour. He panicked, terrified Daddy Lenin had melted away, vanished forever. But then his eyes cleared and he spotted him striding full throttle down the sidewalk, strollers flinching back from the maniac bearing down on them. In a frantic dogtrot, Jack pursued his quarry down College Avenue, the honking of horns and the roar of engines battering his ears. After three blocks, his head was thumping and he was gasping for breath. If this was Jorgensen, the bastard had kept himself fighting fit.

The same couldn't be said of Jack Corbin. Thirty-five years teaching high school had worn him down. Keeping the rowdy elements in check in the classrooms had always been a problem for him; anxiety over disruptions had kept his stomach constantly flipping and churning, turned him into a squeamish eater. But in retirement he had recovered his appetite and all those pounds he had gained were taking a toll.

Suddenly, Jorgensen veered off the busy thoroughfare and disappeared up a side street. Rounding the corner, Jack saw that his prey had slackened pace. Maybe he was looking for an address, or maybe the quiet of this residential enclave, the stately elms spreading a yellow, shimmering vault of leaves above the roadway, had subdued his frenzy. It definitely was a pleasant area, what Jack's wife, Linda, who had acquired a real estate licence after their two girls had flown the nest, would describe as a *mature neighbourhood*. In the 1950s, the majority of the children and grandchildren of the original owners of these houses had removed themselves to the new suburbs, opting for reliable wiring and plumbing.

In time, many of the spacious family homes they had deserted had been subdivided into cheap rental accommodations. But recently the district had undergone a gentrification blitz and was hurriedly being restored to its well-heeled beginnings. "Location, location, location," as Linda was fond of saying. Within walking distance of the university, the river, and the downtown, this neighbourhood resoundingly tinkled the location bell three times. Plus, it exuded *character*, a DINK couple's wettest dream.

Yet here and there a relic still teetered, and Jorgensen was making for one of these, a three-storey with plugged eaves sprouting rusty weeds, windows curtained in dusty sheets and fading Canadian flags, its siding eczemaed with scabby paint. Cutting across a lawn patched with naked earth and dead grass, Jorgensen bypassed the front door and slipped around to the side of the house.

Jack hesitated, ambled up and down the sidewalk, doing his best not to signal to any onlooker his interest in this rotten molar in the jaw of the street. Either Daddy Lenin's run of bad luck had continued, or living in that corroded wreck was his way of defying the soul-destroying *embourgeoise-ment* he had mocked back in the Apollo Room days. Either way you cut it, Jack thought, age does strange things to you. This ghost-hunt was proof enough of that. The only sensible thing to do would be to return to the bank, get his cash, find a place for a cup of coffee, and let the psychological dust that this apparition had raised settle. But instead, he crossed the street, located a side door where a neat, hand-lettered card mounted by the doorbell proclaimed *K. Jorgensen.*

Jack stabbed the button, loosing a strident, nervy buzz. Dead silence. No footsteps, not a rustle of movement. Perhaps Jorgensen suspected proselytizing Mormons or Jehovah's Witnesses. Jack rang again, then again. Finally there came the sound of shoes punishing a stairway. The door flung open. Daddy Lenin's face had lost all traces of the Buddha-like serenity it had radiated in the bank.

"What!"

"Professor Jorgensen. It's Jack Corbin."

Daddy scanned his features, scrutinized them closely, running a thorough identity check. A shrill whistling erupted downstairs that diverted Daddy's eyes. "Shit. The kettle," he said, whirling around and clattering back down the stairs.

One thing Jorgensen had never been known for was courtesy, and Jack took his having left the door open as a tacit invitation to follow him. At the bottom of an unlit stairway a door stood ajar. Through it, Daddy could be seen at the kitchen counter of a gloomy suite, spooning loose tea into a pot. Jack stepped across the threshold, shut the door softly behind him.

A stench of mouse, sewer gas, and mould burrowed into his nostrils. The place was tiny and sparsely furnished. An Arborite table and two chrome-legged chairs took up most of the floor space in the kitchen. An air mattress in the living room sat on a ratty carpet stained with blotches of god only knew what sordid liquids. There was a bum-hollowed armchair, a floor lamp, a small bookcase painted midnight blue. A simple wooden crucifix hung on the wall above the bookcase, witness, perhaps, to Jorgensen having finally consummated his flirtation with Catholicism. Back in the day, Jack could remember Daddy paraphrasing Charles Maurras, something along the lines that he preferred to give his allegiance to the learned procession of the councils and the popes rather than put his trust in gospels penned by four obscure Jews.

That statement was typical Daddy. *Épater la bourgeoisie* had been Jorgensen's style from the moment he had arrived on campus as a young professor newly graduated from the Sorbonne, reeking of worldly Left Bank sophistication. An American army brat, his father had been attached to NATO headquarters in Brussels where a preteen Daddy, contrary to expatriate custom, had insisted on attending a French-speaking school where he had become fluent in the language.

It hadn't taken long before the new addition to the History Department was a focus of interest, gossip about him flying thick and fast. Edna McElroy breathlessly confided to Jack that Daddy had liberally sprinkled the word *fuck* in a conversation she had had with him about a research paper she was working on. And then the juiciest of juicy stories broke, one concerning the philosophy prof George Carson. Apparently, one night when a lovesick Carson had rung Jorgensen's doorbell, it was answered by a naked coed, her thighs streaked with semen. How anyone knew any of these very intimate details was never explained. Nor was the source of the rumour that Carson and Daddy were romantically involved ever identified. It was accepted on faith that Jorgensen had decided to coldly terminate his involvement with a male lover by sending a female conquest to greet him at the door.

Jorgensen had been a tough man to get a handle on, not only in regard to his sexual tastes but also his political orientation. A self-declared right-wing anarchist – no one among his students could define what that was – he scorned "suckling-pig free enterprisers," detested liberals and "their masturbation fantasies about welfare mothers," and abhorred "Modern Times Marxists eager to grind every one of us up in the cogs of the state apparatus."

A loud thud snapped Jack out of his saunter down memory lane. Jorgensen had banged the teapot down on the table and was irritably rattling mugs and spoons. "Sit," he commanded and Jack did as he was told.

Daddy dropped in a chair, ran his eyes around the apartment, feigning puzzlement. "No, just as I thought . . . I don't have a telephone. So you didn't get my address from the phone book. So how the fuck *did* you find me?"

"I spotted you in the bank just now."

"You *tailed* me?"

"I was curious. It's been a long time, Kurt." Jack was making sure not to repeat what he had done earlier, humbly address Jorgensen as professor. That was a tactical error. Professor was forty years ago, this was now.

"A blink of the eye in the face of eternity, Jackie."

"Before you left here, you promised to keep in touch. I heard nothing from you." He waited for a response. Jorgensen offered none. "So what have you been up to for all these years? I'm curious."

Daddy Lenin lifted the lid on the teapot and peered down into it as if it were a shaft sunk into a rich reservoir of memory; setting it gently back in place, he said, "Decades of playing wandering scholar, that's what. One-year teaching stints filling in for professors on sabbatical. Holding the fort for nervous breakdowns and alcoholics in treatment or addicts in rehab. But another tenure track job – " His shoulders rose in weary resignation. "After what happened here, no chance of that."

"I'm sorry to hear it."

"I can't offer you sugar or milk. I don't use them. I have my girlish figure to preserve," was all he said, slopping tea into their cups.

"Neither do I." It wasn't true. Jack gingerly sipped the scorching tea and waited for Jorgensen to fake some curiosity about *his* life. But Daddy's gaze was directed to the floor, which seemed to have captured all his interest. Jack had a bird's-eye view of the top of his bald head, jaundiced by the fitful fizzing and stammering of the fluorescent tube overhead. "Me, I became a high school teacher. I'm retired now," Jack finally volunteered.

Jorgensen lifted his eyes. "Yes, chinos – is that the right word? – and a cotton button-down shirt. I assumed from your wardrobe that you had entered the ranks of some conventional, mind-numbing occupation."

Dockers and Arrow shirts were how Linda uniformed him now. Jack surmised she preferred to come home to someone who dressed like her clientele. "I wasn't left with many other options than teaching high school," Jack said defensively. "Not after what happened to me when you left the university. Having you as my thesis adviser was two strikes against me. The examining committee was in an unforgiving mood towards anybody thought to be in your camp. It was guilt by association. Guess what? Their verdict was that my thesis lacked balance. They said I needed to re-examine and rethink my entire approach to my topic. I left without my degree."

"Does that mean you stood by your guns, stood on principle, Jackie? How unlike you. How surprising."

No, I didn't stand on principle, thought Jack. And fuck you too. "The writing was on the wall. It was clear they were never going to pass me whatever I did. It was pointless to continue."

Jorgensen was absorbed in rolling a cigarette. Jack remembered all those nights he had spent with Daddy, chain-smoking, drinking Scotch, he hanging on to Jorgensen's every word, swept along in the dance of ideas, filled with optimism, youthful prospects, and hopes. "I didn't have the luxury of fighting lost causes. I needed to find a job. A year in the College of Education qualified me to teach," Jack said. "After all, I had a wife to support." How apologetic, how pathetically self-justifying that sounded, this making of excuses for failing to live up to the pedal-to-the-metal bohemianism Jorgensen had held up to his disciples as the ideal. Did anyone use the word *bohemian* nowadays? Did the young aspire to that quaint condition anymore?

Daddy Lenin struck a match and held it to the tip of his cigarette. "Poor baby, toiling away in the dark satanic mills of public education. Did the little woman appreciate it? Your sacrifice? Are you and she still together after all these years? What was her name? Don't tell me. Don't tell me. Linda. Was it Linda?"

"Yes, Linda." *You don't remember her name? What a load of horseshit.* "I'm happy to say we're celebrating our fortieth anniversary next month. We have two lovely daughters, Rebecca and Smith. Both professionals, both married, each with a child." He realized this prim description of his offspring was a mistake. It might elicit admiration in the circles he and Linda travelled in now, but it was likely only to incite disdain in Daddy Lenin.

And how right he was. "Smith. Interesting name for a young lady," said Jorgensen. "Of course, there was a bumper crop of female Caseys, Sidneys, and Dylans some decades ago. But somehow Smith conjures up a burly lesbian hammering sheet metal rather than the soccer mommy portrait you paint."

"It's Linda's family name," said Jack. "Smith." He could feel Daddy Lenin edging him further into a corner, driving his back to the wall as he had always done. He tried to counterattack. "And what about you, Kurt? I don't notice any signs of blissful cohabitation here. Any significant other?"

"No, still wandering lonely as a cloud."

"How's that at your age?"

Jorgensen studied the end of his cigarette. "Just fine. One thing at *our age*, there's never a shortage of willing divorcees and widows."

I'll bet, thought Jack. All of them eager for a guy in a stained trench coat to flash them his withered package, scoot them off to his groovy bachelor pad, and send them into transports of ecstasy on a leaky air mattress. Daddy Lenin the lady-killer. How far he had fallen. In comparison, Jack felt he had done all right. It wouldn't hurt Linda to see that. "Look," he said briskly, "we should get together. Why don't you come by for dinner? Weekends aren't great – Linda's a real estate agent now and weekends are her busiest time for showings – but a weekday would be good."

"Ah," said Jorgensen, "I hate to disappoint you, but I'm not in the market for a cozy cottage." He gestured to the suite. "I can aspire no higher than this."

"Nobody's trying to sell you anything, Kurt. All we're talking about is dinner, a few drinks. Talk over old times. How about it? What do you say to this Monday?"

"What time?"

"If you came by for drinks about six that would be great. I can't guarantee Linda will be home exactly then, but she shouldn't be much later. Then we'll eat." Jack took out a pen and his seldom-used appointment book, scribbled down his address, ripped out the page, and laid it in front of Jorgensen.

Before any objection could be raised, Jack bustled to his feet. "Good, it's settled then. See you Monday."

"I'd never have thought you susceptible to *nostalgie de la boue*, Jackie. But it's a bad day when you don't learn something."

"Hardly *nostalgie de la boue*, Kurt. Just a little get-together."

They parted then. Once out the door, Jack unleashed his pent-up anger, savagely scattering fallen leaves with his feet as he marched up the street. Nostalgia for the mud, he thought. That about sums you up, cocksucker. Never happy until you had landed somebody in the muck. For five or six blocks Jack carried on like this until his rage suddenly died, leaving him feeling spent, depressed, and hungover the way he always did the morning after one of those dinners Linda hosted for her boisterous real estate colleagues and professionally hearty business contacts.

Looking around him, Jack realized his anger had swept him in the opposite direction from the bank, farther east along Jorgensen's street. It was déjà vu all over again. There he was right in front of a house that only a few weeks ago he had been peering at from his wife's BMW while Linda chattered away in his ear, flushed by the news that the property's owners were in the process of having their home appraised for the market. But her excitement about the house wasn't professional. Linda was sure it was perfect for the two of them.

There he had sat while Linda enthusiastically enumerated the virtues of the monstrosity before them, forefinger emphatically tapping the driver's wheel. The city had recently designated it a heritage building, which in her books gave it an irresistible cachet. For the life of him, Jack couldn't see why the municipal nabobs had bestowed this dubious distinction except that the house looked *ancient*, even if it was nothing of the kind, hadn't even clocked a century yet. Built in the Gothic revival style, an architectural fad already passé when the eyesore had gone up in the 1920s, this prairie *manoir* boasted a parapet, a slate roof, a duo of marble gryphons mounting guard on the front door, and a cuddly, cute tower nestled coyly up against the east end of the house. The only fucking things missing were a moat, a drawbridge, and a donjon.

In spite of the Ye Olde chintziness, Jack found the place genuinely disturbing. He could just make out a presence hovering behind the stained-glass window at the top of the tower, someone who he sensed was looking fixedly down at him. If whoever was up there was trying to intimidate him, he'd give him as good as he got. He was prepared to enter into a staring contest if that's what the watcher wanted. After all, he certainly wasn't doing anything wrong; the whole *raison d'être* of the house was to elicit attention. So don't act hostile when you get it.

But the feeling of being subject to some cold, probing, clinical examination grew in Jack with every moment that passed, swelling his chest with panic. Heart banging, he lowered his eyes, and before he knew it his feet were carrying him away from the house. For the life of him he couldn't say exactly why this Disney-enchanted-kingdom nightmare filled him with such anxiety and apprehension.

Just one more curveball that life was throwing him. Ever since his wife had gotten her realtor's licence, the curveballs had kept slicing by him while he stood flat-footed, bat lamely propped on his shoulder.

Linda had amazed him with her talent, her flair for hawking houses. And not just houses. Five years ago she had gone into the commercial property sector and had become her office's number-one earner, raking in some very big bucks indeed. Jack's teacher's pension now accounted for little more than pin money in the family budget. Linda was the breadwinner, and she made no bones about letting him know that she and she alone was in charge of the big financial decisions. When the haunted castle hit the market, she was buying it. End of discussion.

How difficult Jack found it to reconcile this ruthlessly driven woman with the girl he had married forty years ago, a girl so unsophisticated and unworldly that he had worried about her fitting in with the self-styled "intellectuals" of the Apollo Room, wincing whenever she said something gauche in the presence of Daddy Lenin. Jack had wanted to *protect* his wife from condescension and the killingly tolerant, understanding smiles that his friends turned on her.

Now it was he who needed protecting from her and her colleagues' condescension. Those bluff, practical men and women who knew exactly where they stood in the realtor pecking order, their rank determined by their sales: Executive Circle, President's Circle, Director's Circle, Rookie Circle. There was no question about Linda's status. She was absolutely top gun Executive Circle. Her title had earned her deference at the office and she expected the same at home.

Jack meant to do something about that. He was tired of riding in the back seat. A visit from Daddy Lenin might take some of the wind out of Linda's sails. Jorgensen had a talent for doing that. Daddy's presence would be a reminder to Linda of what she had done in the past.

As for installing herself as *châtelaine* of the eyesore *château*, at the end of the day Jack would have something to say about that too. The horseshit had to stop somewhere. There was only so much a person could tolerate.

Monday afternoon Jack spent tippling cooking wine, chopping and dicing meat and vegetables. While he did these things, he brooded over questions he had wanted to ask Daddy for forty years. Had his supervisor really encouraged him to examine the fairness and legitimacy of Robert Brasillach's trial because he thought it a topic worthy of historical inquiry? Did he really have so much confidence in the principle of academic freedom that he believed it was possible to argue that the moon-faced, spectacled Brasillach had been sent to a firing squad by a kangaroo court? Because Daddy Lenin had made it very clear that that was the line he wanted Jack to take. Or had he simply sent his graduate student down the academic coal mine to see if the air would be toxic for Kurt Jorgensen if he pursued similar scholarly interests?

Daddy had been cunning, a master at selling himself as a certain winner in the academic stakes race. His colleagues may have resented his arrogance, but they were also a little overawed by his presumed promise. After all, at twenty-seven, the precocious Jorgensen was already the author of two highly regarded articles that had appeared in prestigious journals devoted to the history of ideas. Even more impressive, he had a letter from the distinguished Parisian house, Gallimard, professing interest in publishing his doctoral dissertation on Charles Maurras, once he had finished satisfactorily revising and expanding it to book length.

So why hadn't he been recruited and hired by a university of higher standing? Only Stoyko, who had gotten himself into Daddy's bad books, had ever had the temerity to actually wonder out loud why this supernova had chosen to blaze in the heavens of a prairie backwater. Stoyko liked to speculate that it was the draconian anti-sodomy laws still on the books in many American jurisdictions that had enticed Jorgensen to Canada. Once Pierre Elliott Trudeau had declared that the state had no business in the bedrooms of the nation, Daddy Lenin had assumed the Great White North was, as Stoyko put it, "a pederast's paradise."

But Stoyko's sniping was largely ignored because by then the Jorgensen fan club was in full bloom. His Survey of Modern History was the most popular class in the department, perhaps even the entire College of Arts and Science, Daddy packing the biggest lecture hall on campus to the rafters, stalking the stage, lecture notes abandoned on the lectern, freestyling his way through rambling monologues. Jorgensen, the acid-tongued iconoclast, was perfect for the times. Young parricides who made it an article of faith to trust no one over thirty were happy to hear him slash and burn the reputations of everything and everyone their parents admired.

Daddy liked to point out that as late as 1938, Churchill had declared that if Great Britain ever lost a war he hoped it would find a Hitler to lead it. Was the booze-addled British aristo pining to play führer in England's green and pleasant land?

And Franklin Dumbo Roosevelt, the president around whose head every right-thinking liberal loved to draw a halo, Roosevelt the sainted democrat, was he entitled to all that adulation? According to Daddy, it was Roosevelt who had done more than anybody else to establish the "imperial presidency." Against long-established precedent that no president serve more than two terms, FDR had run for office a third and then a fourth time. A blatant play for absolute power, naked Caesarism.

And let us not forget Senator Harry S. Truman, Daddy Lenin would say, the statesman who had opined that if Germany looked to be winning the war, the United States should support Russia, and if Russia seemed to be getting the upper hand, then Germany should become the recipient of American aid so as to kill off as many Germans and Russians as possible.

Another day, Daddy scrawled a list of names on the blackboard: Dostoevsky, Wagner, Rilke, Valéry, Eliot, Pound, Celine, Hamsun, Degas, Rodin, Renoir, Cézanne. What do all these men have in common aside from being among the most celebrated artists of the modern age? he had asked the class. Why, they are all anti-Semites. Every mother's son of them. Think about it.

Nobody had known what to make of that.

But if Jorgensen was a crowd-pleaser as a teacher, he was equally skilled at navigating his course through the university bureaucracy. With two more years of probation before he was eligible for tenure, Daddy had suggested that Jack request him as a thesis supervisor. But to make this kosher, the History Department had to be persuaded to appoint Daddy an adjunct professor, a bit of jiggery-pokery that made him eligible to supervise graduate theses before he received tenure. All of which had left Jack basking in the warm feelings that he had been hand-picked by the great man to study with him, that he had been the number-one draft pick by the number-one professor in the league.

Dinner was in the oven by four, and Jack had drained the last of the cooking wine and was dipping into a bottle of Macallan. By five-thirty he was anxiously peering through the picture window, searching the street for any sign of the guest of honour. He worried that Daddy might arrive late. He wanted to see him comfortably settled before Linda got home. Jack had decided not to inform her they would be entertaining a blast from the past tonight because she would have vetoed the whole thing; guest and hostess colliding on the doorstep would have most definitely ruined his little surprise.

Just a few ticks short of six, he spotted Jorgensen churning up the street, trench coat billowing and flapping around his knees. Jack made sure to let the doorbell ring a few times before answering it; looking too eager to welcome Daddy wouldn't set the correct tone. After three insistent peals of the bell, he popped the door and said, "Hello, Kurt."

Jorgensen snapped him a nod, walked straight past him into the living room, and hurled himself down on the sofa in his trench coat. From that vantage point he inspected the room with a savage gaze.

Five years ago Linda had given a free hand and a blank cheque to an interior designer. The superannuated artiste had dictated "a mid-century Danish teak look."

"Personality plus," Daddy observed.

"To the max," conceded Jack, reluctant to defend the *look*. "But I'm sure you could use a drink. I think we have pretty nearly everything. But I remember you had a taste for Scotch. How does a bit of single malt sound?"

"I wouldn't say no. Nothing but a few drops of water to break the surface tension."

Well put, thought Jack. He slipped into the kitchen, fixed Daddy a very hefty drink, and generously refreshed his own. When he returned and leaned down to hand Jorgensen his glass, Jack felt himself tilting, and barely managed to correct the list before he toppled into Daddy's lap. No doubt about it, he had taken on more liquid ballast than was wise on an empty stomach. "Let me take your coat," he said. "Stay awhile."

"We'll see," said Daddy. Jack didn't know what that was supposed to mean. Then came the abrupt demand: "Where's Linda?"

"Linda? She often does a bit of paperwork in the office at the end of the day. She shouldn't be too long." Jack didn't fancy Linda as a topic of conversation this early in the game. He was holding that off for the dessert course.

Just then he heard the clunk of the automatic garage door being activated, followed by the expensive purr of his wife's bimmer rolling up the driveway. *Today she decides to come home early. Fuck me gently.* "Why, there she is now," he exclaimed with manufactured brightness. "If you'll excuse me a sec."

He reached the back door just as his wife was shouldering her way into the kitchen, arms stacked with binders, a laptop balanced precariously on top of them. A rust-coloured suit, a string of amber beads, an ash-blond French bun fastened with a tortoiseshell hair comb lent her fluster an undeniable elegance.

"Let me take those," he mumbled, relieving her of her load and dumping it on the kitchen island.

Linda's nose wrinkled. "What's that smell?"

"Beef bourguignon. I went all out for a Monday night."

"No, not that. Has someone been smoking in the house?"

Jack caught a telltale whiff of cigarette smoke threading its way from living room to kitchen. The son of a bitch had made himself at home and lit up. "We have a guest. Somebody unexpected," he said quickly. "You'll never guess."

"Who?" she said. "And who gave *him*, *her*, permission to smoke in the house?" Linda was beginning to wind herself up, and Linda wound up was no one to mess with.

"Jorgensen. Kurt Jorgensen." Linda stared at him blankly. The name didn't seem to register. "*Daddy Lenin*," said Jack excitedly. "Now there's a name you probably never expected to hear again."

Linda's face stiffly set in a mask. "What the hell is he doing here?"

"We ran into each other the other day. I invited him to dinner."

"You're insane, Jack," Linda said in a husky whisper, retrieving her car keys from the counter and heading for the door. "Totally and completely out of your tiny fucking mind."

"Where are you going?"

"Out," she said. "You two have fun." The pneumatic closer softly eased the door shut on her departure.

Out of the corner of his eye Jack caught a glimpse of his blurry reflection on the stainless steel door of the fridge. It reminded him somehow of the ill-defined figure behind the stained-glass window in Linda's new dream home. He felt terrified. This wasn't like the panic attacks that had robbed him of breath in his days of teaching school. Those were of a different order. This, however, was a fucking *attack of doom*.

Braced against the kitchen island he heard the garage door roll up, Linda's much-loved bimmer roar to life, the sharp squeak of rubber as she backed down the driveway at a rate of speed that sounded, to Jack's ears, unsafe and uncalled for. And just like that, as inexplicably as it had poked its head up, his anxiety retreated. Jack took a deep breath of relief and headed back to the living room.

Jorgensen had removed his filthy trench coat, tossed it in a bundle on the sofa, and posed himself in the frame of the picture window, backlit by slanting fall sunshine. He's *unveiled* himself for Linda, Jack thought. There was no other word to describe it. Daddy Lenin's suit looked to be salvage from some Goodwill rack, a Rat Pack number with narrow jacket lapels, tightly tapering trousers. What closet or suitcase had this perfectly preserved fossil been hidden away in for all these years? How to account for its immaculate condition? And how had Daddy managed the same trick, kept himself equally untouched by time? Jack felt a twinge of envy noting Jorgensen's flat stomach, his Sinatra-like angularity, the way he casually took the cigarette from the corner of his mouth, and said, "Was that Linda I heard leaving?"

"Yes."

"But she's coming back?"

"Hard to say. Likely not. She has a real estate emergency to deal with."

"No time for a quick hello?"

"No time for a quick hello."

"What exactly constitutes a real estate emergency, I wonder," said Daddy. Jack had no answer to that. The awkward moment expanded. Daddy directed a withering smile at him. "I think I need an ashtray," he said.

"We don't have any ashtrays. We don't permit smoking in the house."

"You mean Linda doesn't permit it."

"I'll get you a saucer," Jack said.

"You are too good," said Daddy.

Jack went to the kitchen, collected a saucer and the bottle of Scotch, carried both back to the living room, and set them down in front of Jorgensen on the second-hand Danish coffee table that the interior decorator had "picked up for a song" at an estate sale. He ran Daddy's glass half full of Scotch and did the same with his own before flopping into the Finn Juhl easy chair, another of Linda's prized acquisitions from the land of the Vikings.

"I need to bum a cigarette from you," he said to Jorgensen. "I want a smoke. For old times' sake."

After months of long summer days, Jack was always surprised to realize how early dusk arrived in September. It stole over them as he and Daddy huddled in the living room around the Scotch bottle, plates of beef bourguignon on their knees. Jack had suggested that's where they eat. It reminded him of student potluck suppers, those halcyon days when he had revelled in the prestige of having been Jorgensen's anointed. It had been a wonderful feeling to know someone had discerned promise in him, to feel *selected*. And now it was a strangely, sweetly companionable feeling to share a meal with his old mentor.

But to Jack's disappointment, Daddy had no interest in reminiscing. He preferred to talk about some stupid Mediterranean cruise he was off on in October. Not as a holiday-goer but as staff. For four autumns now Daddy had had a gig giving onboard lectures about the glory that was Greece and the grandeur that was Rome to what he described as "a bunch of baseball-capped, pot-bellied smorgasbord-foragers and women of a certain age who have selected purple, fuchsia, and lavender as the colours for their sunset years. Whenever I think of *S.S. Change of Life* and all who will be sailing on her, I am sorely tempted to pack an AK-47 and do a Columbine."

How Jorgensen had managed to keep intact his invincible sense of superiority all these years while in freefall down a garbage chute that had landed him in a basement squat reeking of mouse shit and sewer gas was a mystery to Jack. But Daddy had never suffered from self-doubt. Running into Jorgensen three days ago had been like time travel; Jack had found himself just as intimidated by Daddy's patronizing attitude as he had been in his student days.

"Well," said Jack, "I guess we've both had a come-down. You and me."

Daddy carefully set his plate on the coffee table and said, "Have *we*? Really? Fucking *we*, is it?"

Jorgensen's anger startled Jack. True, they had both put down a lot of whiskey and that turned certain temperaments aggressive, but he still couldn't see how Daddy could take offence to what he had said.

"All I mean is we were pretty much linked once," said Jack. "Identified with each other, so to speak. And when you fell, you brought me down with you. I mean, in the eyes of the department."

"Empires *fall*," said Daddy. "Guys like you don't fall. Because your feet never touched the first rung on the ladder, Jackie. You can't fall from the ground floor." He paused and raked Jack with a hard look. "And you can give it a rest. I mean, the innocent guise. It hardly matters anymore. It's been forty years. And I didn't *fall*, as you so dramatically put it. My legs got chopped out from under me. I've got a pretty good idea who chopped them. You. Because you wanted revenge for Linda."

"You're wrong," said Jack. "I only found out about you and Linda after you left town. That's when the rumour reached me."

"Really?" Daddy slung one long leg over the other, leaned back in the sofa. "I wish she were here," he said. "Then the lovely Linda could confirm your story. Or not."

Jack said, "Ernest somebody or other was the one who ratted you out. Not me. Stoyko told me about him. Ernest consulted with Stoyko about what he should do."

For a moment Daddy looked uncertain. "Ernest? I can't picture him."

"He wasn't a guy anyone noticed. I don't remember much about him except that he had enormous aviator glasses. I think he was studying to be some kind of Protestant minister."

Now Jorgensen was truly baffled. "A theology student? Why would I let a theology student into my seminar?"

"I don't know. Maybe you let him in because you sniffed him giving off moist, sticky, Christian idealism. You liked knocking the illusions out of people and what better target than a Martin Luther King fan? But Ernest had a trick or two up his sleeve." Jack could scarcely stop himself from grinning at the thought of Daddy undone by Ernest. "Earnest Ernest the mole, the secret agent man. Never raised an objection to what you said in class, just sat there looking troubled and pained, until his social conscience got the better of him. Until he asked himself what would Martin Luther King do in such a morally compromising situation? Gandhi? Bonhoeffer? It happens to people in the caring professions, those crises of conscience. Apparently Ernest was a very caring guy."

"Ernest somebody or other," Jorgensen said softly to himself. "Macdonald would never give me the name of the student who brought the accusations against me. Macdonald said he wanted to keep everything as friendly and informal as possible."

When Ernest had mentioned to Stoyko how disgusted he was at having to read Drumont's *La France juive* in Daddy's seminar, Stoyko had encouraged him to take the matter to the head of the department. And that's exactly what Ernest had done.

The fact that he'd been done in by somebody he had no memory of seemed particularly galling to Jorgensen. "I remember the day Macdonald called me into his office for a scolding," he said. "He had a copy of *La France juive* on his desk, passages bookmarked. He insisted on reading each one out to me. When he finally finished, he said one of my students had come to him to object about the book. Macdonald said he was inclined to sympathize with the objection. He wanted my justification for exposing students to such slanderously anti-Semitic statements." Daddy smiled. "I said to Macdonald, 'I, for one, have never *said* anything that could be taken to be anti-Semitic. I have never said anything *slanderous*. The opinions expressed in the written material assigned by me are the author's, not mine.'"

"How politically astute. Playing lawyer, splitting hairs with the head of the department," said Jack.

Daddy ignored that. Some inner compulsion to revisit his struggle with Macdonald seemed to have gripped him. Daddy said that he had told the head that he had assigned *La France juive* because understanding Drumont's influence on French public opinion was absolutely necessary to provide a context for the Dreyfus Affair.

He went on to say that Macdonald had wondered out loud if it might not have been wiser for him to summarize Drumont's views and point out to students how baseless they were. He said the unsophisticated among those who were required to read Drumont's work could very easily misinterpret, think they were being forced to consume anti-Semitic propaganda. That certainly was what one member of the class thought.

Daddy retorted that he couldn't be held responsible for what an idiot thought. And as for giving the members of the class a neat and digestible version of What They Should Think, wasn't it the policy of the department to encourage the future historians they were training to use original documents and primary sources from which to draw their own conclusions?

None of this went down well with Macdonald. Tottering towards retirement at the end of a career that could not in any sense be described as distinguished made him doubly touchy and resentful at being talked back to by a junior colleague. "He turned nasty just like that," said Daddy. "If I wouldn't take the hint then he was going to bring me to heel with the choker chain. You know what the old prick said to me? That above all else he valued a 'culture of cooperation' in the department. This was the sort of situation that could very easily get out of hand. The complainant had made threats about contacting B'nai Brith to inform them that an anti-Semite was being given free rein to spread his poison in the university. If I refused to remove *La France juive* from my reading list there would surely be 'consequences for someone who demonstrates so little concern for the reputation of his colleagues.' Toe the party line or else was his message. He made it clear that if I didn't do as I was told, I would have no supporters in the department when I applied for tenure." Daddy fell into a long silence. Then in a quiet voice that Jack had to strain to hear he said, "I couldn't do it, Jackie. I couldn't back down. Not to that fucking mediocrity. Out of the question."

The living room was almost completely dark now, crowded with shadows. It seemed to Jack that Daddy might be prone to regrets, just as he was. Until that minute he would never have entertained the idea that Jorgensen could harbour second thoughts. He said, "So you slapped his face. Well, you always liked to slap faces. Although I still don't know why you had to slap mine. Linda, I mean."

"There you go being dramatic. Dramatic and bourgeois. Linda and I had a bit of fun. That's all. I wasn't slapping your face."

"But she was my wife. Didn't that mean anything to you? Why did it have to be her?"

"Why Linda? I don't know. It's like when they asked the guy who had decided to climb Mount Everest why he wanted to do it, and he said, Because it's there." He shrugged. "Linda was there."

"That's your fucking reason? *Because she was there?*"

"Not entirely. Linda always had something about her."

"Oh really. There's an excuse for bad behaviour. *She had something about her.* You want to help me understand? Explain to me, as far as you were concerned, what exactly that something was."

"If you can't see it, I can't tell you what it is."

"Okay, if you can't explain what your *something* was, explain this," said Jack, struggling to feign composure. "You wanted to supervise my thesis. You *courted* me. I was the one who was always at your side in the Apollo Room. You counted on me. You believed in me. So why treat me like shit?"

"*Counted* on you? *Believed* in you. Do you think there was something special about you?" Daddy shook his head in disbelief. "Let me explain it to you. The truth is, unlike the rest of the graduates from Bumfuck High and Podunk Comprehensive who made up the student body of this

Harvard of the flatlands, you could read French just compe-
tently enough to research a thesis on modern French history.
I had to make do with what crooked timber I could lay my
hands on. That's it."

"I don't believe that. Not for a second."

"Indulge yourself. What you need to believe is nothing
to me."

In silence, Jack watched Jorgensen roll a cigarette. Focusing
on the fastidious way he manipulated the tobacco and paper
helped Jack to put the brakes on his brain, helped stop it
from testing the truth of his memories against what had just
been said. Daddy began to roll another cigarette; when he
finished it, he passed it to Jack. Was this a kind of apology?
Jack accepted the cigarette and Daddy poured them each a
drink. They lit up, curtaining the room in smoke. After a bit,
they started to talk again; stepping back from the past they
spoke of nothing but inconsequential things: Jorgensen's
upcoming cruise, the possibility that Jack might take some
Spanish lessons come winter. They chatted like retirees sketch-
ing lives chock full of small, discreet pleasures.

At about nine o'clock Jorgensen began to exhibit signs of
restlessness; a short time later he announced it was time for
him to go. At the door, the two men shook hands clumsily.
"We'll have to do this again," said Jack. It was the sort of
thing that he had said to guests a hundred times. The words
left his mouth without a thought.

"I don't think so," Daddy replied. His face grew sombre
under the door light. "Tell Linda I was sorry to have missed
her. Good luck when she gets home." With that gnomic warning, he went down the steps and waded into the darkness.

Jack returned to the living room, stretched out on the suitably hard and penitential Danish mid-century sofa. What had he hoped to gain by bringing up all this old business about Linda? What would an apology or explanation from Daddy be worth? Piss all. Nothing would change. Besides, even in the unlikely event Jorgensen understood his real reasons for acting the way he had all those years ago, he wasn't a man to make excuses or give away anything he didn't want to. Years ago, he had stood firm and refused to remove *La France juive* from his class syllabus. His attitude had been fuck the head of the department and fuck the department too. Curiously, there had been none of the consequences his colleagues had feared, no public scandal. In the end, righteous Ernest had apparently lost his nerve and decided not to denounce the most popular professor on campus. He simply dropped the class.

There were, however, consequences for Daddy. By defying Macdonald, he had made sure he would never get tenure. He had no alternative but to hand in his resignation and begin the search for another job. Jack faced consequences too. Jorgensen's resignation left him sitting high and dry, without a supervisor, and with a thesis topic now irrevocably tainted.

Naturally, Jack had wondered if Ernest hadn't been right when he accused Daddy of being a rabid Jew-hater. It had seemed conceivable, maybe even likely. Why else had Jorgensen been so insistent that Jack examine the legal proceedings that had condemned Robert Brasillach to death if it wasn't to discredit them? Why had Daddy been so fascinated with a man who was no more than a minor footnote in a terrible period of French history?

Jack saw another possibility now. Maybe it was only the Brasillach persona and the Brasillach style that had meant anything to Daddy, maybe the man's opinions had been immaterial to him. Certainly Brasillach had been everything Daddy had longed to be. Brasillach was a genuine boy wonder, reigning *enfant terrible* of French letters, savage annihilator of literary reputations, a real force, not somebody striking bad-boy poses at a second-rate university. Like Daddy, Brasillach had hated everything and anything middle-class, everything and anything that smacked of compromise and caution. Like Daddy he had had an insatiable hunger for attention, and nothing attracted attention like outrageous opinions outrageously expressed. What was more uncompromising and outrageous than fascism? It strutted, preened, scoffed, slandered, and insulted. It dismissed and denied boundaries.

Even when on trial for his life Brasillach couldn't stop pretending there were no boundaries when it came to him. He refused to take back a single word, refused to show contrition for anything he had said or written. At thirty-five, he was executed for being Robert Brasillach.

With Brasillach as his *beau idéal*, with Brasillach as his emotional doppelgänger, could Daddy do anything else but choose self-destruction too?

Right now, Jack was contending with his own doppelgänger. The one he had seen floating on his fridge door just hours ago was now hovering in his peripheral vision. Trying to see it more clearly did nothing but lure him into sleep.

———

The sound of footsteps woke Jack. He listened to Linda pass down the hallway to their bedroom, heard the door gently close. Jack was certain that she was not being quiet out of consideration for him, was certain that she was not doing her best to avoid waking him. From experience he knew that when Linda was most furious, she was softly, quietly furious. That had certainly been the case when, four months after Jorgensen had left town, Stoyko had let him in on what everybody else already seemed to know. That Linda had been sleeping with Daddy. When he confronted her, she had made no attempt to deny it. In a voice that barely qualified as a whisper, she had said coldly, "Face it. You could care less that I betrayed you. It's Jorgensen betraying you that's really got you upset. Well, I just fucked him. Unlike you, I'm not in love with him."

Jack had forgiven her – halfway forgiven her. Not that Linda had asked for forgiveness. She never felt any guilt for things she did. In her mind, what was done belonged to the past, and she had no interest in the past. She was always looking ahead. Maybe that was what made her such a successful realtor.

However, she wasn't likely to concede him the exemption from guilt she granted herself. Springing Kurt Jorgensen on her like a jack-in-the-box was not something she would let go of, he was sure of it.

Truth be told, maybe throwing all this in Linda's face had only been his pathetic attempt to wrong-foot her, to throw her a little off-balance. She had been so confident, flying so high for such a long time. It wouldn't hurt his wife to be reminded that in her day she had done a stupid thing or two.

Her success hadn't been good for Linda, had been even worse for him. Things had been bad between them for a considerable period of time and now they were going to go downhill fast. Not bad enough for either Linda or he to ask for a divorce – there were too many practical considerations for that to be feasible: there were the girls and the grandchildren to consider, and Linda would be hard-headed enough not to wish to contemplate a division of property now that there was quite a lot of property to divide. Most of it earned on her watch.

One thing was for sure, and this he hadn't foreseen, what had happened tonight was going to cut his legs out from under him in the debate concerning the preposterous château. His hating the house would make it even more attractive to her. He supposed the uncomfortable sofa he was lying on now would soon be going the way of the buffalo. The château would need to be decorated with either overstuffed Victorian furniture or maybe a pricey French country antique look.

Jack glanced at his watch. One o'clock. He curled up even tighter on the sofa, knees drawn up to his chest, desperately trying, without success, to hug sleep to him. He began to sweat and tremble. With the cruel clarity of a hallucination, he saw the château in every detail. Above all, he saw the shadowy figure behind the stained-glass window, studying him, scrutinizing him.

In a haze of exhaustion, he recognized who the figure was. It was Jack Corbin waiting for Jack Corbin to arrive home, arrive at the place to which every step and misstep he had ever made had been leading him for years. There he would stand, keeping watch behind a stained-glass window, waiting for Daddy Lenin to pass by on the street where they both now lived, hoping that the only person whose opinion had ever counted with him might break stride, pause, give him a wave confirming that, yes indeed, Jack Corbin had once shown extraordinary promise. A final sign from Daddy, before he resumed his frantic clip and continued on his way.

Acknowledgements

THE STORIES IN THIS COLLECTION were published in slightly different variations in: *Epoch*: "1957 Chevy Bel Air"; *Planet: The Welsh Internationalist*: "The Jimi Hendrix Experience"; *The Walrus*: "Live Large"; *Prairie Fire*: "Tick Tock."

I would like to thank my editor, Ellen Seligman, and my agent, Dean Cooke, for their valued counsel, assistance, and support over many years.